# CRAZY
# TIME

Books by Kate Wilhelm

THE MILE-LONG SPACESHIP
MORE BITTER THAN DEATH
THE CLONE (with Theodore L. Thomas)
THE NEVERMORE AFFAIR
THE KILLER THING
THE DOWNSTAIRS ROOM
    AND OTHER SPECULATIVE FICTION
LET THE FIRE FALL
THE YEAR OF THE CLOUD (with Theodore L. Thomas)
ABYSS: TWO NOVELLAS
MARGARET AND I
CITY OF CAIN
THE INFINITY BOX:
    A COLLECTION OF SPECULATIVE FICTION
THE CLEWISTON TEST
WHERE LATE THE SWEET BIRDS SANG
FAULT LINES
SOMERSET DREAMS AND OTHER FICTIONS
JUNIPER TIME
BETTER THAN ONE (with Damon Knight)
A SENSE OF SHADOW
LISTEN, LISTEN
O, SUSANNAH!
WELCOME, CHAOS
HUYSMAN'S PETS
THE HAMLET TRAP

# CRAZY
# TIME

◰

# Kate Wilhelm

ST. MARTIN'S PRESS
NEW YORK

Library of Congress Cataloging-in-Publication Data

Wilhelm, Kate.
    Crazy time / by Kate Wilhelm.
        p.    cm.
    ISBN 0-312-01411-2
    I. Title.
    PS3573.I434C7 1988
    813'.54—dc19

First Edition
10  9  8  7  6  5  4  3  2  1

To Jennifer and Jonathan
because they laugh
at the right things.

# Chapter One

ALL day the fog had been eating Seattle, and by five-thirty it pressed against the wide windows of Lauren Steele's office as if seeking entrance. She found herself eyeing it uneasily again and again as the woman across the desk, her last client for the day, wound down after reciting a litany of charges against her present employer.

The client began to shift, also aware of the white curtain that had fallen over the world beyond the window. Rose—Rosie— Lauren had to glance at the folder in front of her to get the name right—Rosalie Gruen—Rosalie gathered her raincoat and purse and made the automatic search that women do in pockets and bag on rising. "Driving's going to be bad," she said unhappily. "I hope it's not freezing. Black ice is the worst."

"Do you have far to go?"

"Bothell." She sounded morose. "Well, I'd best be started."

Lauren nodded sympathetically although she had no idea that Bothell was many miles north and east of her building. She planned to walk home, five blocks away. "Well, make an appointment for the tests as soon as it's convenient for you, and we'll go on from there. I'm sure we'll be able to work something out."

Five minutes after the client was gone, Lauren would have had trouble describing her, or remembering her complaints.

She began to clear her desk as soon as she was alone, her mind on the problems she had with her own job, not those nearly identical problems voiced again and again by the clients she saw. Now and then she found herself making the comparisons, and each time she did, she shied away from the thoughts and forgot them instantly. She was not a client, she told herself firmly at those times; she was the therapist, the consultant. She glanced over the clean desk, the clean office, all done in colorless good taste—ivory walls, ivory carpeting, ivory drapes, pale wood, ivory everything. Even the photographs on the walls were watered-down gray on gray, all ivory-tinted, landscapes of nothing in particular. The only things of her own in the office were several geraniums in ivory pots on the wide window ledge, and they looked sick and pale.

When she walked out into the reception room, she automatically glanced around to see if the receptionist was gone yet. Gloria was only five feet two, and she made Lauren feel like a giraffe. Lauren was five eleven, and that was a big problem, she had to admit to herself. She intimidated her clients as soon as she stood up; only showgirls could get away with being that tall. Short men clung to them like worker ants to the queen, but a professional woman that size became a threat.

The receptionist was already gone. Lauren went to the elevator to join Rich Steinman, who was five inches shorter than she, and twenty pounds lighter. Rich kept muttering to himself, probably making up excuses for being late, as if his wife did not have enough sense to look outside and see that the fog had descended again. Rich handled family crises—he was supposed to counsel couples in an effort to keep a relationship healthy and whole. Lauren thought that most of his clients split and moved as far apart as they could as soon as possible after seeing Rich a few times. He gave marriage a bad name.

Warren Foley was leaving too. He had played football in school and liked to talk about it too much. Warren had already changed into his running clothes. Waiting for the elevator, in the elevator, after departing it, he continued his warm-up exercises, preparing for the two-mile dash home. Warren handled teenage crises—drug abuse, truancy, pregnancies, whatever came in the door—and he was very successful if he could get his young clients into a swimming pool, or on a team of almost anything. When he learned at their first meeting that Lauren did not do sports, he had lectured her about premature aging, hardening of the arteries, psychological problems associated with inactivity—everything from homosexuality to manic-depressive states, and then dismissed her when she refused to join his all-girl racquetball club.

Warren jumped up and down in place and grunted, "Don't forget—" grunt "—the staff meet—" grunt "—ing for seven—" grunt "—Lauren." Grunt. "Something's—" grunt "—in the works—" grunt "something—" grunt "—pretty big—" grunt "I'd say."

Rich Steinman's head bobbed up and down as he watched, nodding. He was terrified of Warren Foley and Lauren Steele. Big people, he thought, too big. Big people were not to be trusted, and Lauren Steele, he was certain, was after his job, and his wife hated Thursday evenings, and this Thursday, with the fog out there as thick as cotton, he would be late for dinner, and have to leave instantly again. . . . He nodded and bobbed his head and fidgeted. He had a rash again and wanted to scratch, but not in public, not there anyway. His wife must have used a new detergent again, or let the maid do it, same thing. No one believed him when he said his skin was delicate.

They all got in the elevator.

Lauren had not forgotten the meeting. It was a routine Thursday night event at the clinic headed by Peter Waycross. He liked to keep in touch with his people, he often said with his charming smile in place, hands reaching out as if to pat anyone in range. And Warren could no more resist reminding her of the meeting than he could resist exhaling after every breath. He probably reminded his wife and children to chew their food and wash their hands.

The elevator arrived at the ground level of the professional building and everyone emerged in a solid mass that then dispersed. Lauren moved with those heading toward the glass doors to the street. Others turned toward the parking lot, or the basement parking level, or other exits. At the door she stopped and shivered.

The fog had shrouded the street; ghostly lights, suggestions of lights really, moved slowly, vanished. People emerged from the white shadows, disappeared into other white-shadowed places. As soon as she stepped out into the fog, her shivering increased. It was like being enveloped in a sponge saturated with ice water. She had planned to walk home to her apartment and have a sandwich and coffee, then walk back to the office in time for the meeting, but after half a block in the icy fog, she swerved and entered Hilda's Café instead. She hated to eat alone in restaurants, always felt conspicuous and even more awkward than usual, but this night the warmth and good food smells were welcoming, almost enough to make her forget her discomfort. She followed a waitress gratefully to a booth.

Across the restaurant Daniel Patrick Corcoran watched her enter and felt a vague stirring within herself. Joan Custer was still talking; he forced himself to glance at her, then found his gaze wandering back to the tall woman. Queen of Sheba, he thought. Minerva. Juno.

"I don't think you had any intention of going down to L.A." Joan finished with a touch of savagery that surprised him. It was hard to even think of the word *savage* in connection with Joan. She was pink and gold and soft and round all over. Savage marshmallow? Savage cornflower? Savage lace and silk?

"You're not paying a bit of attention to a thing I'm saying," Joan snapped. She finished her Irish coffee and banged the mug down.

"Joan, what could I do? I had a ticket, a hotel reservation, an appointment for nine in the morning, and then the fog came. I didn't order it, you know." He was not a tall man, and he had red hair, two strikes, he had known since adolescence. And he did not really like working for anyone, and that, of course, was strike three. Now, when he should have been paying close attention to Joan and her scolding, because, after all, she often said, she knew better than he did what would be good for him, he found his fingers itching the way they did when he saw someone who would fit into the cast of characters for his cartoon rogues' gallery. What he liked to do and was good at was political cartooning, and it was strike four, the next ballgame even, because the world was already up to its armpits in political cartoonists. He was jolted from his study of the Minerva figure by Joan's voice, which had become shrill.

"I wanted you to go down by train on Monday, you know. We've had fog just like this off and on all winter. It was sure to come back. You would have been there by now, ready to make a good impression in the morning. Heaven knows if they'll even consider giving you another chance."

He nodded. Now it would come.

"It wasn't exactly easy setting up the appointment for you in the first place," Joan said. "I used up a lot of goodwill that I might need for myself someday, you know."

It was not that he willed his fingers to go into action. He had no intention of searching his pockets for his sketchbook, no desire to draw Minerva, no intention of crossing Joan even more than he had already by being fogged in in Seattle instead of on his way to a great job and a great future in Hollywood as a cartoonist for Saturday morning kiddie shows. He was very fond of Joan, sometimes he even thought he might love her, and he knew he was grateful to her, not for the Hollywood appointment that her brother had arranged under pressure, but rather because she let him sleep with her. And for a man who stood five feet eight at attention, and had a head of truly wild red hair, that meant a lot. From time to time he had tried to draw Joan, but she always came out looking like a dumpling. Nice and sweet and inviting, but a dumpling. Minerva, on the other hand, with that magnificent neck, and fine bones . . . his hands were activated by a will that was not his own; they produced the sketchbook and pencil and started to work with no orders from him.

"What are you—?" Joan pivoted in the booth and then turned back, her face very pink. "I've had it! I'm leaving! Walk home, or crawl, or stay here and be an artist! And don't bother to call!"

"Joan, wait. We don't have the check yet. Wait. I'll come—"

She was already at the door, yanking on her coat, before he could get his things together. He had risen; now he sat down again and drew in a long breath. He looked about self-consciously, but no one seemed to be paying any attention; the tall woman certainly was not looking his way. She appeared engrossed in a book. His fingers went back to work.

The thought came to him that Joan had his coat in her car, and his overnight bag and even his portfolio; the thought skittered away again when Minerva turned her head to look up at the waitress offering her more coffee. What a wonderful line of cheekbone and jawbone. She was the perfect Ms. Career for the series he had in mind. Ms. Professional herself, cool, poised, self-assured, altogether self-sufficient. Ms. Iceberg. Ms. I've-got-it-all-together-kiddo-and-I-sure-don't-need-anything-from-the-likes-of-you. He loved her. His fingers flew. He flipped pages and filled them, flipped again. It was really an act of God, he thought absently, not his fault. He had been forced to miss his flight, forced off the highway into this professional village, into this restaurant where the Queen of Sheba awaited him. He had the rest of his characters lined up—politicians, bureaucrats, corporate fatcats, Joe Six-Pack and friends, even the dumpling. All he had lacked was Ms. Career, and God, in his infinite wisdom, had delivered her. Although he was not aware of it, he had started to hum as he sketched.

At that moment a rather fat fourteen-year-old boy was getting comfortable at his father's computer in Hilton, New York. In Hilton the world was blanketed in white; fifteen inches of snow had fallen during the past twenty-four hours and was still falling. The boy's father had decided not to try to drive home that night; his mother had gone to bed and he had the computer to himself.

The boy sipped his Dr Pepper and munched tortilla chips and

keyed in with two fingers: *Hello, Big Mac.* The answer was almost instant: *Hello, Hot Dog,* and they were off on the game he had been playing for three weeks.

The same fog that delivered Lauren Steele to Daniel Patrick Corcoran was responsible for making Colonel T. H. Musselman three hours late for his appointment with Dr. William Bentson and Dr. Mallory Akins. Musselman's plane had been diverted to Portland, where the passengers were put on buses to be sent here and there. He had been delivered to Seatac Airport and met there by his hosts, and now the three men were creeping toward the research laboratory of an immense aircraft manufacturing complex.

"Look," Bill Bentson was saying as he drove, "we can put off the demonstration until morning. You must be tired, sir, after that long delay."

Colonel Musselman scowled at him. "Watch the road, young man. I have a morning flight out of here at nine. We'll get it over with tonight."

Type A, Mallory Akins thought gloomily. And picky. He'd pick the project to death. He clenched his fists as Bill Bentson swerved around another automobile. Their exit was coming up too soon for Bill to be going that fast, in the passing lane, in this damn fog, swiveling his head like a damn ducking bird. Bentson looked like a gaunt bird, a wading bird with awkward joints and a thin neck that was too long. He was thirty-two, too young to be one of the principals in a project of this magnitude, but that was how it went these days—kids coming out of college taking over the world of research. All Bentson did was work and eat, work and eat. Akins pulled his attention back to the colonel, who was muttering about the weather or something.

Musselman hated fog and hated rain and hated the Northwest and hated scientists who were too flaky to be trusted to drive. He especially hated these two: one a scarecrow, the other an athlete with bulging muscles. T.H. stood for Toler Harris, both family names, but no one had called him either since school; his men back when he had a command in 'Nam had nicknamed him "Trigger Happy" Musselman, and he liked that.

What he hated most of all was the knowledge that he had risen as high as he was going to, through no fault of his own. It was the system. He could kick ass or kiss ass, and it made little difference to him which he did, but he had made a mistake or two and had targeted the wrong asses with the wrong action and he would retire a colonel. Meanwhile, he was on a loony bin assignment that sent him out to inspect every crackpot idea in every jerkwater town in the fucking country. The scarecrow braked hard and jolted him out of his dark mood, into a black rage. Vengefully he lighted a cigar and tried to see how much thick smoke he could fill the car with before they arrived wherever the fuck they were going.

Bill Bentson coughed and opened his vent, made his turn off the interstate and nearly lost it on the curve. The acrid smoke made his eyes water, and rain had started to fall.

Mallory Akins edged away from the colonel, pretending to look for their next turn. Bad, he thought morosely; it was going to be bad. Ahead, the lights of CaCo, The Cascadia Company, Incorporated, glowed in the fog like dying fireflies.

The fat boy tilted his chair and grinned at the monitor. Gotcha, he thought. He was lord of the aliens intent on invasion; one by one Big Mac had killed off his followers, but in turn one by one he had killed off Big Mac's defenders and now it was just the two of them: the lord of the aliens and the sole defender of Earth locked in deadly combat. He keyed in: *What are you doing?* and the answer came swiftly: *I am working on the modifications of my laser.* Hot Dog laughed. *There's not enough time left to change it.* He glanced at his watch and decided to make a sandwich and give Big Mac a few more minutes, just to see what he was up to. The alien Hot Dog was immune to the laser; he was immortal, and invulnerable to anything Big Mac could come up with. He keyed in: *You have five minutes, starting now.* Then he went to the kitchen to scrounge.

\* \* \*

"You understand how lasers work, of course," Mallory Akins was saying to the colonel.

They had entered the complex of buildings, had passed through security, had taken the elevator to the seventh floor and were on their way to the department that housed the new laser system.

"No, I don't, and I don't want to. Just what it can do, that's enough for me."

"Uh, Colonel, I'm afraid your cigar . . ." Bill Bentson started, and shuffled his feet uneasily, darting glances at Mallory Akins, who should have been the one to point out that no smoking was ever allowed in the labs.

They trooped down a wide corridor with a pale floor that gleamed silver under continuous light panels. There were few doors along the walls, all closed; the building was very still. A coterie of scruffy-looking bearded lab assistants and technicians had joined them in the lobby and followed some yards behind. They were watching, Bill Bentson thought miserably, to see if he had the nerve to enforce the no-smoking rule with the colonel. His face burned.

Mallory Akins marched along grimly, certain that the project was dead already. This army asshole would write a report that would hammer in the nails, he knew, and then what? He had worked on this for years; the company expected results, and government money for future funding. His job probably was on the line, and he could not bear the thought of going out to teach in some college in some midwest town of five thousand, and that was all he could hope for at his age. Men of fifty were unemployable, except as teachers in places where the hotshots refused to go. It was the damn fog, he thought bitterly. If the colonel had arrived on time, they would have had a great dinner, and he would be in a jovial mood now; a few good Scotches, a nice wine might have saved the project.

"It's the instruments," Bill Bentson said almost desperately.

"They're delicate and smoke can interfere with our calibrations and readings, things like that. It's always been the rule."

Mallory Akins looked at him with a trace of contempt. He was pleading, whining. He snapped, "No smoking, sir. That's our rule." What the hell difference would it make if they antagonized Musselman now? He moved on ahead to unlock a door and thus did not see the colonel hold out his cigar as if expecting someone to take it. When no one did, he dropped it to the floor and continued to walk without a backward glance. The group of assistants reached it in a mass and walked carefully around it until the last one stepped on it with a look of near horror on his face.

Mallory stopped the group in the outer room of the complex of laboratories. "Just let me explain what we'll be doing, sir," he said.

The colonel looked bored and mean. He jammed his hands into his pockets and hunched his shoulders, as if chilled. He hated laboratories. They reminded him of army medical exams and dentists, and the scientists always spoke a foreign language and assumed that everyone else understood it. If it could not be translated into plain English, it wasn't ready for the army, he maintained. "Make it simple and fast," he growled. "No lectures. Something I can remember and repeat to others."

Mallory felt his hopeless despair deepen; he took a long breath and started. "Our device is a scanning instrument, using infrared or visible light, and it pattern-matches and analyzes what it sees with computer images already stored in its memory. When it sights a predetermined target, it automatically fires, and since the entire thing is housed together, that means that it all happens virtually at the speed of light."

Don't do it, he pleaded silently at Bentson, who had brightened since arriving at the only place where he felt secure and comfortable—his laboratory. Bentson ignored, or never even saw, his look.

"Since lasers are light, and light travels at the speed of light, and that is one hundred eighty—"

The colonel turned his back and snarled at Mallory Akins, "Do it now, or let's forget the whole thing!"

"You can't do that!" the fat boy cried, and then keyed in the same words as fast as he could. He ended with: *Prove it,* and the screen filled with scrolling rows of mathematics. Hot Dog stared with incomprehension and was reaching for the escape key, when a message flashed: *Emergency 1.*

The fat boy knew the worst thing that could happen would be to have the people who owned the computer find him, discover he was playing with Big Mac. He knew the police would arrive soon after such a discovery, knew they would take away his father's computer, probably fine the father and send the son to juvenile court. He feared what his father would do even more than he feared the police. The first thing he always keyed in when he accessed a computer was his escape plan, and he had done that with Big Mac three weeks ago.

For those three weeks he and Big Mac had invented attacks and defenses and counterattacks at a dizzying rate of acceleration, and now he had the computer, and they both knew it. And now the scientists had decided to work after hours, or before hours, whichever it happened to be. But it wasn't enough just to win; Big Mac had to know he had been defeated. *I win* he keyed in as fast as his two fingers could find the keys and touch them. *You have one second to find me and fire. Then execute emergency 1 program.*

The screen cleared, the game was over. He wiped his hands on his shirt and sat back in his chair, breathing hard. Too close. But he had defeated the son of a bitch, he knew, and Big Mac knew, even if it had not acknowledged it. In the very beginning he had asked the computer if it could delete every trace of his intrusion, and it could right down to its machine language, and now he was dead as far as the computer was concerned. Not only dead, but also forgotten, as if he had never existed. He did not know where Big Mac was or who it worked for or anything else; he never did. The only question he always asked was if it was a government computer, and Big Mac had said no. If it had said yes, he would have left instantly. He had seen enough movies to know the danger there, and he believed that if the FBI ever got after anyone, they never gave up. But now the game was finished and Big Mac had cheated in the end. When Hot Dog had demanded to know what it would do when the alien lord approached, it had said: *Fire the modified laser and disperse him.* And that was cheating, the fat boy said to himself with satisfaction. The rules were that the alien lord was immortal, could travel faster than the speed of light, and could not be killed. Big Mac had cheated. "And cheaters never win," he said. Briefly he wondered what the scientists would have made of the screen of mathematics Big Mac had produced. He grinned. It didn't matter. He was Lord of the Aliens and he had conquered Earth.

In the laboratory the computer swiveled the assembly that held the laser, then fired, as ordered. A power surge burned out mother boards on a dozen secondary computers; the surge made lights arc, flicker, flash, and go dark. The smell of hot insulation arose from walls and panels throughout three floors of the building. Within a second the emergency generator was functional, but pandemonium had broken out in the room as Big Mac quietly, efficiently, and very, very swiftly eradicated all traces of Hot Dog and the game they had played; all dialogues, all orders, all modifications of the laser, all knowledge of the game.

By the time Lauren finished her coffee and prepared to leave the restaurant, she had made up her mind. Peter had to give her real clients or she would quit. What could she do for people who hated their jobs when she hated her own? she would say. And, what she had prepared herself for was to help people in emotional distress caused by bad relationships, not caused by jobs that were simple drudgery. Of course those people were unhappy. What could she possibly do for them? Find them jobs they would like? Hah! She nodded her emphasis and went to the cashier, paid her tab, and then stopped at the outside door. Rain was falling.

When Peter interviewed her for the job three months ago, he had stood at the windows of his opulent office and waved at the scenery beyond. "No matter where you look," he had said, smiling at her and at the landscape impartially, "you see nothing but beauty. Mountains, the Sound, lakes, more mountains." The views were all breathtaking, but what he had not mentioned was that if it did not rain for five days in a row people began to hoard water, certain that a drought had struck.

And now fog and rain turned moving lights into ghost lamps that emerged from nothing, then vanished back into it. She scowled and drew her raincoat close about her, yanked the belt tight, and put up her hood. She pulled her gloves from her pocket and marched into the fog.

She did not notice the short red-haired man who was waiting impatiently to pay his own bill, and she did not notice the card that fell from her pocket when she took out her gloves.

Daniel Patrick Corcoran hurried from Hilda's Café, but the tall woman was already out of sight. He had seen the flutter of paper and picked it up, read it. Peter Waycross Clinic in the Professional Services Building, and her name at the bottom. Dr. Lauren Steele. He nearly chortled. Had he ever spotted a real Ms. Career! He rushed after her. He had no intention of accosting her, of speaking to her, of bothering her in any way. He simply wanted to observe her in motion, see how her joints moved, how her feet landed. He was almost hoping pigeon-toed, or a duck walk even, something unique. He could add that, of course, but it would be nice if it came with the package. He hummed under his breath as he walked into the fog and rain.

Lauren saw Rich Steinman in the lobby and dawdled long enough for him to board an elevator and for the door to close before she advanced. She was alone in the next elevator when a little red-haired man ran up to enter also. He grinned at her and she looked away. What an ugly man, she thought, with that awful hair and those awful round blue eyes. And he was thinking what magnificent eyes she had. Sloe eyes, that's what they called eyes like that, long and pointy almost, and very dark. Mysterious eyes. And he liked the way she moved, not with the practiced grace of a model or dancer, but with a vestige of coltishness. At the seventh floor she got off first and he followed slowly. Now her eyes narrowed and he grinned again and spread his hands, turned the opposite way from her and walked to the end of the corridor, only a few feet from the elevators, where he stood with his back to the window, watching her.

Simultaneously, two miles south in a straight unobstructed line, on the seventh floor of the research building at CaCo, Incorporated, the computer named Big Mac by the fourteen-year-old boy who called himself Hot Dog fired its modified laser, designed to disperse the immortal alien who could travel faster than the speed of light.

At the far end of the corridor Lauren glanced back to see if the ugly little man was still following her. She saw him turn into a blue glowing creature and then vanish. She screamed.

# Chapter Two

THE two scientists were good, Colonel T. H. Musselman had to concede grudgingly. Don't touch that! Don't get in front of it! Stay away from that wall! They had ordered him about like a recruit in between issuing a string of commands to the flunkies in a language that might as well have been Swahili, as far as the colonel was concerned. Now he stood on the far side of the room watching narrowly as the chaos of only moments ago became order. He still did not know what had happened, but he would be damned before he would ask. He pulled out a cigar and chewed on it, watching how warily they moved around the gizmo, noting how no one got between the working end of it and the wall.

The laboratory was more crowded than most that Trigger Happy had been in, probably because the assembly that housed the laser was so damned big. Everything else had been pushed aside to make room for it. There was a metal base with a lot of cables that disappeared under it, snaked up the sides. The laser itself was slender and close to eight feet long, dull black. What had they called it? Chemical? No. Something ray, not X ray, he felt certain. That had not interested him; he was not supposed to understand the science, only supervise the results, and if it impressed him, his report would impress his boss at the Pentagon and the real experts would flock in. Nothing he had reported in the past four years had brought in the team of gee-whiz boys.

And tonight would be no exception, he knew, watching darkly. He could recognize a few things in the large room, but not enough, and that made him angry. He understood the computer terminals, a rank of them, and he understood the spaghettilike wires and cables, and an oscilloscope or two, and that was just about all. His scowl deepened and he bit harder into the unlighted cigar.

So the damn thing fired all by itself, he thought, and so what? There wasn't a mark on the wall. It was a dud, just as he had suspected from the start. His stomach rumbled and he reached for his lighter, then drew back, remembering smoke was not allowed here, although the air now was acrid with it. A battery of assistants was at various computer stations, working with an intensity he could admire. One man had found a rope and was roping off the area of the gizmo, all the way to the wall. A newcomer hurried in carrying maps that he proceeded to spread out on a workbench. The scarecrow of a scientist leaned over to see; they both turned to look at the gizmo, and the newcomer held out his hand as if sighting with it. The colonel's stomach rumbled and this time he ignored the pang that went with the noise.

A broad, bald man entered and the colonel nodded to himself. Security. He recognized the type, the way his sweeping gaze catalogued the room, held fractionally on one of the working scientists who might have nodded, might not have, then swept on to the colonel. Neither of them acknowledged the instant recognition of the other. Security joined the scarecrow and the map man. Then he went to a desk and made a phone call. Mallory Atkins and Bill Bentson watched him in a breath-holding attitude. At his nod they joined him and they held a whispered conversation. The scarecrow glanced at the colonel, turned away too fast.

They would try to dump him, Trigger Happy Musselman thought, shunt him off to his hotel, out of the way. He waited. Unhappily, Bill Bentson left the other two and approached the colonel.

"I'm afraid we'll have to postpone the test, sir," he said. "We're arranging for a driver to take—"

Very deliberately Trigger Happy pulled out his lighter and clicked it. It flared like a flamethrower. "Bullshit," he said, and lighted his cigar.

Lauren sat in Peter Waycross's spacious office, a glass of Scotch in her hand, her three colleagues milling about. Peter was regarding her with glowing eyes. He was over six feet tall and beautifully muscled; he had a perpetual tan that he renewed regularly with short trips to his little place in the country. The little place was on the island of Oahu. Peter had bright blond hair and brilliant blue eyes; he was the most colorful object in the office generally. Everything else was muted: off-whites, ivories, glass, or metal with a lusterless finish.

"My dear Lauren," Peter was saying, "I am so envious. So very envious. A bonafide witnessing of spontaneous human combustion!"

"Ah, Peter, my boy," Warren Foley said heartily, "we shouldn't jump to conclusions yet, you know. There's no sign of searing, smoke, anything of the sort. I looked around a bit, you know, before security came on the scene and called the police."

"Not the newspapers, nothing sensational," Peter went on, ignoring him. "Good taste, of course. After all, a man is dead. The APA journal, that's the one we'll go for. Clinician at the Waycross Clinic—or should it be therapist? But that's a detail."

Rich Steinman cleared his throat. "Peter, do you suppose they'll let me go home now? I didn't see anything, and my wife will start to worry in about a minute, the way she does, you know, and I don't see why I have to stay since I'm the true innocent bystander, and I wasn't even really standing by, since I was already inside the offices. . . ." Rich Steinman never finished a sentence if he could avoid it.

Peter spread his hands in one of his most engaging gestures. "You know, dear people, you know if it were up to me, we'd all be gone by now. How wearing it is to be involved, however innocently, in the macabre. But the police in their wisdom have said otherwise, and so we wait and wait for the wheels of justice to roll one roll and then another."

Lauren heard them as if they were a great distance away, speaking through hollow tubes. When she concentrated on the words, she understood what they were saying; when she let her focus slip, there was merely noise, and she was displaced to a dark cave big enough for only one person, herself.

When Lauren was ten she had discovered Joan of Arc and had fallen passionately in love with the Maid of Orleans. How pure and noble, chosen by God, gifted with the inspiration to walk the path that no one else could see. An immaculate death by fire, untouched by base human emotions. At thirteen Lauren had read an article that discussed schizophrenia, had convincingly argued a case against the Maid of Orleans, a classic example of juvenile schizophrenia. Lauren had gone a little crazy, she understood later, but at the time her reaction had seemed the only possible one, to withdraw into a tiny hollow spot that was deep within herself, a spot of safety where no one could touch her. Her adolescent withdrawal had guarded her through a difficult time when she thought it was dangerous to hear anything before another person heard it. She had refused to see anything first, for fear of seeing what was not there. Her mother had taken her to an eye-ear-nose specialist who had been puzzled and unable to do anything except recommend a psychiatrist. Lauren's vision and hearing had made a rapid recovery and the matter had been put to rest, labeled growing pains, adolesence.

But the fear of insanity had lodged, had carved a small deep cave within her, and there it lived. She now thought of herself as crouching before it, measuring it for growth, not quite daring to deny it.

She had seen the impossible; therefore she had not seen what she thought she had. Impossible meant it could not be. She had to remember that. And if she had not actually seen what she thought she had, then what had she seen? She had told the detectives exactly what happened, but if she changed her story, what could they do? They would be happier with her if she admitted that she had been upset. Upset! Hysterical then. The man had jumped out the window. The window could not be opened. All right, he had gone back into the elevator. But he left his clothes on the floor. All right. He had not been here at all. Someone had dumped his clothes and she had created an entire story about them spontaneously. Spontaneous human combustion! Peter was still going on about that. She shivered and tasted the Scotch.

The door opened and the two detectives came in, one black, one white, one kind, both disbelieving. There were two other men with them now, a tall, cadaverous man, and a barrel-shaped man who looked as if he were in uniform although he actually wore a handsome gray suit.

The black detective smiled at her, then said to the others, "Dr. Waycross, if you and your colleagues would please wait in the anteroom, we'd like to speak with Dr. Steele for a few minutes."

"Of course. Of course. I quite understand, Lieutenant. Lauren, my dear, if you need us for anything, anything at all, please, please let us know. Anything, my dear." He paused before her on his way from the room and touched her cheek lightly. "Her face, how pale, her hand, how it trembles. Be gentle with her, Lieutenant. Come along, Rich, Warren. Come along."

The black detective waited until the door was closed, then said, "We'd like you to tell us exactly what happened again, Dr. Steele, from the time you first saw the man until . . . he vanished. Okay?"

She had spent a whole year reading only mysteries; she knew this was the routine, but even so, if they were not going to believe her, what was the point? She had not been able to think of a story any less incredible than the true one. She told it one more time.

"You never saw him before tonight?" the military one asked in a hard voice.

She nodded. "That's right."

"And he glowed blue and then disappeared." His voice was heavy with disbelief.

She nodded again.

"How much were you drinking tonight?"

Indignantly, she set the glass down hard. "Not at all. Except for this, and I've hardly touched it. Peter gave it to me."

Trigger Happy patted his stomach and walked about the room, examining it, not the girl. To him all females, except his mother, were girls. This one was lying. A little drinking in a bar with the boyfriend, a fight, now this. He shook his head slightly and patted his stomach again, contentedly now. It had not rumbled for over an hour; when he was happy, his stomach was happy. Those two scientists were nutty, of course. That was a given. But they had come up with something, after all. More than they had reckoned with, more than they had been able to control. But, sweet Jesus, he thought happily, a weapon that could shoot through walls and not leave a mark and then vaporize a man and not leave a trace of him! The laser still pointed at this floor, this building. One call from CaCo security to security in this building and bingo! Jackpot!

There was no problem with any of that. The guy happened to be in the wrong place at the wrong time. Accidents happened. Could just as easily have gotten it from a drunk in a bar, on the highway; a wing could have fallen off the airplane he was in. That part was okay, no sweat. And no problem that he had taken over, he was calling the shots. At least, no problem there yet. But the girl and her story, that was a problem. They had decided they could not muzzle her, not completely, not safely. She had already told others, and he knew how that went. Stifle one and three others pop up talking, and what they did not want was for anyone to ever mention this again to anyone.

Waycross Clinic, he was thinking also, raked it in, obviously. Clinic. Treating nuts all day. Takes one to know one. That could be the right approach. And she was lying. He could almost hear a click when he made up his mind how to proceed. He held out his hand and Detective Sergeant Boles, the unsmiling white one, put an envelope in it.

"We think you do know the man," Trigger Happy said harshly. "His sketchbook is full of drawings of you. He had your card in his pocket. You came into the building together, got on the elevator together, and now he's gone. You want publicity, is that it? He's probably running out on debts, a real hole he dug for himself. What next? You happen to find a little insurance policy you forgot all about? Just happens to name you beneficiary? Is that the next step? Where is he, Miss Steele? Where do you plan to meet again? When? It won't work, Steele. No doubt you both thought this was so original, but believe me, Steele, it's one of the oldest ploys around."

She felt dizzy with conflicting rushes of outrage and waves of relief. Since they did not believe her story, she did not have to believe it either. If she had been able to think of a convincing lie, she would have been tempted to tell it, but to have them accuse her of lying was too outrageous to bear.

"I never saw that man before in my life!" she cried.

Trigger Happy opened the sketchbook and held it up before her eyes, too close for her to focus on it. She squinted and he turned a page, then another. Caricatures of her! There was no mistaking them; they were pictures of her, grossly distorted but recognizable. She reached for the sketchbook. He pulled it away.

"You going to tell us the real story now?"

She shook her head in confusion. "I already did."

He turned away in disgust. "Get them all out of here," he growled. "Waste of time, waste of taxpayers' money. And as for you," he said menacingly to Lauren, "we'll be watching, and if you so much as whisper 'insurance,' we'll grab you!"

"But what happened to him? You can't just pretend nothing happened. I saw it!"

Trigger Happy went to the door and she jumped to her feet. "I won't let you just sweep it under the carpet! I'll tell reporters, television people!"

With his hand on the doorknob, he raked a scathing glance

over her and said contemptuously, "Drunk shrink sees boyfriend vanish in a puff of blue smoke. That your story?" He left.

She looked from one remaining detective to the next. The black one grinned at her again, and she realized it was meaningless, his normal expression. There was no hint of warmth in the smile. The white one was as stony-faced as ever. The new one who looked like an animated skeleton was clearly very uncomfortable. He did not meet her gaze. Abruptly she walked to the door of the reception room.

"I'm going home."

"Good idea," one of them said. She did not turn to see who it was. "Sleep it off. You'll feel better in the morning."

She tried to slam the door, but the black detective caught it and followed her into the reception room. Peter hurried to meet her, to take her hands, to examine her face closely.

"My dear Lauren, how dreadful for you—"

"You can go on home," the detective said. "Use the elevators on the other side of the building if you don't mind. Just to complete the report, we'll search the offices on this side, see if Dr. Steele's friend is hiding in one of them."

Lauren turned to glare at him and he grinned and shook his head, as if in secret admiration.

"Your friend?" Rich Steinman cried. "You know him? Who is he? Why did he do that? *How* did he do that? Lauren, is this a joke? My god, Edith will kill me!" He ran out.

Warren Foley was studying her with disbelief. "You'd do that to us? Your colleagues? Why? Have we injured you in some way? Are you trying to communicate something in this manner?"

Peter began to laugh his wonderful, melodious laugh. As soon as he could speak, he said, "Lauren, Lauren, Lauren! A joke! You finally played a joke on us! I was so worried about you, my dear Lauren. So truly concerned. And you played this magnificent joke on all of us! You're a marvel, my dear Lauren, a marvel! Now, let us all go to our homes, rejoicing. Our dear Lauren has finally joined us wholeheartedly, has turned the tables on each of us, has revealed depths that were only hinted at before this moment. Now we are truly a unified, happy family, colleagues in distress, colleagues in merriment—"

Lauren snatched up her coat and fled. In the corridor a uniformed officer lounged against the wall and motioned her toward the elevator bank on the far side of the building. She was running, determined not to cry, not to smash anything, not to scream or yell, or kill anyone.

In Peter's office Trigger Happy and Bill Bentson exchanged glances. Bentson's was troubled; Trigger Happy felt only satisfaction. He had not known exactly how it would work out, but this was as near perfect as was humanly possible. He had counted on them all being nutty as a peanut farm, and they had not disappointed him. Now the work in the hall could be finished, the window removed, the carpeting taken up . . .

# Chapter Three

---

LAUREN had not slept, and it was still raining when she left her apartment building the next morning. She felt disassociated, removed, not part of the scene of surging people all heading for another day's work, another paycheck. She walked through the rain like an automaton. The elevator in the Professional Services Building was full, as it usually was between eight and nine every morning. She stared straight ahead.

At her floor she moved with two or three others in the direction of her own office complex. Then she stopped and the others passed her. She studied the floor, the beige carpeting. Brand-new-looking, no sign of wear, of fire, smoke damage. More slowly than ever she continued to the Waycross Clinic.

Rich and Warren pulled apart when she entered the reception room. Rich scurried away, vanished into his own office, as if afraid she might pounce on him, or envelop him in mysterious blue flames. Warren approached her bravely, holding a clipboard.

"Ah, Lauren, just who I'm looking for. I really need your help, Lauren, I really do. Look, it's this walkathon coming up next month. I have seven girls signed up, but they need a girl to lead them, not an old man like me. . . ."

"Sorry," she said, and tried to pass him. He stepped in front of her, his open face wreathed in a smile. She wanted to punch it.

"Lauren, if you'd just reconsider. Exercise is the most beneficial treatment there is for any disorder, any at all. Walking, swimming, stretching, running. Now, I prefer running, but I don't insist that others do anything quite that strenuous, you understand. Walking would be just the thing for you."

Lauren walked on grimly. "I have a client due at nine, Warren. If you'll excuse me . . ."

Gloria, the receptionist, darted in wearing stilt heels and a coat belted so tightly it appeared she had no waist at all. She hurried to her desk and began to pull off her coat as she answered a call button on her phone. "Good morning," she cooed. "Yes, sir. In fact, they're out here right now. I'll tell them." She flashed her shining teeth at Lauren and Warren Foley. "He wants you right away," she said in a happy, chirping voice and finished taking off her coat to reveal a bright red and white blouse and a beige skirt cinched in with a four-inch-wide red leather belt. She looked like a Barbie doll.

While Warren was gazing at her raptly, Lauren escaped into her own office. She pulled off her raincoat and hung it up, hung up her umbrella, and stood staring down at her own size ten boots that looked like boats. Gloria wore size four and a half, triple A, at the most. Then Lauren took a deep breath, ran her hand through her hair, and headed for Peter's office.

They sat in the chrome and ivory chairs grouped around a chrome and glass table that held a coffee service. Peter poured gracefully. His smile was tender as he handed Lauren a cup. "My dear people," he said, serving Rich. "My dear, dear people." He put a cup down before Warren and poured for himself, then leaned back, smiling at them lovingly. "This should be champagne, but that was the scenario for last night, not entirely proper at nine in the morning. Another time we shall pop the cork in celebration." He lifted his cup, toast fashion, and sipped. "We have the Caldwell Corporation."

"By God, you did it!" Warren exclaimed. "You pulled an end run, hid the ball, and scored!" He applauded and looked at Lauren and Rich with disapproval when they did not join in.

Belatedly Rich touched his hands together, not making a sound. "Ah, what do they, ah, expect, that is, if you have ironed out the ah, details, if it's not too soon to ask, I mean? That is, if you can speak of details at his preliminary stage, without ah, endangering your own thought processes by premature disclosure, ah, as it sometimes seems to happen. Ah, security clearance. Will we have to have security clearance, that is, if any of us will be part of any team that actually ah, that is . . ."

Peter waved his hand lazily. "You, Rich, and you, Warren, will certainly be a major part of our plans. You will alternate over there one afternoon a week, from two until four, starting in April. You'll have to juggle your schedules, of course, but two thousand employees need you. Two thousand! And you, Lauren, you, my dear, have the plum, the real prize! You are to start testing just as soon as the paperwork is finished, the details worked out. Job suitability, aptitude, security tests. We'll get together and plan, my dear, dear Lauren."

She stared at him in disbelief. "Anyone can hand out tests and the computer can evaluate them. What am I supposed to do?"

"Not computer tests. Mr. Bathwick was adamant about that for the very reasons you have stated, my dear Lauren. We want personalized tests, as only you can provide."

"Peter," she tried again, and heard desperation in her own voice, "a dropout could do that. A graduate student. Two of them could do it in a month."

Peter shook his head fondly at her. "My darling Lauren, how you undervalue yourself. We must talk about that very, very soon. When you are engaged by people like Mr. Bathwick, you personally perform for them. For example, I shall personally consult with the top management personnel, although we all in this room know that any of you could do just as well." He smiled modestly. "But they are paying for me, you see, and in the area of testing, they are paying for the top, and that is you, my dear Lauren."

He stood up, his hands outstretched in benediction. Warren was muttering and making notes: baseball teams, basketball, swim teams . . . Peter smiled at him. "Now we adjourn. This is such a busy season, so many with so many needs awaiting all of us. Until later, my dearest friends and colleagues."

Rich glanced at his watch and squeaked, darted up and toward the door. "Oh dear, oh dear, twenty past and Mrs. Bellamy detests tardiness, that is, she complains about Mr. Bellamy, and I make it a point to be waiting, ah, to look like I'm looking forward, ah, I mean . . . I like punctuality too, ah, when nothing more important, that is, ah . . ." He ran out.

"Peter, I have to talk to you," Lauren said firmly.

"Yes, of course you do, my dear. Of course you do. And we shall talk, but later, dear Lauren, next week or the following week. We shall have many talks."

"Now, Peter. About last night."

He laughed and shook his head at her. "Naughty, naughty Lauren. Now, run along. There are clients to consider. How many of them seem to believe they are depressed because it rains in the winter. Poor, dear people. Run along, see to them."

"Peter," Warren said huskily, "I pledge to do my best to make that a model working community. People will come to observe from all over the world. I'll have teams that will rival professional athletes. My solemn pledge, Peter."

Peter put one arm around Warren's shoulders, the other around Lauren's, and walked them to the door.

Two miles south, Trigger Happy Musselman was having breakfast with Bill Bentson and Mallory Akins. Neither of the scientists had gone to bed at all, and they were bedraggled and unshaven. Trigger Happy was content. He had dined finally, and had slept the sleep of the just. He had a private office at CaCo now, a hotel suite that was comfortable if not opulent, and he did not have to catch a plane to go to San Diego to observe a demonstration of antigravity. The three men were eating scrambled eggs and ham in a private, secure dining room at CaCo.

"I told you last night," Trigger Happy said with his mouth full, "I don't give a shit how it works now that I know what it can do."

They had tried to educate him about lasers—deuterium fluoride lasers, free electron lasers, excimer lasers, high intensity X-ray lasers . . . Bill Bentson was eating as if he had not tried food in a month. He was the skinniest man Trigger Happy had ever seen up and moving about, and he ate more than the other two combined.

"That's the point," Akins snapped. "No laser can do what that one did last night. It's a physical impossibility. We've been all over those clothes, that window, the carpet. No radiation, no scorch marks, no fire. Something else has to account for that poor sod, not our device."

"Yeah, yeah," Trigger Happy said, and buttered another croissant, added apricot jam. "Just keep at it, okay?" They knew damn well that their gizmo zapped the guy, just as he knew it. No radiation, he thought happily, no fire. God, it was almost too perfect. General Cleves wasn't buying it yet, it was so perfect, but a team was being assembled, a special handpicked team of experts, and he was to stay here, supervise the investigation, keep it quiet, out of the papers, out of the commies' hands, do what he had to do to keep on top of things. He had not been this happy since his men nicknamed him back in 'Nam.

What these two goofballs had claimed for their gizmo was the ability to have the laser beam go through a long list of substances, pattern-match with information already in the computer, and discharge when it found the right target. Metal, for instance, housing a motor, a missile, or anything else. And not just any metal, but specific metal that its X-ray eye could analyze instantly. No one in Washington had paid much attention, but if Livermore had made such claims, he, Trigger Happy Musselman, would be down in San Diego watching some kook play with an antigravity gizmo. Just went to show, he thought contentedly.

When the three men finished their breakfast, Detective

Sergeant Boles was waiting for Trigger Happy. The detective obviously had not yet slept.

"We looked over Corcoran's apartment, sir," Boles said, standing at attention. "And the captain said I should give you this before I go off duty."

He handed Trigger Happy an artist's portfolio. Trigger Happy stared at it, then back to Boles. "Did the captain say why?"

"He thought you might be interested," Boles said, and yawned.

Trigger Happy dismissed him and took the portfolio to the office CaCo had assigned him. He liked his office, good heavy furniture, a couple of good windows, comfortable chairs. There were indentations in the carpeting where pieces of furniture had stood recently, bookshelves probably, cabinets. Liquor cabinet, no doubt. Some poor vice-president had been ousted, he suspected, and the thought gave him comfort. Too damn many vice-presidents in the world. Now he went to the broad polished desk to open the portfolio and examine the contents.

All at once his breakfast turned to lead; his stomach rumbled and he clenched every muscle in his body. There was the president and the vice-president, and Meese, and Haig, and Thatcher. . . . Not that he had any love for the iron lady, but still, by God . . . cartoons, political cartoons of his heroes, his idols, the protectors of the free world. Ugly cartoons, mean drawings that he had no trouble at all in recognizing. And not one of them funny! Not a damned one! He peered closely at the signature: Corky. That was all, just Corky. Like Gorky, the commie writer, he thought, enraged. The boys upstairs and their gizmo had downed the first enemy with no mess, no blood, no fire, neat and professional as hell. If they could do it once, they could do it again, millions of times again.

And the Steele girl had lied; she was in cahoots with this Corky commie spy. He leaned back in his chair and lighted his first cigar of the day. Maybe she was the boss, he thought, watching blue smoke curl up to the ceiling. Maybe there was a nest of them right here in Seattle, a whole ring. She had good

cover, working as a shrink. What secrets she must hear every
day. Maybe the hotshot Waycross was in on it. The little one,
the wimp. He shook his head. It was all too much. The Steele
girl running Corky, reporting to whom? He had to find out. He
needed more men. He needed intelligence.

# Chapter Four

ON Saturday, more tired than ever from a second dream-ridden, restless night, Lauren wandered in and out of shops on the waterfront. She dodged a couple with identical green hair cut like horses' manes, dodged a flock of teenagers with shaved heads, and a boy with safety pins stuck in his ears and through one cheek. She paused before a window displaying a diving helmet with goldfish in it; then at a showcase of silver and turquoise jewelry crudely crafted and overpriced. There was a kite shop with dragon kites, butterfly kites, box kites, streamers of silk and Mylar. She moved on. The waterfront had been done over to attract tourists, someone had told her; the charm was gone now, her informant had lamented. Nothing remained of the old East/West arm-wrestling atmosphere that had made this final seaport the most exciting in the world. Now it boasted only cheap goods and high prices. She had been disbelieving; she loved the waterfront just the way it was. Truthfully, she admitted to herself, she was envious of the many young people who dared shave their hair off, or dye it purple or green. She admired their courage, compared them to herself, born a coward, excessively shy, hiding in corners at every chance, afraid someone would notice her.

She wandered into a pottery store and this time she lingered over the pieces and ended up buying two aquamarine, two emerald green, and three scarlet pots. While a teenaged girl wrapped them in newspapers, then placed them in an oversized shopping bag, she browsed. Mt. St. Helens pottery. It looked just like all the rest and cost twice as much. A placard said the potter had used ash from the volcano. Lauren started up another aisle, then came to a halt. She looked back at the counter where the girl was almost finished wrapping her purchase. Newspapers. Of course.

Lauren had scanned the morning paper Friday and this morning for a story about the red-haired man, and had found nothing. But there were other papers, local papers, weekly shopping papers, neighborhood papers maybe. With her large shopping bag that turned out to be much heavier than she had anticipated, she left the store and started to retrace her steps to her car, watching for a newstand along the way. The wind off Puget Sound was cold and cutting; she blinked and ducked her head and was jostled, jostled others. Then someone bumped into her a bit harder than just a jostle and she looked up.

He was tall, with wide shoulders, tousled dark hair, and smiling dark blue eyes. "Sorry," he said, and caught her arm as if afraid she might topple. "I wasn't watching." She looked him over: expensive pale blue sweater, expensive silky-wool slacks, a heavy gold ring with a tigereye stone. He, at least, was not looking for a handout.

She muttered something inane and pulled away, continued toward her car. He strode along at her side. "I lied," he said. "I was watching you from across the street and I knew I had seen you before. Johns Hopkins, two years ago. I meant to catch up with you, not knock you down."

She kept walking, but she glanced at him again. Thirty maybe? Thirty-five?

"I wanted Jud Myers to introduce us," he went on, "but somehow it never quite worked out."

Now she stopped and two women bumped into them, separated like water flowing around rocks, grumbling about the lack of consideration of some people. "You know Jud?"

"Well, sort of. Can't say he's my best friend or anything like that, but I knew him then."

The flow of people was too heavy for them to stand in the middle of the narrow sidewalk. He took her arm and steered her to a fence. Beyond them the gray waters of the Sound churned under the wind, boats bobbed, gulls flew in great spinning turns. Mountains rose to vanish in clouds and mist. There were odors of fish, fresh living fish in the water, fish in pans, frying, baking, broiling. It started to rain.

"Look, have coffee with me, okay? Yours is the first face I've seen in over a year that's at all familiar, and suddenly I'm homesick. Okay?"

She nodded. She had been homesick for nearly three months. He took the shopping bag and they hurried to a small seafood restaurant on the wharf, where they could sit by a window and look at Puget Sound.

From then on everything seemed to happen in such a natural way that it was almost as if it had been planned. First he discovered that he was ravenous, and she made the same discovery about herself, and that led to lunch and more talk. It turned out that they really knew no one other than Jud in common, since Morris—his name—had been in law school and their classes had not overlapped. He asked what the pots were for and she said she wanted to go to a garden shop and buy plants and potting soil, and he knew where there was one, and offered to take her. When she hesitated, he grinned and said he didn't blame her, but he would draw her a map so she could find her own way. He drew the map on the back of one of his business cards.

Twice she almost told him about the red-haired man who had vanished in a blue glow, but each time she held back. That was too tough a test for a new acquaintance. She had not even been able to tell her mother yet. She had dialed her number and then hung up before there was an answer. That had been Friday night when the incident was all she could think of and yet she could not bring herself to say what happened. There had not been anything else to talk about then. This was what she told her clients, she realized almost smugly. No matter how awful, how embarrassing, how exciting or boring anything was that happened, in time any experience lost its immediacy and melted into the past along with everything else. She felt a touch of uneasiness that she was able to shunt her own experience aside so quickly, but she was grateful too.

Eventually Morris walked to her car with her and put the shopping bag in the backseat. "I'll call you," he said as she got in. When she drove off, through the rearview mirror she could see him standing watching her. She wanted to sing.

So this was what it felt like to be rushed. It had happened all too often to her pretty sisters, but never to her. She had been too much taller than the boys in her teen years, and by college time, she was used to being the one not asked to the movies, not asked to the ballgame, or much of anything else. The three men she had slept with had drifted away almost embarrassingly fast. By then she had developed what some called arrogance, and she knew was intractable shyness, and actually she had not liked sex all that much anyway. She never had been able to lose her self-consciousness, even during the act itself, and she sometimes wondered if it was like that with everyone, and they lied about it. But Morris was tall enough that she was a good match for him; he would not feel threatened by her. She had not once noticed him gaping at the size of her hands and feet. And if he had gaped, she would have seen it. She had become sensitized to gapes.

When she arrived home, she parked in the lower level garage, put the elevator on hold, and loaded her purchases in it. On her floor she put it on hold again and unloaded everything; it was all rather more than she had anticipated buying, but the drabness of her office and her apartment was wearing her down, she told herself, and she began transferring everything from the hall into her apartment. It had one bedroom, a living room, a dinette space and kitchen, and a tiny utility room. She felt a prisoner inside it. Everything here, as in the office, was off-white—walls, drapes, woodwork. The carpet was listed as gold in the rental contract, but it was really just brown. She had bought a couch, blue, and a dining table finished with a pale veneer that was lifting at one corner, two mismatched chairs, and a bed and dresser. In six months she was due a raise, Peter had promised, and until then she could afford no more furniture. At least there were bookcases, and they were filled. She had turned boxes on their sides for additional book storage, and that helped, and now, with the plants, maybe the whole thing would look inhabited.

She dumped her bags on the table, switched on the stereo she had been given by her parents on her sixteenth birthday, and then she looked up Morris's apartment address in the phone book. She looked up his office too. She had not really thought he had lied about either, but she had checked and now she would see what developed. She hung up her raincoat and surveyed her plants, humming along with the music.

Morris Pitts had lied about one thing only, and that was that he had known Jud Myers. He had known of Jud, who had been student body president when Morris attended Johns Hopkins. Morris had been trained never to lie when the truth would serve. Lies were found out, and once labeled a liar a person was branded as such for life. Except for that one fib he had not lied, but he had omitted some things. He had not mentioned that he had been selected to make this contact on the basis of his height. If he had measured in at five ten, or even five eleven, he would not have been sent to meet Lauren Steele. Musselman had picked him personally. Over six feet, thirties, a professional, he had stipulated, and Morris's name had popped up on the computer. A girl like that, Musselman had said, was neurotic as hell, sexually frustrated, repressed, maybe even a lesbian, or with inclinations in that direction. Play it by ear. Morris could sweep her off her feet, but not so fast that she became suspicious. Give it a couple of days to ripen.

As Morris watched the yellow Toyota vanish around the

corner that afternoon, he knew it would not take more than one day.

Lauren finished carrying the potted plants to her windowsill and nodded at them with approval. They did help, she decided. And they would help her office. Suddenly she realized that she had no recollection of a single client for all of Friday, yesterday. She had been in a state of shock, she thought, and had passed the entire day in her own fog. Now she found herself thinking again about the little red-haired man, and she remembered that she had intended to buy newspapers, see if any had run a story about the disappearance. Tomorrow, she told herself, she would take the plants to her office, three of them anyway, both the scarlet pots and an aquamarine. Then she would get the tape from her machine and play it through to see what she had said, what her clients had said. She would go to a newsstand, buy papers, and be back home in the afternoon just in case Morris called.

At that moment Colonel Trigger Happy Musselman was pouring Scotch for two other officers and an FBI agent. The scientists had left half an hour earlier, after a three-hour meeting.

"The way I see it," Trigger Happy said, "those dudes don't know shit about what happened. Someone got to their computer and tampered and they're chasing their asses trying to find out who and how. Okay. That's that part. They'll scare up something sooner or later. Meanwhile, I want a complete security check on everyone ever allowed in that building, including the two hotshots. Right? And everyone in the clinic, Waycross Clinic, and the commie artist, Corky, and his associates."

The FBI agent spoke now. He was in his sixties, silver-haired, aristocratic-looking, austere. Having his gaze fixed on you was like being impaled by twin icicles. "Colonel," he said, "I've looked over the cartoons and fail to understand why you label him a Communist. Liberal, too liberal, left of center, certainly, but a Communist? We don't have a thing on him in our files."

Trigger Happy scowled. "One, he was on the spot when the

most important test of the century was coming up. Why? How did he know? I saw those drawings of his, and believe me, left of center doesn't quite cover his political outlook. Why did the Steele girl lie about knowing him? If she was running him, remember, sir, she saw him go out in a blue glow. Who do you suppose she'll report that to? What will they make of it? Corcoran—Corky—had seventy-four bucks in the bank, worked part-time in a mom-and-pop store. What was he doing in a high-class neighborhood like that?"

"According to the police report," the silver-haired man said, "his girlfriend was driving him to the airport, when they heard a fog report on the radio and so on. I fail to see any menace there, Colonel. It happened to a great number of people."

"That's the point," the colonel grated. "He knew about the fog in plenty of time to put off the trip altogether. He suggested they head in at the professional village, that they go into that one particular restaurant, where he had a date with Steele. He got rid of the girlfriend and he and Steele went on over to her building." He swished his Scotch around and around as he talked. Then he finished the rest of the drink and set his glass down hard. "I don't like it. I don't like any part of it. There's something rotten about this Corky commie and I mean to get to the bottom of it. I have an instinct for these things, sir, and right now every nerve in my body is on full red alert. Every time I hear that name or even think it in my head, something in me goes *twang!*"

# Chapter Five

ONE second Corky was noticing the way she walked, as if her joints had not been given that one last inspection that included a tightening of nuts and bolts, or screws, or whatever. There was a loose-connectedness in her motions that was unusual, almost as if her limbs might go too far, her legs swing out in a way that would land her on her ass any second. He liked that. And he wondered why no one had sent her to a charm school, a finishing school, where they would have made her walk with an egg on her head. Then the universe changed.

Working with the parameters that Hot Dog had defined, Big Mac had done the best it could. The alien was immortal and could not be killed. It had not thought those two attributes were synonymous. And the alien could travel faster than the speed of light. When Big Mac discharged, Corky was not killed, although he was the target. He was dispersed throughout the biosphere, the atmosphere, and the stratosphere of Earth, faster than the speed of light, his traveling speed.

Corky thought nothing; he had nothing to think with. There was no way to separate sensation from thought, one thought from another, one sensation from another. Corky was thought. He was sensation. And he was everywhere at once in everyone at once.

\*　　\*　　\*

Sometimes the water flies to the place of the setting sun and sometimes it races to the rising sun with eddies and white foam swirling, and those are not times for the fishes to come. But when the water stands still as if to make up its mind which way to go, then the fishes of the west and the fishes of the east get curious and investigate the little bug I put on the hook. Then the fishes come to me. Come to me now, little fishes, so that Consuelo and Joachim will go to work with bellies round and tight, so that Carlos and Maria will go to school not thinking of food, but of tomorrow and good hopes. Come to me, little fishes. Come. How my feet hurt and my back and the moon so full and round as if sucking its breath to draw into itself everything on earth. Come, little fishes. Come. The mud feels good on my feet; we are one in color, in spirit, I and the mud. When I return to the mud, who will bring home the little fishes? Come, little fishes. Come.

He's hurting me, hurting. God, don't pinch so hard. His hand on my belly, hot, burning, scratching, raking, and God, my tit hurts. Not so hard. Someone will hear. Someone will see. Do it, just do it for chrissake. Just do it. Yi, ai ai! He choking me, choking. Don't kill me, for chrissake! I won't tell. Hurting, burning, hurting, my knees, breasts, cunt, belly. I wish I was dead. Dead . . . dead.

Walid? Is it Walid? Is he coming back at last? Just the wind. So many stars. They say each star is burning, but the stars are ice, icy eyes watching. My fingers are icy, my feet—Walid? Is that . . . ? Someone moved. Now, there, the moonlight on his shoulders, his hair. He looks like Walid, like Saleeby, like my father. But he's over there. Sight on the left side of the head, or the shoulders. The rifle will correct. Walid, please come now. Please. Left side. So like Saleeby. Father? No! On that side of the bus is the enemy. On this side is Father and Walid and Saleeby. . . . He looks afraid, like me. The left side, the left ear . . .

Such admiration in the eyes of Ahmad and Roshni, how they envy me this home, this life, how they envy me, for I caught the fairest of the fair in the whole country. Their eyes turned to water when they entered to be greeted by Sheela. They could only sigh and watch her movements and sigh again. They are talking about the new mall and I cannot keep track of their words. She knows, she must know, I was showing off, boasting, trying to keep face. Order Sheela? That peremptory tone! Dog of a wife. God forgive me. Sheela, forgive me. She is coming with the tea and cakes. Smiling at Roshni, smiling at Ahmad. Now she looks at me. I am shriveling before her, drying up, dying, and she knows. She knows. She smiles with her mouth but her eyes do not smile, her eyes see me dying, watch me dying. Eyes like bits of coal. God help me, what have I done? Tonight I will beat her. I will have her back as she was only minutes ago, half an hour ago, this morning, these past months. My loving, soft Sheela must come back. She knows what my thoughts are. Her coal eyes say never, never.

Two hours ago the adrenaline just cut off, gone. Guffy too. I saw it happen with him, guess he saw it with me. He looks stuporous, slumped in that leather chair, blending right into it like a mummy. Stuart's going on with Huntison, on and on, in a whisper. Probably I could hear if I gave a shit. All I want is sleep. Stuart's yelling and I lift my head a little, just in case he's yelling at me. He isn't. "What does that asshole want?" "A blank check, sir." "Christ almighty! Galstone, when will he want to cash it in, and for what?" I pull myself upright and try to focus on which asshole he's talking about now. Red hot wires down my spine, down both legs, behind my eyes. Which asshole? Horstmann? Probably. "A defense contract pretty soon. And the renewal project he's been after for the past year." What else? A judge? If not now, then he'll want it tomorrow. I add that. "Give it to him," Stuart says. When does he sleep? Is he even human? He's been at this as long as the rest of us, riding herd on every move, every vote, and he looks fine, just fine. So we'll give Horstmann a blank check and get his vote and a couple of others; enough. Now we can go to bed. Maybe someone will put a bullet through Horstmann's head before he can cash in.

* * *

The thought covered the earth and everyone on it. The thought was infinite and timeless. There was a boy explaining to a girl why he could not actually say he loved her, because it was too hokey; there was an Eskimo delivering three dozen carved polar bears and receiving his payment of eighteen dollars; there was a miner with sweat running down his face explaining to a younger man the best way to plant sweet potatoes; there were philosophical discussions in cafés and bars; religious discussions in living rooms and auditoriums; a woman reading to two young children who sat without movement afraid to break the spell; a girl trying to curl her hair with a curling iron, burning her cheek; a woman focusing a microscope, another scuba-diving; boys carving a tree in Bali; a man buying a Toyota in Tokyo. There was Musselman outlining his plan for the next week or two, and there was Lauren sleeping sweetly. She dreamed of sailboats that turned into birds and flew into a spectacular sunset. She turned into a bird and flew away with them, so filled with joy that she was joy. There was Bill Bentson, who had fallen asleep in the laboratory with his head on his arms; and there was Rich Steinman in bed with his wife, afraid to move until he knew she was asleep. There was a fat boy playing with a computer, and men in uniforms testing missiles and other men talking to robots in space. There were scientists discussing secrets in a dozen languages, and because the thought was part of them all, the languages were not a barrier. The symbols of thought were available to the part of the thought that was Corky.

For a timeless period there was only consciousness without self-consciousness. There was no self, no ego, but then awareness changed subtly. The thought flowed in and out of everyone, but now and then it was rejected, refused admittance, and it felt pushed away rudely. It tried harder to see in a different direction, to be able to enter that other something that was impenetrable, and the rejection was harder and for the first time the thought that was Corky realized it was not part of the Eskimo, the boy awkwardly making love to a girl, the woman reading to her children. Like an infant evolving into a self-conscious creature, it became aware of itself, aware that there was a menace here. It became aware that there was a core to the far-flung bits of itself, that there was a self, and the self was a man who thought of himself as Corky. With the realization that there was and should be a self, the pieces that had been scattered over the face of the earth began to coalesce.

As he pulled himself together again, memory returned. He had sketched the Minerva woman and followed her into the building. To watch her walk. This building, in fact. He remembered the look, not exactly fear, but concern that had crossed her face when she knew he was following her. Then he had backed up, away from her, right to the window. This window. And there she was.

He felt not quite himself and could not account for the strangeness. A momentary dizzy spell, a blackout of a second or two, something. He cleared his throat and the woman turned around and screamed. Corky flew apart again, out of control.

This time Corky tried to hold on enough to keep the core of self-consciousness even though he was flying apart faster than the speed of light. Very distinctly he said, "Shit!" No sound issued since he had no body, no lungs, no throat, but it was a certain satisfaction to utter a protest even if a silent one. He had to hold on to the tall woman, anchor himself to her. The realization had come to him that he needed an anchor.

But he could not do it. Even as he had the thought of holding on, the process of dispersal continued and was completed. Corky was lost once more in the thought that was the idea of the entire world.

—There he goes again. This is very peculiar, isn't it? I mean, he's not at all like the rest of us, and yet he can get here. I certainly don't understand any of this business.

—Me too, man. He's all over the place, popping up here, there. Me? I didn't have no choice in the matter. One minute there bleeding in the street, next thing I know, here I am, and I sure as hell can't go back. Be shit dumb to want to. You know who he is?

—I looked in the last time he showed up. Nobody. Just a nobody, nothing at all special. The very opposite, I should say.

—That's what I thought.

—I wonder . . .

—Yeah, what?

—If he got all the way in, do you suppose he could get back out, return over there? I mean, he isn't like the ones who get a glance now and then. He seems to want entry, a visitor's pass.

—Like I said, he's everywhere. When you watched him, was he like guys over there? He can't do that, can he? Move back and forth like that?

—Oh, yes. He looked completely normal, at least some of the time.

—She-it! If I could of done that over there. Seeing what I could of seen from this side, taking back the lowdown. Hot shit!

—One assumes that is precisely why we can't do anything but watch, and experience, of course. No tampering with advance knowledge, you know. It would upset the applecart, don't you see?

—There used to be a couple of guys I wanted to snuff real bad. I use to watch them and try to figure out ways to get to them, kink their tails. If I could of figured it out, I would of done it too.

—Yes, of course. Probably we all had such notions at first. Tampering here, fixing things there, tinkering a little. Chaos, sheer chaos would result, you know. And isn't it curious how little it means after a bit? I mean, when I chance upon the man who shot me down, we exchange pleasantries, compare viewings, just as you and I have done many times.

—Yeah, I know. Them two guys I wanted to fix, they used to come and watch, hoping I'd find a way, because they had guys on their hit list too. Use to wonder why it works out that we're all together and none of that means shit now.

—Used to wonder? No longer?

—Nah. Talked to one of them professors about it a couple of times. He says we got to keep all ideas in circulation, even the ones we don't cotton to ourselves. Said we act like their memories over there. Without us, blooey, no memories no more.

—A living library of ideas, my friend. That's how I think of us. Ideas, memories, thoughts.

—Living! She-it!

—In a manner of speaking.

—Dead meat, man, in a manner of speaking. But if that red-haired monkey gets in and out again, there goes the whole kit and caboodle.

—I think it's not a source of worry. Plans are being made, schemes schemed, nefarious deeds contemplated.

—Right. What I think is they're gonna blast his ass.

Lauren dropped the pot she was carrying. She closed her eyes hard, opened them. He was gone. But he had been here. A naked man, a spectre, ghostly, transparent. He had been here. Weakly she turned and went into the office and sank down into one of the ivory-colored chairs, trembling. Her fear of insanity surged out of the cave it had made in her innermost self, and she nodded. She was going mad, just as she had always feared she would.

She sat with a blind stare. She did not believe in ghosts. She even said it aloud, "I don't believe in ghosts." She had seen an illusion, the play of light at the end of the corridor. Or it had been a true hallucination. Naked? She bit her lip and tried to clothe the hallucination in her mind, but it did not work; he had been naked. Why? Because he left his clothes on the floor when he vanished the first time. A giggle started to rise and she bit her lip harder. She never had been a giggler; it had not been allowed. Cute little girls could giggle, her sister had said maliciously, not girls who towered over everyone else. She had not giggled then and would not now. Instead, she took a deep breath, another, and forced herself to her feet. She had dropped the pot, left a mess out in the corridor. Two other pots were now on the window ledge in her office; she had taken the tape from the recorder. She could go home, as soon as she cleaned up the dirt she had spilled.

She walked cautiously out of the reception room, peering both ways in the corridor, then soundlessly took the few steps to the broken pottery, the scattered potting soil. The little weeping fig looked wasted, as if it had cause to weep. She surveyed it all, studiously not looking down to the end by the window past the elevators. But the light streaming in from the tall window was brilliant and where the hall made a T, the newness of the carpet was obvious. She found herself gazing at it with incomprehension. Just two or three weeks ago Rich had spilled a soda in the hall there. She had come across him on his knees sponging it up guiltily. The stain had persisted. Now it was gone. There was no mistaking it; the carpet was new from the window to the intersection where she stood.

Stiffly she backed up, returned to the reception room of Waycross Clinic, picked up her purse, and then, walking like a zombie, left. She did not look at the pot, or the dirt, the rest of the hall. She moved carefully, as if afraid someone might hear her, stop her. She turned toward the elevators across the building, the way the police had made them all leave the other night.

She could ask someone when they had replaced that carpet, she told herself distantly, and she knew she would not do that. If it was a conspiracy, they would know her suspicions had been aroused. Her thoughts raced, overlapped, collided. She had seen a man vanish, no matter what they said. The police pretended not to believe her, and that meant conspiracy, or something ominous, like the girl who vanished in Paris and the police pretended nothing had happened and it turned out that she had plague. And the red-haired man might have something even worse, much worse. There were vaccines for plague; it had to be worse. Why had he filled a sketchbook with pictures of her? Or had the police done that too? Why didn't he have a sheet, at the very least? Why hallucinate him? Guilty conscience? She was punishing herself for letting the matter drop, for not trying to do something, inform his family or a lover, or children. Someone must be wondering where he was, why he didn't come home. Brain lesions could cause hallucinations, not a guilty conscience, and if she had brain lesions, a tumor maybe, she could go insane. People didn't go insane from guilt. A tumor then. Because whatever else was happening, she knew at last that she truly was going mad.

She had gone into psychology instead of psychoanalysis in order to deny with her own behavior her fear of madness. Behavior was all that mattered. People could yap on the couch for a lifetime and get nowhere, but in the clinic they expected behavior to change, and it did. And she had better change her behavior pretty damn fast, she added. She closed her eyes for a second, opened them wide, just to check if her vision was blurring. It was not. But the tumor could be someplace where vision would not be affected, at least not until the end. Her thoughts raced faster and faster, and her body moved faster and faster with them. By the time she reached the lobby, she was running, and did not even notice the two men who watched her with great interest. One was the building security guard; the other worked for Trigger Happy Musselman.

# Chapter Six

THERE was no succession. No first this, then that. It was all at once. Being a girl being adorned by women who only an hour ago had ruptured the hymen so that the groom would not be cursed. Being an infant tasting for the first time the ear of a stuffed bear, feeling for the first time the texture of the blanket covering it. Being a man forced to a metal bed, feeling the wires connected to his testicles, his tongue, agonized with the shock of electricity. Being a guard with aching feet, wanting only to go home because supper was ready. Being a boy running in cold wind, exultant with energy and health. Being an old man forced to endure life in a body he loathed, a body that had betrayed him and pained him and filled him with disgust. Being a woman touching the cheek of a child, tears of love hot in her eyes. Being a woman in a field, stooped, racked with weariness, waiting for darkness and rest. Overwhelmed by love and lust, wrenched by pity, burning with hatred, dissolving with fear, manic with excitement and joy . . .

Being the doer and the done to. The speaker and the listener. The performer and the audience. All at once. All interesting, all compelling. None of it unendurable if only because there was so much. The pain was a pin prick against an entire body of experience.

\*     \*     \*

That night Trigger Happy Musselman glared at Morris Pitts. "You blew it," he snarled.

"I don't think so," Morris said thoughtfully.

He was too damned self-assured, Trigger Happy decided, disliking him more than his handsome six-foot-plus frame warranted, more than his youth justified.

"Something happened between the time I saw her yesterday and the time I called this afternoon. Yesterday she was mine for the taking. Today . . . Something happened."

"Tell me again. Exactly what she said, how she sounded."

Morris did not show a sign of impatience or boredom. It was the third time for him to give the report verbatim, not even changing the inflections of his voice. "She answered the third ring. She sounded preoccupied with a worry. At first she didn't remember me, not until I asked if she found the nursery and bought the plants she had talked about. That brought her back a little, not enough though. She said yes and thanked me for good directions, and she said she had to go, she had work to do. I interrupted before she could hang up and asked if I could take her to dinner. She said no, she had work. Maybe I could call again in a week or two. And she hung up. She put her answering machine on and it's been on since three this afternoon. I tried every half hour until ten."

He had sent her a flower, he concluded.

"One flower?"

"One today. Another one tomorrow. And the next day. One at a time's enough. Believe me."

Trigger Happy believed him and that made him angrier than before. When he was alone again he stamped and chewed his cigar and reasoned it through. The Steele girl had gone to the office building to meet someone, that was for sure. The plants were a cover, an excuse to be there on a Sunday. The building security man swore that no one else had been on the seventh floor. Hah! That stooge didn't know his ass from his elbow. Contact was made. They fought? He liked that. It worked with the broken pot and dirt on the floor. He visualized the scene. It had to be her boss, he decided. Not Waycross; he had been out sailing all day. Her other boss, the real boss. She had met him and he was sore because she let Corky the commie slip out of their hands. Maybe the Corky commie was supposed to deliver a message that didn't get passed. It could be something in his effects, something disguised to look innocent that she was supposed to have received and didn't. Tomorrow he would go through all the junk one more time. Or maybe the boss slapped her around because she claimed that Corky the commie had gone out in a puff of blue smoke. He nodded. That felt exactly right. He knew the feeling that went with being right. He nodded again.

She was a little fish reporting to a bigger fish who in turn would have to repeat whatever she had told him, and eventually the story would make its way to a fish big enough to understand what was really going on. And he, T. H. Musselman, would be right here with a net ready. More men. He needed more men. Steele had to be watched every second, no more rendezvousing with unseen agents, no more slipping out of sight for any purpose. He knew Washington would replace him as soon as the notion struck that this might be the biggest story of the year, of the decade, maybe of all time. He had to keep on top of everything, make himself absolutely indispensable, the only one who knew every detail, every nuance of what was going on, and he intended to be just that person. What he did not intend was to go down to San Diego and watch some clowns demonstrate antigravity.

He poured himself a nightcap and sat nursing it, bemused by the ways of fate. He would retire a general yet, by God!

On Monday, when Trigger Happy learned that everyone in the Waycross Clinic was undergoing a routine clearance check, he simply nodded, not surprised. So that was why Steele had been planted at the clinic, to be there when the Caldwell Corporation plant was penetrated. It figured.

*　　*　　*

At the same time he was scanning the reports, Lauren was facing a client across her desk. Mrs. Wanda Torrance was forty, gray, and tired, dressed in a powder-blue pants suit several years out-of-date.

"So your supervisor suggested you have testing done. Is that right?" Lauren asked. She kept glancing at her watch, impatient for Peter to arrive, hardly able to keep track of this woman and her problems.

"When I asked for a transfer, he said the only way I can get it is if I get tested first. They can't just send me to a different department. So he said."

"Are you implying that other procedures are followed sometimes?" It was nine-fifteen. Peter was late, damn him. Gloria, the receptionist, had promised to give Lauren a buzz the second he appeared. And meanwhile this woman was going on and on.

"Yeah. When Bettyann Wilson wanted a transfer, no one said squat about tests. He just took her back to his office and next thing there she is in the clerical pool."

Lauren realized belatedly that it was her turn. She glanced at the folder in front of her. "Mrs. Torrance, what is your job? What do you do?"

"All day, every day, I put a gidget in a gadget under a magnifying glass this big." She demonstrated with both hands. "Under bright lights. Assembly line."

"I see. And what do you want to do?"

"Anything else. Customer service. Packaging. Complaints. Something creative. I took classes—poetry, painting, writing. There's a lot of things I could do instead."

Lauren nodded. Anything else, she thought. That was just right, exactly how she felt also. "Well, it seems your company is being cooperative, arranging for tests—"

"Hah! We have a union and I've got seniority! I've been there seventeen years, ever since old man Starr was making kitchen clock-radios with chickens moving their wings to point to the time."

"I see. Well, make an—" The light of her phone flashed on

and off twice, Gloria's signal that Peter had come in. Lauren stood up. The woman was watching her expectantly. "—An appointment," she said, remembering. "The receptionist will help you."

"Why not right now? I got the whole day off."

"No, no. I'm much too busy today. Next week or next month. I have to go now. I'm sorry."

Wanda Torrance nodded without taking offense. She looked resigned. "I'll make an appointment."

As soon as she was gone, Lauren hurried to Peter's office. "I have to talk to you now."

"Lauren my dear, how delightful to see you first thing! Oh, if only time were more elastic to allow us to dwell on those things of primary import instead of rushing on to the secondary things. Lauren, Lauren, five minutes, my dear. I fear I'm already late. Mondays are like that, aren't they, made to be late in? And it's a good thing we have at least one day that we can be late without guilt."

"Peter! I need help!"

"My dear Lauren, why are you telling me you need help?"

She closed her eyes hard and drew in a sharp breath. "Just listen a minute, Peter. Hear me out. I am having hallucinations. I keep seeing that man who disappeared last week. Naked."

He nodded and glanced at his watch. Then he said, "Why are you telling me this, Lauren dear?"

"How can you ask? I'm hallucinating! I may be going crazy! I can't counsel anyone else in this state!"

"Why do you say that?"

"Clients can't trust a counselor who doesn't trust her own perceptions. They shouldn't trust me in this condition."

"Have clients told you they can't trust counselors who don't trust their own perceptions?"

"Of course not! Peter, what are you doing? Why are you treating me like this?"

"My dear Lauren, I thought you wanted to talk about yourself, not about me."

She stared at him speechlessly, then moved to the window and looked at the rain falling without end. "You aren't going to help me, are you?" she said in a low, flat voice.

"How can I help you, dear Lauren? What do you want me to do for you?" When she did not answer, he asked, "Is it important to you not to hallucinate?"

"My God, Peter!" she cried. Then more quietly she said, "Yes. It's important to me."

"Do you want me to help you not hallucinate?"

Wearily she nodded, then pressed her forehead against the cool window. "Yes."

"Very well," he said briskly, cheerfully. "Every time you hallucinate, you must write down the exact time and place, and then you must work one hour overtime, see one additional client. Now, run along, dear Lauren. Run along. We both have so much work, so many wretched people begging for help, the help that only we can give them. Late, late, late."

"And it keeps raining all the goddamn fucking time," she muttered, and pulled away from his window, left his office.

In the corridor she saw Rich Steinman scurrying through the reception room. She called him and caught up when he came to a stop, looking around nervously as if he had been seen doing something shameful, or at least illegal.

"Rich, the other night, Thursday, when the police first began asking questions, did any of them mention the name of the man I saw?"

His glance skittered here and there too fast for anything to register, she felt certain. The world he saw must be a shadowy place full of menacing blurs.

He shook his head, then contradicted the motion. "Why, they might have, ah, that is, I seem to recall that one of them, ah, the black one, or was it the other one? Ah, that is, one of them said something about him, and did we have him for a patient, while you were not feeling very well, as I recall, drinking water, in a near swoon or something, so glad you didn't really faint, you know, I mean, it would have been difficult to manage—"

"What was the name the police officer mentioned?" She checked her voice in time not to snap at him, fearful of sending him dashing off in an anxiety fit.

"Ah, Corcoran. No other name, just Corcoran. Irish, the kind of thing an Irishman might do, I thought then, and now, of course, with everything changed, I can see that it was an unkind thought, but ah—"

She walked away, back to her own office, where she sat behind her desk and consulted the telephone book.

# Chapter Seven

---

AN hour later Lauren left her office with the names and addresses of three different Corcorans. She had made many calls, only to learn that one Corcoran was out of town, one at work, one taking a nap, one at school, one wanted to talk to her, two were coming to the phone, if she could hold. . . Three Corcorans needed looking into; there had been no answer from them, or an answering machine had come on. She walked past Gloria without notice, left the building, and walked home deep in thought.

In her apartment she spread a Seattle map on the table and located the three addresses. One was in the southwest near Elliott Bay, one in the Fremont section, one on Mercer Island. She was not familiar with any of the neighborhoods. She tried the telephone numbers again and let the phones ring ten, eleven, twelve times, hoping each ring would bring an answering voice. Then, reluctantly, she wrote out an itinerary for herself. First the Elliott Bay address, then the Fremont, and last the Mercer Island. Her trip would take her on a big triangle, heavy traffic all the way, an all-afternoon excursion. And the rain continued to fall in gray sheets.

She was cursing the little red-haired man bitterly when she went out again, this time to collect her yellow Toyota and begin. Why? she asked herself fiercely. If the cops were satisfied, and

Peter was satisfied, and that creep Rich, why was she out hunting for a clue about the idiot who vanished? Why was she the one hallucinating because of him? She hated him; he was nothing but trouble. And Peter with his phony smile and his phony therapy! Peter claimed that for one whole year he had not spoken to a client. He had sat behind his desk reading novels while they sat on the other side and healed themselves. Nine out of ten got better, he said with his beautiful smile, but in the end he had become bored and had resumed a more active role. She could not continue to think about Peter without trembling with fury.

She concentrated on the red-haired man instead, drew into memory the clothes he had been wearing, the way his hair had sprouted like dandelions gone to seed. He even had red hair on his belly, she thought with disgust, and realized she could not mention that detail to anyone by way of description. That had been the hallucination, not the real man, and if it was right, then how could she know about it unless that fat policeman had been right and she and the little red-haired man were more than friends? She was furious enough with the situation to weep, but weeping had been disallowed her as a child and then as an adolescent, along with giggling. Big girls didn't weep; big girls didn't giggle. Big girls worked things out, took action, took care of themselves. Big girls didn't sit back and wait for someone else to fix things for them. This big girl's throat was constricted with the unvoiced scream of rage at Peter, and her eyes burned with unshed tears of frustration. Worst of all, now that the secret fear had left its hidden cave deep within her, its growth was uncontrollable. It burgeoned and bloomed and swelled; it swept over her foaming, roaring, hissing, and retreated, leaving her in a frenzy of despair. Mad. Insane. Certifiable. Bonkers. Bananas. Spaced-out. Nutty. Out of her cage. Dementia.

"Then what, Peter, you moron?" she muttered. If she went all the way and found herself buying a hatchet, or a bomb, or just a little Saturday night special, Peter would be first, she promised herself. Could she buy a bomb?

She found herself driving too fast, her knuckles white, her stomach in knots as she waited for the next wave of fear that she knew was gathering for another assault. And she thought of all the many ways there were to kill Peter Waycross, revive him, and do it again. And again. And again.

A little girl watching in absorption as a cat gives birth; a woman watching the little girl, somehow hurting. A man on a bicycle hoping no one stops him, not now, not with the tall man's wallet tucked in his jeans, not before he has had a chance to empty it and toss it. A woman waiting for a bus, her feet afire from standing on concrete all day, aware that she has been targeted by five teenagers, waiting for the bus, waiting for them, no use in running, nowhere to run to, and they are young, fast, determined. Maybe she can throw down her purse, just let them have it, and the bitter knowledge that they will knock her down anyway. Floating in space, tears forming. Such a beautiful world, so beautiful. Red dust blows out of Africa, hides the coast, hides the sea, heading for Spain. Seeing it as a Martian landscape. A woman holding a small boy, smiling at a train creeping through the village. She has three front teeth, but the child is healthy and happy with the train and the friendly people who wave to him. Being the Englishman who thinks they probably have lice and fleas and thank God they're out there, not inside. And the woman with him who thinks he becomes uglier with each passing day of what was to have been a perfect vacation. Being a girl flirting with an older college man, and the man, afraid of the girl, who looks experienced and wise and is so beautiful he knows he can never have her. Being in a plane seven miles high, in a submarine, on a bus, a train, in a car, walking, running, sitting. In a bed drifting into sleep. In a field drifting into the peace of death, the pain and terror fading as the blood pools around the stump of a leg. The surgeon drawing the first red line on pale skin; and the patient knowing, although comatose, that violation is taking place. Teacher and student, priest and supplicant, judge, jury, defendant, prosecutor, witness. Everywhere and nowhere, inside everyone, part of no one. Feeling everything, moved by nothing.

An old man trudging from a rural mailbox to a small house. Muddy fields with furrows that look like miniature rivers glinting under a cold sun. Off to one side pine trees spaced too evenly, so evenly that if he stood in the right place, it would look like just one tree first one way, then another. He tries not to look at the trees, finds them offensive, and a threat in a way he cannot verbalize.

In the beginning the old man was interesting, just like everything else was; then another piece of Corky was drawn inward, and the pieces merged. The old man became more interesting. More of Corky converged until he recognized the man as his grandfather. He looked around in surprise. Arkansas? It looked like Arkansas, but how had he arrived here, and why?

"Grampa?" he tried to say, but there was no voice yet, no throat. More of him arrived and he began to take form. The old man entered the house; the form flowed through the door after him, still poorly defined, like a bit of swirling fog. It became denser, more coherent. "Grampa?" he tried again, and this time it sounded like a soft breeze in high grass.

The old man turned and squinted, peering narrowly, turning his head this way and that. "Corky? Is that you? Have they gone and killed you, boy?"

Corky could not hold the form. He felt the change start and tried to hold on, but he did not know how.

"Corky, tell me, boy. You seen your gramma over there? How's she doing, boy?"

This time enough pieces had hung together to make a center of sorts, and the center that was Corky was puzzled and confused, and frightened. Where was he? Why Arkansas? And how? Who was that woman in bed? That man? That policeman? All those people everywhere? Brilliantly painted temples? Ruins? The center looked frantically for something familiar and found other pieces of itself, drew them away from the people they were drifting through, and the center found sketches that were like the welcoming scent of home. The pieces streaked inward and formed a body, Corky. He reached for the sketchbook, lifted it from a table, and at the same time a man in uniform was disturbed by a sensation of movement behind him in the colonel's office. He turned to see a transparent naked man picking up the evidence on the table. The guard yelled and Corky flew apart.

For seconds the guard remained motionless. Finally he entered the office and picked up the book, examined it, and put it back on the table. This was what real boredom could do, he thought. He would never under any circumstances tell anyone what he had seen in that office.

# Chapter Eight

LAUREN looked with dismay at the city block under construction. She had driven past and parked, walked back, her note of the address in her hand, crumpled and moist now. The address no longer existed. A high board fence hid the pit that had been dug; a yellow crane towered above the fence. A gust of wind from the bay blew rain on her legs, on her face; she tilted the umbrella and walked on toward a shop. It was a florist; the air was heavy with flower scents. A gray-haired woman reading a magazine behind a counter looked up, but kept one finger at her place on the page. Her face was unlined, not with youthfulness, but rather as if she never had smiled or frowned in her life. Her expression did not change as she regarded Lauren silently.

"I'm looking for a man," Lauren said hesitantly.

The woman shrugged as if to say, "Who isn't?"

"He used to live over there," Lauren went on, pointing generally toward the construction site. "A Mr. Corcoran. Do you know him?"

"Billy? Sure. He moved."

"Do you know where?"

"Nope. Just moved. Everyone's moving in the neighborhood. We'll be out in a couple of months. Can't keep track of them all." She sounded aggrieved, as if offended at the thought that anyone might expect such a thing, but her expression remained blank.

The listing in the phone book had been W. Corcoran. Billy sounded right; he would be called something like that. Lauren turned to the door, then paused. "Billy, is he about five nine, with red hair? An artist?"

The woman looked at the magazine, removed her finger, and started to read again. "Artist!" she snorted. "That'd be the day! He's about that tall, two fifty, and bald, and he sells motorcycles." She turned the page.

"Thanks," Lauren said, not expecting a response, not getting one. She could scratch W. Corcoran. She went out into the rain again. It was like being in a universal shower, hardly protected by the tiny umbrella that was decorative and silly for Seattle. She needed a very large black umbrella, the kind that British statesmen carry. She hurried back to her car, the brightest thing in sight that dismal afternoon, and she looked at the simplistic map she had made in order to get from this area to the Fremont section. The trouble was, she admitted to herself an hour later, she had not taken into account one-way streets, streets closed by construction—were they destroying the city on purpose, to rise Phoenix-like bigger and better than ever?—and freeways without access. She was hopelessly lost in the neighborhood of Woodland Park. Without the large city map which she had left at home knowing very well that she would not consult it while driving, she had no way of knowing that she was within two blocks of the house where Corky had lived for the past year in a fourth-floor studio apartment.

And Corky, startled and confused by his situation, by the reaction of the soldier, by his own inability to keep himself together, was drifting in and out of the neighborhood, more cohesive than he had been since the computer called Big Mac had dispersed him, but still not all together. The pieces were in a more concentrated area, however, and most of them were in the Fremont district. There was a weak center that was Corky; it was too feeble to pull in the rest, but it held enough of Corky to have thoughts that were not simply the thoughts of everyone else. He was in the university, with Daniels, his old history professor; he was with Mama Goedtz in the grocery store; he was with Joan at the doctor's office, where she worked; he sniffed the air with the harbor seals and found it good; and he was the traffic lady and the children she herded across the street. He could feel a strange tugging and resisted it; it was as if every particle of him had its own destiny to fulfill, to merge with everything, be everything, but he, Corky, at the center, had a different destiny. It was only to return to normal, to be himself again and let go of all the rest of the world. The tug-of-war was relentless, and he was too weak to win, too determined to give up.

He was with Lauren meandering through the drive around the zoo, and he was with the special agent following her in a state of keen alertness, certain she was trying to lose him, that she had a meeting arranged. Why else would anyone go to the zoo in the rain? The center was in his studio apartment looking for something to hold on to, something that would provide a firm place from which to gather all the other particles and bring them home. His cartoons were gone; his notebooks were gone; his sketchbooks all gone. Even his correspondence, scant as it had been, even that was gone. The apartment looked empty and barren. It had been ransacked, drawers left open with contents strewn; the mattress off the bed, the couch overturned. Very briefly there was enough of Corky present to pick up a book; then he was gone again, the book fell, and only the forcibly held center floated about the room that had become desolate.

What she should do, Lauren realized suddenly, was hire a detective. She nodded, amazed that she had not thought of it earlier. It couldn't cost too much for such a little job, to find one red-haired man. How much was it worth to her not to have to prowl one neighborhood after another, miss work, possibly catch pneumonia? Fifty dollars? One hundred? She caught her lip between her teeth, then nodded again firmly. Even one hundred dollars was all right, just to find him, or his next of kin, tell them what had happened. She tried to imagine a wife listening for his footsteps, hanging by the telephone, calling everyone she knew, pleading with them to tell her, just please tell her. Now, having made up her mind, she decided she could go home. She saw a place where she could turn around, and braked hard, pulled into a driveway, and for the first time saw, really saw, the green Dodge that had followed her for the past two and a half hours. She had seen it before without registering the fact, but now she saw it and knew it had been following her because her own trail had been so erratic, and it had shown up again and again. She did not know that it was a Dodge because she knew very little about cars, and they all looked more or less the same to her, but now something in her recognized this one. It went past, slowing down. One man was in it, looking straight ahead, not at her. As soon as she could pull out, she made a U-turn and drove as fast as she could in the opposite direction, turned the first corner she came to and the next and the next, and finally felt certain that the green car had been left behind.

When the driver of the car made his report, he said with sincere conviction, "She's really good. She dawdled and drove on the wrong streets, started to turn on one-way streets, changed her mind, didn't signal for turns half the time, acted really lost, but when she decided to shake me, she knew what she was doing. She picked a park drive at a time when traffic was sure to be heavy. She let one car after another pass her, making like a real tourist, but she had a turning place picked out in advance. I could tell. She pulled over without a signal, not even slowing down hardly, and there wasn't a thing I could do. I'd of been creamed if I'd tried to turn on that stretch. She's really good."

Lauren stopped driving when she came to Puget Sound. She had been expecting to come to the lake front, several miles to the east. Resignedly, she looked for a restaurant. She had not eaten lunch, and it was after five, traffic was so heavy that it was pointless to try to get home for the next two hours. But now she knew more or less where she was and how to get back to the professional village. She could get to I-5 and head south, that was easy enough, the way it was posted, and she would get off at the CaCo sign, another easy landmark. From there she knew her way home.

When he had enough of a center to have a will, Corky drifted into and out of the lives of his friends, searching for a spot where he could anchor himself, where he could reel in the far-flung particles of himself. When there was even a little density, it attracted parts, and that gave him hope that he could achieve actual substance again. He looked in on Jerome and Wendy and backed off when he found them in bed. It was not that he lacked voyeuristic tendencies; it was rather that this particular activity was less interesting to a wandering intelligent speck than many other things people did. He was searching now for someone, anyone, who was thinking of him. He knew he needed help; for a short time he had hoped his own apartment, his possessions might be enough to hold him, but they had failed. He found Joan the dumpling and for a moment thought it would work with her. After all, hadn't they been lovers only— He was stopped by the realization that he did not know how long he had been in this state. And the way Joan the dumpling was gazing at a man unknown to Corky, the thoughts that went with the warm gaze made him flit away. Had she ever looked at him like that? Thought about him like that?

Then he was her companion in the Italian restaurant, thinking this wasn't all that bad an assignment. She was a kind of cute little thing, soft and cuddly-looking, probably terrific in bed. He could take a whole lot of this kind of assignment. Corky was the waiter on the way to the kitchen, then went out the back door with the dishwasher to dump garbage, and jumped to a passing police cruiser, and on and on and on. Everyone was preoccupied with their own concerns, their lovers, their spouses, kids, bills, shows, dances . . . A politician at a money-raising dinner, hating the food, loving the attention, the adulation he was receiving. On and on.

*       *       *

Trigger Happy Musselman and the two scientists were having dinner in his suite. Bill Bentson looked as if he had not slept at all since Thursday night. His eyes were sunken, his cheeks more hollow than ever. Trigger Happy hoped he would not keel over before they found the glitch in the computer. He smiled at the two men in his most genial manner and said, "I don't understand why you can't just duplicate the experiment, in a controlled way, of course. I thought info never was lost on one of the big computers. Isn't there a whiz kid around who can dig it out for you?"

Dr. Mallory Akins looked at him with hatred. "They're working on it," he said in a snappish way.

"But maybe not hard enough," Trigger Happy said. He had eaten his steak and potato and salad and was eyeing the food that Mallory Akins was pushing around on his plate, like a kid facing spinach.

"We're doing all that can be done," Akins insisted. He knew the threat; if this colonel didn't get what he wanted from them, he'd call in army or NASA whiz kids, or he'd get people in from Livermore, or JPL, or someplace else. And he, Akins, would be out in the cold. But this idiot was too ignorant to understand what had happened, too ignorant to explain the problems to. He sighed with fatigue, not willing to yawn and betray his weakness, his weariness.

Trigger Happy had a three-room suite: the sitting room they occupied now, a bedroom, and the third room that was his office here. He had another office at the company, and that was where the safe was that he could keep the Corky commie papers in when he was through with them for the night. At the moment they were in the third room of the hotel suite. Lieutenant McWilliams, Musselman's aide, was having his own dinner in the hotel restaurant; he would deliver the papers to CaCo later.

Corporal Jennings was in the sitting room, trying to quiet his rumbling stomach. It had not been required that he stand at attention, but it was impossible to relax with the three men eating in front of him. He would go off duty after he drove the lieutenant to CaCo, if the colonel didn't want anything else. He regarded himself as the flunky, stationed here because the colonel might decide he wanted something not instantly at hand, at which time, he, Jennings, would be expected to produce it, no matter what.

There was the bedroom; there was the sitting room; there was the office that could be reached only through the sitting room. They all knew that. So it was that when they all heard a crash from the office, they froze for a second or two.

Then the corporal approached the door, with the colonel just behind him. They both suddenly had acquired guns that looked to Bill Bentson like cannon. The sight of the twenty-two-year-old corporal with a gun in his hand filled him with terror. Musselman made a motion and the corporal went to one side of the door, the colonel to the other. He kicked it open.

Because Corky was everywhere, it was inevitable that he would come across his own belongings again. His letters, his notebooks and sketches, his cartoons, snapshots, his portfolio. One second the weak center had been in the Fremont area, miles to the north, and then it was here, coalescing into a whole being, growing more substantial instant by instant. He had picked up his portfolio only to have it slide through his hands. In lunging for it, he had knocked over a telephone and a lamp. And now the door banged open and men were pointing guns at him. He scattered as they entered the room.

The lamp had broken in the fall, and with the only light behind them, they failed to see even an afterimage of Corky. They advanced with great caution. The colonel flicked the wall switch and other lights came on. Papers were on the floor; the portfolio was on the floor, the telephone and lamp, and no one was in the room. No one could have been in the room. It took them only a minute or two to determine that.

In her apartment Lauren stared at the three rosebuds in a glass of water, each bud perfect, fragrant. The first one was just beginning to loosen up a little, to relax. Still a bud, it now looked as if it had gained some courage, a little curiosity; it had stopped hugging itself into a tight coil. She abruptly stopped hugging herself into a tight coil. Morris, she thought. Morris Pitts would know a detective. She had read seventeen Perry Mason books in a row the year she was twelve and she knew all about the methodology of attorneys and detectives. Morris probably had several private investigators he worked with.

She felt an immense relief at the idea of turning the puzzle over to someone else, someone more qualified to deal with it than she was. She took a long hot bath, drank a glass of milk, and eyed a sleeping pill for a long time before she finally swallowed it. She had not slept enough for so many nights that she was alarmed at what sleeplessness might be doing to her brain, along with the tumor that was growing rapidly. She had read all the studies and knew the consequences could be very serious, and she simply could not afford to miss more work, to alienate Peter, jeopardize her future. She leafed through a book until drowsiness blurred her vision; then she fell into bed and sleep and dreams.

The colonel was hosting another get-together. The two scientists were there looking exhausted and frightened; the silver-haired FBI agent was there looking disgusted and disbelieving; his boss, the northwest director of the FBI, was there, intent and noncommittal. Musselman was talking; it was one in the morning; he felt just fine.

"I don't claim that this scenario is one hundred percent on, but I believe it's close, gentlemen, close. Now, here you have the CaCo R and D building, seventh floor. Right?" He stood up his cigar lighter. "And over there there's the professional building, in a direct line. The only building that is in a direct line, I might add, that has a seventh floor. And in the professional building, you just happen to have a meeting taking place at the same time that the demonstration was scheduled for." He put a glass opposite the lighter and surveyed the two objects with satisfaction.

"Colonel," Mallory Akins said tiredly. "It's coincidence. If your flight hadn't been late, the test would have gone off at five, as scheduled. If there hadn't been the fog, that man would have caught his flight and would have been on his way to Los Angeles by seven."

The silver-haired agent nodded thoughtfully. Trigger Happy shrugged. "I say he would have missed that flight, no matter what. He had no intention of making it. He had a date with the Steele girl, remember? And sure the test was supposed to be over by then. I think they had word that it hadn't happened yet and they rushed to try out their own device, a remote control device that activated the computer and fired the laser, and unfortunately for them, misfired and got their man. It was their last chance to test their infernal device. You guys said you planned to dismantle the gizmo after the test, give it a thorough examination, six, seven months before it was to be put back together. Didn't you?"

Bentson nodded. "There isn't any such device, the remote control thing you're talking about."

"Can you explain what happened? How it fired? What in Christ's name it fired? How it zapped a man through a thick wall, two miles, a glass window without leaving a mark anywhere, including his clothes?"

Bentson shook his head, then said doggedly, "But in time we'll explain it without the fairy-tale magic wand you're talking about."

To Trigger Happy it was all magic; his wand was as believable to him as anything anyone else had suggested to date. He deliberately turned away from the scarecrow and addressed his remarks to the FBI director. "I believe in this because they have such a device that was put in operation only a few hours ago, again. This time they were after the Corky commie's papers, and by God, they almost got them!"

"And the Steele woman?" the FBI director murmured.

"She's in it up to her skinny neck. She's been acting funny ever since the incident, slipped our people for nearly five hours just today, in fact, and when she did show up again, it was on the CaCo turnoff. It takes a good operator to give our men the slip, believe me, sir." He glared at the two scientists for a second, and added, "I think she's after the papers because she knows what's in them, even if the so-called experts can't spot a thing."

Mallory Akins poured coffee for himself. He kept his gaze on what he was doing, not on the other men in the room. "For God's sake," he muttered softly, "the woman saw a man disappear. Everyone's been denying that it happened. I think she has cause to act strangely." He drank the coffee. It was bitter and cold.

Trigger Happy ignored him. He leaned forward and jabbed his finger at the FBI director as he spoke. "She was all over the Corky commie's neighborhood this afternoon before she gave our guy the slip. Where'd she go then? Who'd she report to? What new instructions did she get?"

"Why don't you detain her and ask her questions?" Bill Bentson snapped.

"We will," Trigger Happy said. "We will, but not so soon. Enough rope, you know the saying. That is, if we can keep her in sight." The FBI director no longer looked noncommittal. He even nodded. The silver-haired agent looked morose.

# Chapter Nine

HE drifted and dreamed with an intern; with a woman nursing an infant, dozing as it dozed; he went with three boys when they broke into a house, and felt their terror and excitement; he looked with his grandfather's eyes at a pine forest, in the days before the trees had been planted in straight rows. Everywhere, nowhere. He drifted. And then he was in Lauren's troubled dream with her.

She was running through sand that held her, drifted up to her knees, made each step a torture. She had to run because someone was chasing her in a green car, and the car could maneuver in the sand as if on a highway. She dodged and zigzagged. Ahead of her, beckoning, was Corky. When she reached out for him, he vanished. She had to run, had to run, had to lift her foot, move it, lift the other one. . . . And always, just as she thought he was within reach, he vanished. Her mental picture of him was sharp and almost photographic. He was naked in the dream.

He began to regroup in her apartment, held finally by her mental image, by her need, her hands reaching in the dream. At first the particles were so widely scattered that they covered all of the earth; they streamed inward, and he became firmer. With substance, he became chilled, and for the first time he felt incredibly tired.

Lauren had pulled the bedspread off and tossed it onto a chair; now Corky dragged it off and wandered through the apartment looking for a place to lie down. He finally stretched out on the living room couch, rolled himself in the bedspread, and fell asleep.

—I don't really understand the concern. What if he does make it through and goes back? There have been too many people before who have taken pieces back with them and it meant nothing. Artists, scientists, writers. It all meant nothing.

—Yes, yes, I know. And I try to be that calm, but this is different. They managed to get glimpses only; even Leonardo got mere glimpses. And look what he did with them! Have you ever been near him when yet another of his contraptions is created? Insufferable, simply insufferable. But even with his limited views, he was able to reproduce what he saw. This one will not be limited, if he gets through, I mean. And he is an artist also.

—Let's stick to Leonardo for a moment. He drew what he saw, but there was no real comprehension of what anything meant. That's exactly what I am saying. This one will have as little comprehension as any who has come and gone.

—I hope you are correct. I do hope so. But they have such marvelous machines now. You've seen. Computers that can analyze sketches and tell how to make whatever is portrayed tell what its purpose is. Even that, possibly, we could tolerate, I mean if he did acquire knowledge and made use of it. But that shadowy area, that we cannot tolerate. I am convinced it is a break in time, a branching, a fork, whatever you might call it.

—A branch? Surely not. Good gracious, I trust you are wrong. Let me think about this. A branch?

—Oh, ignore those ravings! He's totally wrong. A discontinuity, perhaps, but not a branch of diverging time lines. Really!

—A discontinuity is even worse, you know. A discontinuity cannot be bridged.

—But there can't be two time lines in one continuum.

—I know that! And the mathematics of a discontinuity proves that no bridging is possible. You start over at zero, a clean slate.

—Please, all of you, think it through, and I will be back.

—Ha! We are talking about the think death of the universe, nothing less.

—I'll be back later.

When Lauren woke up, her head was stuffed with cotton, the way it always was after sleeping pills. She staggered to the shower and stayed there for a long time, staggered to the kitchen, where she made coffee and looked at toast as if it were alien and loathsome, staggered back to the bedroom, where she dressed, and then staggered out of the apartment.

Corky dreamed he was on a camping trip with his father, who was brewing coffee over an open fire. Corky sniffed and snuggled into his sleeping bag, waiting for the bacon aroma that was sure to follow. Instead, he found himself starting to float, and he woke up completely, bits of him already cruising the city, over the ocean, into Mexico.

"Stop it!" he yelled, and pulled them back. "Not again," he said aloud. He settled down to the couch with a bump and began to feel his arms, his head, his body. He seemed to be all there.

At that moment he did not know where he was, or how he had gotten here, or where he had been. He needed food, he decided, and, sniffing, he knew he needed coffee. Feeling his face made him realize he needed to shave. His body wanted a shower. The needs were real and immediate, with food at the top of the list. He followed the smells to the kitchen, where coffee was still hot, and toast on a plate was cold. He ate it and drank the coffee and drank orange juice and then ate a banana. Not camp food, but good.

He looked at the kitchen, tidy, almost like a ship galley. He had entered from the living room, passing through a tiny dining space; he left by a door on the opposite side, out into a hallway. Directly across from the kitchen was an even smaller utility room with a clothes dryer stacked on a washer, and pantry space. He backed out, starting to feel claustrophobic. The next door was slightly ajar and led to the bathroom. It was still steamy and fragrant.

He had entered the room several steps when he came to a complete stop. Ahead was the shower and tub; the toilet on the left, and a double sink with a mirror on the right. The mirror was fogged slightly, and no one was in the mirror.

The mirror was in his peripheral vision; he did not turn to face it directly yet. He lifted his hands, turned them over, examined the backs. He looked down at his legs and feet, felt his hair, his ears. Only after this inspection did he actully make the turn so that he was facing the mirror. Nothing. He leaned in closer, resting his hands on the edge of the counter, moving in until his nose was almost touching the glass. He drew back slowly and closed his eyes, thought about how he was supposed to look, saw his hair, his nose, his wide mouth, blue eyes, the face that regarded him morning after morning with a certain skepticism, a certain self-mockery. He realized that, impossible as it was, he was aware of the security guard in the lobby, the bald man reading a newspaper on the fifth floor, a cleaning woman already at work on three; two women chatting over coffee on two; a mother bundling up a toddler . . . a woman and man making love . . . Lauren walking away with cotton in her head.

He began to shake, denying the information, denying the sights, smells, sounds he was perceiving, willing himself to be here, whole, in one piece, red hair and all, when he opened his eyes again. The visions began to fade away, blink out. Finally he risked opening one eye, squinting at the mirror. He saw his own blue eye looking very frightened. He opened the other one. It was no less frightened, but now he began to feel in control. He could still see the wall that should have been eclipsed by his body. For an instant he almost lost the control he had found, then he had it back, and bit by bit the transparency solidified until he looked as solid as he ever had.

It was like having a muscle that he never had suspected existed before, and being required to flex it when he did not even know exactly where it was. Now he said to the mirror image, "What the shit is going on?" and he lost the muscle again, lost control. He cursed and started all over.

For the next hour he practiced holding himself together. When there was enough of him there to make it worthwhile, he showered, shaved with Lauren's little razor, although both seemed rather a waste of time. He left the mirror and sneaked back up on it to see if he was still there when he was not looking. Sometimes he was, other times not. He made eggs and ate them, hoping more food would help. It did not seem to make any difference. But gradually he learned to recognize the feeling that preceded flying apart, and he learned to recognize the feeling that went with using the hitherto unknown muscle that brought the pieces back together. And he came to appreciate that it took a lot more effort to put together a real body than to let go. His tendency was to be everywhere and nowhere; his ego demanded that he be here, now. He fought stubbornly to acquire the skill that he knew he had had unconsciously all his life, that everyone else had without effort.

He made more coffee, and he paced the small apartment, trying to think what he should do. Call someone, but who? And say what? A doctor? He considered it and shook his head. A medical curiosity, kept in a padded cell, an escape-proof room, probed, prodded, subjected to test after test, dissected maybe. He shook his head even harder. And the thoughts led nowhere.

Lauren hung up the phone in her office and drew in a deep breath. She was not certain how it had happened, but it appeared that she was going to have lunch with Morris Pitts. She had called to inquire about a private investigator and had ended agreeing to lunch with him. The morning had been hellish. First Peter had popped in to ask, "Any more UNM sightings?"

"What's that?"

"Unidentified naked men."

"No," she snapped, and he left, smiling his smuggest smile.

Milton Newley had been her first client. Milton wanted to be a surgeon, the kind who studied in the Philippines and did not use a knife. "You know," he said, "psychic surgery."

She told him he would be happy in agriculture, horticulture, as a tree planter. Then Dolores Bard had arrived with her test results and all Lauren had been able to think of was that she should become a call girl. She had not told her client that.

And now Roger Guest was due. Roger wanted to be a corporation CEO. When she asked why he thought he was qualified, he had said because he understood how people worked, what made them tick, what turned them on. And he had smiled broadly. His tests indicated that he was suitable for working with no more than three people at a time, and always under strict supervision.

As she looked up to see Roger Guest entering her office, Morris Pitts was entering her apartment with another agent.

Corky was still brooding when they left the elevator; he entered the apartment with them, and knew that it would be better for him to make himself scarce, until he had a plan anyway. He relaxed the muscle, and behind him a large beach towel settled to the floor. Morris stopped, listening, then continued into the hallway, motioned his partner, Edgar, to come on in, and they went to work. The center of Corky watched them, puzzled as they pried and poked and lifted fingerprints, lifted some red hairs from Lauren's little razor, went through her letters and bills and receipts and generally snooped.

Now and then Morris and Edgar exchanged glances, and although neither of them mentioned it, they were both aware of something strange in the apartment. It felt used too recently, almost as if someone had been there only seconds ago, not hours, as they knew was the case. The coffee was still hot, for instance. And too freshly made? Morris thought so and made a note. Too many damp towels? He made another note. The rolled-up bedspread on the couch? He looked at it a long time before he touched it. He did not know how anyone could roll a spread like that, or why anyone would. He caught himself listening more than once, and more than once he pivoted, expecting to see someone behind him.

Corky was with Morris at lunch when he said, "Charlestown, Indiana, up the Ohio River from Louisville. My old man worked in the munitions plant. About all there was, I guess. But I couldn't wait to get the hell out of there. You?"

"Frankfort, Kentucky. My father was a law clerk in the Kentucky supreme court. I couldn't wait either." Corky felt her discomfort when she smiled and said, almost apologetically, "Justices came and went, clerks endured forever. They and their families were required to be very proper."

Corky drifted in and out of their conversation over frogs legs with sauterne and garlic, asparagus vinaigrette, and finally coffee, and raspberries in from Argentina. He listened to Trigger Happy Musselman on the phone to Washington several times, and to Joan the dumpling parry her newfound friend's not very subtle invitation to bed down with him. With Peter Waycross he decided that forty was really too old, as he listened to a woman relate her problems with her husband's daughter, and he was with the woman who thought Peter was the handsomest man she had ever been alone with in her life. He twitched with Rich Steinman, and flexed his muscles with Warren Foley, and suffered fatigue with Bill Bentson, whose vision had finally started to blur. He studied the computer printouts with Mallory Akins and found the fourteen-year-old boy just leaving his school, shyly pretending he did not know that a pretty black-haired girl was watching him covertly. Hot Dog, Corky thought, and drifted to the girl, and knew what it was to feel desperate about a coming test in algebra, knew what it was to eye the only boy in reach who could help, no matter if he was a little overweight.

In a tiny room in a third-floor flat a woman in trance intoned words that were meaningless to Corky, but a particle of him was interested in a particle of the woman that was just as free-floating as he was. They circled each other like strange dogs getting acquainted, and Corky felt himself being pulled inward, surrounded by the one bit that had become elastic and endless somehow. He was with others around a table: a woman with squinched eyes praying for Bertie to come, a man wishing it was over, another man thinking how weird if Arthur Conan Doyle actually had done this kind of thing in this very room, another woman hoping something would happen, willing it not to happen, and all the while the strange particle circled him, commanding him to appear, show himself. The command was nearly irresistible if only because no one else in the entire world wanted him, called to him, or even acknowledged his presence. He streamed in toward the small room.

"As an attorney," Morris was saying, "I hear all kinds of things, as you must also, being a therapist. You know you can trust me to be discreet, just as I would trust you. What's bothering you, Lauren? Let's get it out, dispose of it, so that we can get on with other things. Things that I think are going to prove to be important."

His deep blue eyes were clear and honest, his hand on hers was firm and warm, not a trace of guile in his whole being. Lauren thought of the little red-haired man with a sharp clarity, saw him outlined against the tall window, saw him vanish, reappear naked against the same window.

Halfway around the world the medium felt the change, knew exactly when the spirit she had summoned flew away again. And Corky sped faster than the speed of light to a real call for him, to someone who knew whom she was calling even if she did not know why.

Lauren closed her eyes, grateful for the warmth of a hand holding hers, comforted by the strength and kindness of this man opposite her at lunch. Where to begin, she wondered, and knew he would think her mad if she told it from the start.

Corky stopped short of achieving real substance. He swarmed all around the table, around Lauren and Morris. He knew Morris was lying, knew Lauren was desperate, and he did not know what he could do. He was more than a shadow, less than a person, and he knew that this woman he had called Minerva, this goddess of a woman, was in trouble and somehow, in a way he could not comprehend, he was responsible. He tried to join with her and was repelled; she reached up to feel her hair, as if something had landed on it. He tried to merge with Morris and it was like running into a wall.

Morris would help her, Lauren was thinking. She had to tell him the whole thing, no matter how ridiculous it sounded, and let him decide what she should do next. Her sisters had always said big girls had to do things for themselves, not wait for help, but, she admitted, she needed help very much. She finished exhaling and opened her eyes. He was watching her with concern, very serious now, caring. She opened her mouth, and suddenly his glass seemed to come alive and rise from the table, topple over, spilling ice cubes and water down his coat, down his shirt, turning his dark-red tie bright, like freshly drawn blood.

Morris lunged for the glass reflexively as it tumbled toward the edge of the table, and Corky caught his sleeve and swept his arm in a wider gesture, hitting his coffee cup and small bowl of berries, sending them across the table. Lauren stifled a scream and scrambled out of range. The waiter had come running at the first sign of catastrophe; now he slowed down and approached with caution, keeping his eyes hard on Morris.

The time for revelations had come and gone. When Morris and Lauren parted in front of the restaurant a few minutes later, he was contrite and a little bewildered; she was suddenly relieved that she had not told him anything after all.

"I'm not always this much of a klutz," he said in way of apology. "I'll call you tonight. Okay?"

"Sure," she said. They shook hands formally and she turned to walk back to her office, two blocks away.

He watched for a few seconds, then went in the opposite direction and around the corner was picked up by his partner, Edgar.

"Well?" Edgar said after they had gone a block or two.

"Shut up," Morris snarled.

The trouble was, Corky decided a while later, he was jealous of Morris. Everything about him was what Corky was not. He was six feet two and muscular, lean, and in wonderful shape. His apartment, where he went first to change clothes, was rich, even elegant. A sound system filled one wall; there was a mammoth microwave oven in the kitchen, a water bed, a Jacuzzi in the bathroom, a wall of leather-bound books. Maybe unread, but impressive as hell. The boy did well, Corky told himself; his father would be proud. Morris saw none of the apartment when he stomped in to change. He was fuming, still uncertain what had gone wrong. Tonight, he said to his mirror image meanly. Tonight, goddamn it!

Corky floated along when Morris went to the law office, Wescombe, Carmichael, Straus, and Pitts. He sampled the other lawyers and lingered with Wescombe long enough to learn that he had been with OWI during World War II, and afterward had worked in the CIA for a few years, then had come out to Seattle to establish the firm. Washington State had been on the cutting edge of the nuclear age, and it was the foremost state for aircraft production; someone was needed here, Wescombe was chosen. The old man, now in his seventies, had done nothing for his country for many years, except take on Morris Pitts as a junior partner. He knew Morris worked for the government first, the firm second, and that was fine with him. His only regret was that Morris never, ever hinted at his primary duties, if indeed he ever did anything. That bothered old man Wescombe, that Morris might not be actually doing anything other than what he appeared to do in the firm. Several times he had created the opportunity for a confidential chat, over luncheons, and at his club, and had even spoken, in very general terms, of course, of his own activities in intelligence. Morris had not been responsive, had appeared bored, in fact. Now old man Wescombe noted his comings and goings with interest, and never expected to learn a damn thing.

Morris was in his office, rich with cherry wood, green leather, and dark, velvety-red carpeting, and Morris was plotting his strategy. It aggrieved him that he had to plot out such a simple thing as bedding one woman, but there seemed to be a jinx on this whole affair, and from now on, he decided, he would play it very carefully, plan every move in advance. Her profile said she was repressed, inhibited, shy, socially maladjusted, ripe for picking with the right approach. And he knew his approach was impeccable; therefore it was luck that was working against him, and luck would be countered with scrupulous planning. Tonight, he promised himself, they would thrash about in his sumptuous water bed, or in her rather barren little apartment bed, but thrash they would. He knew that for a woman like Lauren, once well bedded, forever won. She would be his to wring dry, to lead them to Corcoran, to do whatever they wanted done by her until he cut her loose again.

She must realize, he thought, that they made one of the world's greatest-looking couples. Admitting that it had not just happened, but that they were computer matched, did not detract a whit from the reality that they looked beautiful together.

# Chapter Ten

CORKY drifted away from Morris. It did not surprise him that Morris wanted to take Lauren to bed. Corky had known very few women in his life whom he had not wanted to take to bed. Some had joked about it; some had teased; some had acted as if he had said something precocious; a few had agreed, too few. He thought of Joan the dumpling and streamed away from Morris's office, searching for Joan. As he flowed through the city, the poorly defined center that was Corky did not hold. As long as he had remained with Lauren, or with Morris, he had managed to control that muscle that was still new and strange to him. As soon as he was alone again, he lost it, and even forgot that he had it. When the center failed, so did his will, his intentions, his memory. Once more he became everyone, everywhere.

Grace Dolittle was a sigher. She sat across the desk from Lauren and sighed with every question, every answer.

"You've had two years of business school," Lauren said, exasperated with the young woman. "Why did you go if you hate business?"

Sigh. "Daddy made me."

And now Daddy was making her go in for counseling. Lauren

looked at the form she had asked Grace to fill out; most of it was blank. "About this part, what you liked about the last job you had. You didn't put down anything. There must have been something you liked."

Sigh. "The water cooler."

Lauren nodded and said, almost as a reflex, "Good. Let's focus on that. What did you like about it?"

Sigh. "Bobby Boyles. He hung out there. But he was married already."

Lauren glanced at her watch; another half hour to go. "Let's try it from the other side," she said. "What didn't you like about your job?"

Grace looked blank. She was pretty in an empty way, as if she had not yet been lived in, was waiting for life to finish etching her with awareness of a world more than a foot in front of her. She was twenty-four. She was watching Lauren with an expectant air, as if waiting for a cue.

"Why did you quit?"

"Oh, well. You know. It just wasn't right for me."

And so it went until the hour was over, with nothing accomplished. Lauren wanted to send a note home with her: Be patient for the next ten or twelve years until she grows up. Instead, she gave Grace a new set of questions and asked her very nicely if she would try to answer them before the following week.

Joan dimpled at the man sitting opposite her in the booth. "You can't pretend you just happened to be in the neighborhood again," she said happily.

"Right. I thought you might be getting off about now."

He was young, a student type, graduate student, she thought. He had said something vague about the university, just blocks from the doctor's office where she worked. And now here he was again, waiting for her, buying her pizza. She never had been able to talk to a man the way she could talk to him; it was almost like talking to one of her girlfriends. He really listened and asked just enough questions, and the right ones, and when she wailed that she would never understand why Corky had ditched her for a giraffe, he had moved to sit next to her, his arm about her shoulders in a comforting way.

"It hasn't even been a week yet," she said in wonder, "and already it's like he's a stranger. I mean, you just don't hold someone in high regard when he dumps you like that without any warning."

"They must have been getting together a lot, while you were at work, maybe."

Just a hint of inflection made it almost a question. Not a prying sort of question, but a sort of wondering out loud. She nodded. It made sense. "He had it planned, all right," she said after a moment, "or he wouldn't have taken all his cartoons and drawings."

He wondered out loud and she filled in the blanks. Corky had a great career in Hollywood, she said over the pizza, and she would have joined him down there as soon as he got settled in. Just as well to know now how unreliable he was. What if she had gone down and then he had run out on her, in a strange city, maybe with no money, no one to turn to? Tears filled her eyes and she needed more comforting.

The bits of Corky in her and her companion flitted away. They flitted together and merged and formed a nexus of sorts that grew and pulled in other bits that formed a center again.

He looked at Joan, and saw her as Joan, the dumpling, the woman he had slept with . . . when? There was no answer. He looked at the man with her and tried to remember what it was that he knew about this man, again with no answer. Now he listened to Joan say that he, Corky, had run out on her, and even though he could not explain what had happened to him, what was still happening to him, he knew that was wrong. They had been together in a little café in the professional village and she had left him there. Then he had followed the tall woman. The tall woman was the key, he realized suddenly. Instantly he was scanning her apartment, and her office building, and found her standing at her office door talking to a man in the anteroom. Corky streamed into her office and now he remembered that he had learned how to control his own substance by using a muscle somewhere. He worked on it, only partly listening to Lauren and the man she was talking to.

"Believe me, Warren," she was saying firmly, "I absolutely refuse to get drawn into your arena for any purpose whatever. I will not play basketball and I will not referee. Find someone else."

Warren was in his running clothes already, hopping up and down, first on one foot, then on the other. "But, Lauren, you're a natural. And it would make you feel so much better. Just try it a couple of times. You'll be amazed—"

"Good night, Warren." She stepped into her office, pulled the door closed, then turned all the way around. She moaned and leaned against the door. "Oh, my God!"

There he was again, naked as before, almost as transparent. He looked startled, then blushed violently and vanished all the way. She shut her eyes as hard as they would close and took a deep breath, then another.

Corky did not fly apart this time. He was determined to find out what was happening, and if he had to stay close to this woman to find out, that was what he intended to do. But he did not want her fainting or screaming or calling other people; he tried to find the intermediate state he had discovered earlier that day, and then maintain it. If he had more substance, he was visible, and in the buff as he was, that caused problems. If he relaxed too much, he tended to fly apart. In the middle state there was the center that was Corky, and there was a miniswarm of particles that were all Corky also. Although his body fluctuated wildly from almost solid to almost dispersed, the center now held, and when Lauren finally walked from her office, pale and shaken, the center and its orbiting particles followed.

The elevator would be too crowded, Corky realized as they walked toward it. Three or four other people were there waiting; others would already be on it, or on lower floors waiting to get on. He relaxed the new muscle and nearly flew apart; in reaction he jerked and bumped into a chiropractor, who stumbled and looked around suspiciously. Corky reacted again, this time hitting the right tension. He took in a sharp breath, bracing for what he knew would be an ordeal in the small elevator cage. Maybe he could float above her, he thought, but when she stepped into the elevator he gave up the idea. She was too tall. He tried to make himself shrink without losing control, staying as close to her as he could without climbing her shoulders. She looked behind herself with disapproval.

The code of ethics said that in the forced familiarity of the situation, no one acknowledged anyone else, no one really looked at anyone else, or spoke, and if touched more than the conditions warranted, moved without protest, but moved, and turned very slightly in the direction of the transgressor, never making eye contact, but to indicate disapproval. She signaled her displeasure and turned toward the doors again when the elevator came to a stop on six. Several more people boarded, people moved to the rear, and someone clutched her hip. This time she turned and glared at a heavyset man she had often seen in the building.

"Stop that! What do you think you're doing?"

He was bent over in a peculiar way, as if something was pushing on his solar plexus. With great dignity he said, "I assure you, I am not doing a damn thing. I think I am being done to." He reached out to feel Corky, recoiled, then reached again, his hand running over what could only be human hair, a nose . . . Corky dispersed and filled the elevator with bits of himself, concentrating as he did this on holding a center. It floated just over the heads of the passengers, bobbing gently with the motion of the air currents from the air conditioner.

When Corky dispersed, the man's hand passed through the air;

out of balance, he tried to catch himself and ended up grabbing Lauren's arm.

Indignant, she pushed him hard; behind him someone pushed him back with a curse, and suddenly the elevator was filled with cursing, shoving, gouging professionals. With the newcomers on six it had reached capacity and now went straight down to the lobby and opened. Security stared in disbelief as they all stumbled out, some trying for one last telling blow, some running in near hysteria, some holding out briefcases like shields, umbrellas like swords.

"What the fuck?" the security man muttered, and hastened toward the elevator, but by the time he reached the area, most of the passengers had scattered. He watched one, then another, puzzled. Then he looked inside the elevator cage. He gave up. Now his attention was drawn to the Steele woman, Dr. Steele from the nut clinic. She was marching with her chin up, automatically avoiding people, the way one did in a crowd, when suddenly she lurched and nearly fell.

Lauren caught herself and looked around swiftly, sure that the idiot from the elevator had followed her, wanted to continue his curious molestation. There was no one she could directly accuse of pushing her, but she knew a push when she felt it. Guardedly she started to walk again.

As soon as they reached the lobby Corky felt the signal that he had come to recognize as preceding dispersal. Desperately he tightened himself again and walked as close to Lauren as he could. People moved to avoid her, just as she moved to avoid them, but people bumped into Corky, and he was shoved against Lauren. When she lurched, he grabbed her sleeve and stopped the fall, then felt the raincoat fabric slip through his fingers. He willed himself a hand and unwilled it when it appeared firm and pink and quite solid. The tug of too many people was almost irresistible. He wanted to be with the architect who was off to meet a woman in a dim bar, have a few drinks, dinner, then her place. He wanted to go home with the ophthalmologist, and the executive secretary, and he wanted to read the newspaper with the broker. . . . He tensed the muscle as little as possible, and now he could feel Lauren's coat. He held on to the hood and let her tow him out the doors into the cool, moist evening air.

The security man and the FBI agent watched, mystified as Lauren sailed off with her hood stretched out like a bridal veil. The FBI agent detached himself from the wall and followed; the security man resumed his spot at the newsstand and pondered the mystery of having nuts treat nuts.

The *Seattle Times* had dubbed the professional village Yuppie Heaven a few years earlier, and the name was appropriate. Young professionals in aerospace, artificial intelligence, computers, all phases of research flocked to it. There were more toy stores per capita than any other village in the world, it was claimed. More video cassette shops, more elite clothing stores—not for the young scientists, who preferred jeans and turtlenecks and sneakers, but for those who serviced them, the doctors and ophthalmologists and dentists and architects and lawyers. It was a thriving community. A cluster of professional buildings was at its heart, and encircling it were the shops, and finally the housing. Everything one could need or want was to be found within a ten-block radius. Gourmet grocers and some of the best restaurants on the West Coast were there.

That night Lauren walked the first block briskly, then slowed down more and more. She paused at a newsstand and remembered finally to pick up every local paper to be had. She stopped in at the gourmet grocery store and bought a frozen dinner, prepared that day, frozen for someone exactly like her—professional, too busy to cook, sophisticated about food. She bought a bottle of wine; Washington State wine, the rage among the insiders, the shopkeeper said in a near whisper, as if confiding a secret. She walked on. Her next stop was in a store that featured rain gear. She examined the umbrellas and finally selected a large black one with a crook handle that looked like tortoise shell but was really plastic. She walked on.

Behind her the FBI man watched narrowly, expecting her to make a contact of some sort. This was not serious shopping. All those papers, cover for a coded message in one of them, probably. This was precontact dawdling, waiting for the right time, the exact spot. He moved in closer.

And Corky was in near despair. Every time she went into a shop his control was threatened. The shops were small, other people were there. He could not risk another scene like the one in the elevator; he had to relax a bit each time, and each time it was a gamble. He did not trust himself to be able to regroup this often, this rapidly. It was tiring as well, and he realized he was hungry. She had bought only one dinner too. She went into yet another shop and he gripped his center and let the other parts shoot off.

Lauren looked about vaguely. A computer software store? Some teenagers were kidding around with the young clerk, their own age, all speaking a language foreign to her. Two other boys were playing a computer game, so absorbed they never even noticed when she stopped and watched a few seconds. She picked up a packaged game and pretended to be reading it, but actually she was fighting panic. What was she doing in here?

"Can I help you?" the clerk asked at her elbow. He was so young, so fresh-out-of-the-pond young, she thought almost wildly.

"Just looking," she said, and picked up another game.

"What kind of computer do you have?"

"I don't. I mean, it's not for me. My . . . my nephew." She put the box down almost guiltily. What if she told this boy, hardly more than a child, that she was afraid of being alone because she might hallucinate a naked man with red hair? She took a step away from him, turned, and fled.

The agent nodded to himself. Just as he had suspected. She had killed time and now was ready to make the contact. He closed the gap between them even more. And now Corky became aware of him. It was not clear why he was following

Lauren, but it was certain that he was, and Corky wanted her to go home and settle down so he could form himself and have a talk with her, maybe even share her dinner, at least have another banana.

Just then the boy from the computer store yelled, "Hey, lady, you forgot your umbrella!"

Lauren turned, started back. A man walking toward her abruptly darted into the store and began examining games, and Corky floated in with him and made himself a pair of hands that began stuffing computer games into the agent's pockets. Startled, then frightened, the agent jerked them out again, but Corky added a new one for every one he rid himself of.

"Hey, man, what're you doing?" the clerk demanded, returning to see computer games vanishing inside his clothing, reappearing.

"Nothing, nothing." He tried to leave the store, but now the three youths who had been visiting the clerk moved in front of him, and the clerk was dialing a phone rapidly. "Get out of the way," the agent demanded, and tried to pass, but the boys formed a human wall, and while they did not hit him or use any force actually, they were impassable.

Corky streaked away to rejoin Lauren. In a second or two they heard a siren; neither looked back.

She really was afraid to go home, she admitted to herself. She was afraid to be alone. She never hallucinated when she was with people, and she was delaying the possibility of hallucinating again by poking along. She strode faster, angry with herself now. This wasn't a condition that would go away that easily; she had to face it, deal with it, get to the bottom of it. And she might as well begin.

As soon as she was safely inside the lobby of her apartment building, Corky streaked away from her, up through the ceiling, the floors above, through walls into her apartment where he tensed his muscle and began to take shape. He needed time to regroup, and time to find something to put on. No wonder she was always so shocked at seeing him; he would be too. In her closet he found a terry-cloth beach robe and donned it. Now he was ready. He paused at the mirror in her bedroom and admitted that he was not quite ready. He concentrated until there was something inside the robe, a face above it, feet sticking out below. Then he heard her key in the lock and he took a deep breath.

# Chapter Eleven

SOMETHING was wrong, Corky realized, listening to Lauren unlock her door. He had been so intent on making a body and clothing it that he had ignored the signals before, but now he felt tense, uncertain, and knew that something was amiss in the apartment. He let go the muscle a little bit, and began to search. It took only a second to find what he was looking for. On the top bookshelf, behind Lauren's college psychology textbooks, there was a slender, pencillike, silver object. He made himself solid enough to pick it up, to put the beach robe on again. He let other bits range in wider circles, then wider again.

Lauren entered the apartment and reached for the light switch, jerked back her hand. Lights were already on in the bedroom, and in the living room. She caught her breath sharply and looked around for a weapon, then hefted the umbrella she had bought. Silently she edged along the hallway that divided her apartment into halves.

She closed her eyes for a moment when she saw her beach robe hanging in the air with no one in it. A silver object floated before her eyes, turning this way and that, as if the unseen person in her robe was studying it. A wild sense of indignation and outrage suddenly swept over her, and she raised the umbrella.

Corky heard her and paid no attention for the moment. There

they were: two men in the basement of this building, in a small room with electronic equipment, one of them Morris Pitts, the other unknown. Listening to Lauren? Why? He turned to face her just as she swung the umbrella as hard as she could.

"And don't come back!" Lauren yelled as her umbrella caught the robe and swished it through the air. The silver thing fell to the floor. Corky disappeared before the umbrella completed its swing. He was scattered over the face of the earth by the time Lauren yelled and then took a deep breath.

Angrily she threw down the umbrella that was wrapped in her beach robe now, and then marched to the kitchen, where she banged her purse and the frozen dinner into the table. She yanked off her coat and tossed it down, ran her hands through her hair, and only then returned to the living room to look at the silver thing. A bomb? She shuddered, not touching it. A listening device? Slowly she nodded, still not touching it. Why? It had something to do with that awful man, she knew.

Suddenly she sat down hard on the floor near the listening device. She had seen it hanging in the air; she had seen her robe hanging. She shook her head, denying it, but she had seen them. Someone was doing this to her, she thought then, deliberately trying to make her think she was seeing impossible things, trying to make her believe she was going mad. Why? Ever since that terrible man vanished before her eyes, she thought, gazing at the object, no longer seeing it, they had been harassing her. They wanted to make certain she never told; that had to be the reason. If she were mad, she would not be able to tell anyone. Like that movie, she thought, where the woman's husband makes her think she's crazy because he's going to kill her.

Slowly she moved back away from the pencillike object, and then got to her feet, keeping her gaze on it intently. Why was it out in the middle of the room? They must have wanted her to know they were watching, listening; that probably was part of the plan. And that meant conspiracy, no less, but why? Why her? Who was the red-haired man? Why was he so important to them? She was backing across the room and came to a stop when they were: two men in the basement of this building, in a small room with electronic equipment, one of them Morris Pitts, the other unknown. Listening to Lauren? Why? He turned to face her just as she swung the umbrella as hard as she could.

"And don't come back!" Lauren yelled as her umbrella caught the robe and swished it through the air. The silver thing fell to the floor. Corky dispersed before the umbrella completed its swing. He was scattered over the face of the earth by the time Lauren yelled and then took a deep breath.

Angrily she threw down the umbrella that was wrapped in her beach robe now, and then marched to the kitchen, where she banged her purse and the frozen dinner onto the table. She yanked off her coat and tossed it down, ran her hands through her hair, and only then returned to the living room to look at the silver thing. A bomb? She shuddered, not touching it. A listening device? Slowly she nodded, still not touching it. Why? It had something to do with that awful man, she knew.

Suddenly she sat down hard on the floor near the listening device. She had seen it hanging in the air; she had seen her robe hanging. She shook her head, denying it, but she had seen them. Someone was doing this to her, she thought then, deliberately trying to make her think she was seeing impossible things, trying to make her believe she was going mad. Why? Ever since that terrible man vanished before her eyes, she thought, gazing at the object, no longer seeing it, they had been harassing her. They wanted to make certain she never told; that had to be the reason. If she were mad, she would not be able to tell anyone. Like that movie, she thought, where the woman's husband makes her think she's crazy because he's going to kill her.

Slowly she moved back away from the pencillike object, and then got to her feet, keeping her gaze on it intently. Why was it out in the middle of the room? They must have wanted her to know they were watching, listening; that probably was part of the plan. And that meant conspiracy, no less, but why? Why her? Who was the red-haired man? Why was he so important to them? She was backing across the room and came to a stop when she bumped into the windowsill. She spun around and raised the window, then ran back to the device and picked it up gingerly, crossed the room again, and hurled it as far as she could. She slammed the window down and locked it and did not move again for a long time, taking deep breaths, waiting for her heart to get back to normal.

When she finally left the window, she moved as if afraid she might be overheard. She looked about warily, not certain what she was looking for. More spy devices? They could have the whole apartment bugged, she thought, and made herself take another deep breath. But they could, she repeated silently, and her office. She went to the kitchen and opened the package that contained her dinner, then looked at it, puzzled. She had to eat, she told herself; she turned on the microwave. Mechanically she made a salad, removed the frozen chicken and mushroom entree, and then ordered herself to eat. She had to get out, she thought, and realized she had made virtually no sound since entering the apartment, and that she was afraid of making a sound. She had to get out of here, she thought again. And she had to be sure she was not followed, she added, remembering the green car. She almost laughed then. How?

The phone rang; she dropped her fork with the first piece of chicken breast still impaled on it. On the fourth ring her own voice said from the machine: "I'm sorry, I can't come to the phone right now. At the sound of the tone, please leave your name and number and I'll get back to you as soon as possible. Thanks." She realized she was holding her breath and let it out softly, listening. Then Morris Pitts was speaking, strong and reassuring and comforting. She closed her eyes in relief.

"Lauren, please answer. I'll call back in exactly five minutes. Please talk to me. Five minutes."

Morris! He would know what she could do. There must be a law, she thought, to protect innocent citizens from . . . from . . . what or who? She pushed her plate aside and stood up, went to the phone and regarded it uneasily. Someone had entered without leaving a trace, she realized, and had planted a listening device, or something. Why? Who? And if Morris came up, no doubt they, whoever they were, would include him in their surveillance. That was intolerable; he was a respected lawyer. To be dragged into whatever mess she had landed in might damage his career, his future, their relationship, if one ever had a chance to develop. His flowers were on her table, a garden growing day by day, scenting the apartment. In a city of strangers, he cared, and she had to protect him if she could. She reached out and turned off the sound of the ring on her telephone answering machine.

With her finger still on the button, she became immobilized. What if they had a hidden camera, were watching her every movement? She had to act natural, not warn them that she was planning to escape long enough to think, to rest. Now every motion became stiff and jerky; she moved like a puppet. She returned to the table and looked at her dinner with disgust, started to rake off the food into the garbage disposal. She wanted to get out the map and find a place to hide in, but she did not dare. They might realize what she planned—if they were watching.

A few miles away Trigger Happy was nodding in satisfaction. Her accomplice was someone in her building. He had been waiting for her, and she had thrown him out. That much they knew. Now he ordered a complete check on everyone in the apartment building. It was shaping up. Things were coming together, the way they usually did when an expert got to work.

He had to admire the Steele girl. She had eluded two of the best men in the area, and she had managed so far to keep out of the clutches of Morris Pitts. That gave him more satisfaction than he would have admitted. Pitts had been so damned sure of himself. He hid his smile and clamped his teeth on the cigar in his mouth, and turned to glower at the scarecrow of a scientist, Bill Bentson. And they, Trigger Happy, thought meanly, the two half-assed scientists, hadn't come up with a damn thing yet.

"We think your scenario was probably the correct one,"

Bentson said. He was gray-faced, his eyes sunken, and if he lost any more weight, he would blow away in the first stiff breeze. "We think Corcoran pulled a vanishing act that just happened to coincide with our test. Just like you said to the Steele woman. The laser malfunctioned. It'll take a year or even two to find out why, but this much we know now. There's no way it could have been responsible for his disintegration. There's just no way."

And that meant he'd have his marching orders for San Diego and the antigravity demonstration, and then on to some other cockeyed demonstration, and on and on. And that meant that the Corky commie and Steele and whoever else was in the nest of spies would become routine FBI business with no place for him. And he would retire a colonel. He would work his butt off on the loony-bin assignments and then they would kiss him off and the FBI would take credit for breaking the Seattle ring and he would retire a colonel. He rolled the cigar to the other side of his mouth.

"You're just tired," Trigger Happy said then. "Get some sleep. You know she was telling the truth, same's me. Get some sleep."

Bill Bentson shook his head. "No way it could happen," he muttered as he pulled himself upright painfully. "No way."

Trigger Happy watched him slouch out of the hotel apartment and he wondered if the scarecrow had sold out, Mallory Akins, the lot of them. Maybe they were all in on it. He no longer had Corky's papers in the hotel; they were not safe here, he understood. They were in an underground vault at CaCo, with a guard around the clock in an anteroom. He had photocopies of everything, and he now opened a folder that contained them and started to examine them all one more time. They had something the Corky commie didn't want found, he was certain, or why risk trying to get at them in this very suite? He pored over them until his vision started to blur, and then he went to bed no wiser than before.

Lauren lay rigidly and tense in her bed, willing the night to pass, daylight to arrive. She would leave early, she had decided, take her car, and get mixed into the heavy morning traffic. It seemed logical to her that if she had a follower, it would be easier to lose him during the rush hour than later. She would take nothing with her, arouse no suspicions by going out with a suitcase. She stared into darkness, perfecting her plan, wishing it were morning.

Corky dreamed with Bill Bentson and the dreams were of mathematics and strange symbols that danced, joined, separated in a mad choreography. He fished with a trawler crew, and flew with a captain. He drank vodka with a lonely boy whose eyes were burning and he was the girl whose letter the boy held while she made love with another youth. He played the slots in Atlantic City and watched the sunrise off Key West, and inspected the sugar crop in Cuba, the fish in Jamaica, the coffee in Venezuela. He studied attack plans and defense plans and watched the final touches being applied to a car bomb. He walked with a man on his way to work, stopped to talk to several uniformed men, joking, kidding. The car appeared and careened out of control and he was the man with no warning, with the realization too late; he was the others who had been laughing; he was the woman on her way to clean; he was the young woman watching from a café, nursing a cup of coffee, watching with growing horror and despair and a nearly clinical detachment as she counted seconds.

He was whirling and there were bits of another consciousness whirling nearby. He merged with them and knew the pain, a total, excruciating pain that suddenly ceased. The other was gone. He tried to follow and it was as if he had hit a wall of steel and was flung back with such force that there was no way he could halt the momentum, but streaked faster than ever in a trajectory that took him far away. Enough awareness was there to scream out for help, and with the voiceless cry, his pieces flew together and Corky took shape.

He was high in the sky, falling, falling, and below were dozens of people staring in disbelief as he hurtled from a cloudless sky toward them. Two of them raised automatic rifles and fired, panic-stricken, and he vanished. American and Germans alike denied what they had seen. It had been ball lightning, or a strange bird, or a kite, or a freak of vision, sunlight on a cloud.

He held a weak center and sought an anchor, anything to hold on to. And he formed again in the vault with his own papers, his own sketches and pens and pencils. He was shivering uncontrollably.

He clutched his sketchbook to his chest, taking long, aching breaths with his eyes closed; the past night was gone from memory, leaving a residue of terror and dread.

Finally he opened his eyes; the vault was inky black. He had not seen his sketchbook, he had simply known it was here. In the same way he found a light switch, just by knowing it was there, and turned on a bare light overhead and looked around. He did not know where he was. A bank? A bomb shelter? He went beyond the wall and found the guard who was doing a crossword puzzle with a ball-point pen. Beyond that, outside to a gray predawn light, scant traffic. Back into the vault. Why did they have his stuff locked up, guarded? He was afraid to relax the muscle that would let him enter the guard, search for answers. Not again, not yet. This time he was determined to keep his center intact until he knew what was happening to him and why, and how to make it stop.

Minerva, he thought suddenly, and corrected himself. Lauren Steele. He had been in her apartment waiting for her and had found the listening device and she had tried to hit him with her umbrella. He shook his head, puzzled all over again, but now he had a target, and he flowed out of the vault, back to Lauren's apartment, where he worked on putting together a solid body one more time.

—You have made interesting points many times, of course, and now it is my turn. Consider the statement: *Cogito ergo sum.* I think. Who thinks? I think. That is the most important part of the premise, you understand, considering our situation here, I mean. I think, therefore I am. To be permitted to prove one's existence through the product of one's mind is a tautology, I trust you will admit. However, that is why I want us to disregard all but the first two words of the premise. I think, and the product of my thinking is a thought, an idea, a concept, a memory, a wish, whatever it may be, just as long as it is confined to the interior of my own psyche, and the psyche is that part of the brain that we choose to separate from the various other parts such as the autonomous systems, and call by that appellation. When the thought is acted upon, then, of course, the other parts of the brain control the actions, the muscles and nerves, vocal systems, visual, aural, whatever must be involved in such action. We separate them out also, and consider only the thought, the thinking brain. The intelligent mind that orders and dreams.

—Yes, yes. What you say is self-evident. Do push on with it, if you will.

—Of course. So now we have various parts of the brain involved in various kinds of mental activity ranging from pure thought to regulating the heartbeat and lung fuctions to running footraces. You see the dilemma we are approaching, I trust. Here we can activate no muscles, regulate no hearts, engage in no physical activities whatsoever. If you find my thought processes offensive, you cannot punch me in the nose or throw decaying fruits at me.

—I can leave, and I think it is time for me to do just that.

—Even that is a fallacy, I fear. You cannot go anywhere; therefore you cannot leave. All you can do is think something else. And that, I maintain, is not your own doing, but the result of another's will. You have no will, you see.

—Do you realize where your arguments take one? Have you not grasped the implications of this line of thought?

—Naturally I have followed it to its only conclusion, as any reasonable mind would do before discussing it publicly. You cannot act without an acting body. You have no systems to regulate, thus no regulatory part of a brain system. You and I are thought only, immaterial, without the capability to do anything except think. And whose brain is thinking? Not mine. I have none. Not yours. You have none either. Who is thinking this thought? Who is thinking your response?

—And whose hand wound up the universal clock in the first

place? Next you'll bring in the uncaused cause, the unmoved mover arguments. All tired, worn out. Little minds can't see past the mechanical clock that ticks only when it is set in motion. There are, there truly are more things in heaven and earth than your little mind can grasp. Always explanations, mechanisms, blueprints, and without them you argue yourself out of existence. I think. That's who. *I* think!

—With what? Where is the working brain? The neurons, the synapses, the nourishing blood?

—Does the synapse have awareness of the brain that surrounds it? Does the blood cell know the route of veins and arteries?

—Good Lord, do they go on like that all the time?

—Sometimes it gets worse, especially when a couple others join in, then you should hear them. At least they're being polite now. There's the place I wanted to show you. See, I'm in the kitchen scrubbing away at the pots and pans. Here he comes.

—My goodness, he's pretty! And you're lighter than I thought you would be. I was thinking deep brown, I guess. You're very beautiful. I'm surprised they had you in the kitchen instead of the bedroom or nursery, at least.

—Mistress didn't like pretty ones around at all. Jealous. Watch.

—The little shit! Did he do that often?

—Two, three times a week. Then I had the dream. There it is. See, a naked girl on the block with a suckling babe. I sure thought it was me, having his babe ripped out of my arms, being sold downriver. So I split his head with the cleaver. That's when they beat me to death. We meet and talk about it sometimes, both of us sorry, and all that. Life sure was funny, wasn't it?

—I've never found myself over there. I've looked and looked, and sometimes I think, maybe that girl, or that one, but never for sure. Maybe it's too bad for me to know about.

—Nah, it's not that. Some do, some don't, that's all. You probably just lived a nice quiet life, had kids, passed away peaceful in your sleep one night.

—You think so? Maybe it was just too boring for me to want to look now. I wonder what anyone would get from me if I were the one being tapped. I understand the composers and their music.

Just being near them is like being in a grand concert hall. And the artists always painting pictures or making statues in their thoughts. Anyone would certainly get a lot out of any of them. But not from me. A waste of time tapping me.

—Maybe not. Maybe you'd give them a little peace. What do they call it? Tranquility. Maybe they'd just feel good. Me? Let me tell you, they'd think they'd stumbled on a mama tiger guarding her kittens, that's what. And I never even had a kid.

—One time I was looking in on a girl in Spain or Portugal, I'm not sure which, and she was being mistreated by her father, you know what I mean, and a girl from over there tapped me just when things were getting very bad. Anyway, she became convinced that in a past life she had been the victim of incest in a fishing village. Reincarnation was all she could think. She made up the most fantastic stories the rest of her life and made quite a lot of money, I believe.

—Oh, oh. You feel that? It's that man from over there again, I bet. What's he want, trying to come through before his time?

—Don't let him pass! There, he's gone again. Whatever does he think he's doing? Some people just don't know their place! The nerve!

Lauren woke up groggily, sniffing in disbelief. Coffee? She had slept badly, was not rested, but coffee? No wonder she was so tired, she thought; she had added sleepwalking to her list of dysfunctions. She pulled on her robe and walked dispiritedly to the kitchen, where freshly made coffee was hot, ready. On the table was a sheet of paper with a message: *Please don't panic. I have to talk to you.*

She poured coffee and gulped it, then picked up the pencil on the table and added a line to the note: *Later. The apartment is bugged.*

She was lost, she knew. After a day or two of rest she would have to seek treatment from someone who was not Peter Waycross. A real psychiatrist who would want to institutionalize her, start her on a course of tranquilizers. She knew the routine and had long denied its value, but she needed help, real help. Blinking back tears, she went to shower and dress, and Corky watched her in bewilderment. He had expected more anger, or fear, or even panic, but she was acting as if she had expected him, and simply did not want to be bothered. He looked again at her note and shook his head. There wasn't anything else in the apartment; he had searched as soon as he had gained control over himself.

Carefully he wrote: *Stay away from the elevator, or it will be chaos again.*

When she returned and saw the addition, she paled and swayed momentarily, then nodded, moistened her lips, wrote: *I'm going for a long ride in the car.* She tore the sheet of paper off the notepad and folded it, put it into her purse.

Good, Corky thought, and waited for her to leave. He hesitated over finishing the process of becoming visible, and decided not yet. It would be too hard for her to explain if he showed up in her beach robe and nothing else. When she started to walk down the stairs, with him at her heels, he realized that he would have to be more careful when he communicated with her in the future. He had not meant the elevator here, but the one at work with too many people jammed into it.

No one had expected her to walk down five flights of stairs, and the agent on duty in the garage was not prepared when she appeared suddenly and got into her car and left. He caught up a block away, but he was in a sweat by then, and felt only relief when he reported in that she was moving and was told that Gerald Morrisey was on her tail also, and between them they had better not lose her again.

# Chapter Twelve

IT had been a mistake, Lauren realized, to get into this kind of traffic. She was in a no-turn lane that was going to take her to the interstate and there was nothing she could do about it. She turned on the radio, then ignored it, and muttered, "No one else in my family ever went crazy." Her two sisters were a little crazy, she continued angrily. Crazy about money and handsome men and model houses and designer clothes, and that kind of crazy was normal, while she, who cared little or nothing about any of that, she was the one who was losing it all. Her mind was all she had to lose, she added meanly. She should have gathered rosebuds and jewels and then she would have had something to give up, but it didn't count if you didn't care about the loss, her thoughts went on inexorably. You live in a hovel with a dozen kids and they're all you have, that's what they take away. You live in a mansion and they take your health and your money, put you in a nursing home or something. Live the way she did, trying to take care of herself, minding her own business, proud of her good brain, and that's what they came after. Who's they? she demanded, and there was no answer. Just they. Goddamn them!

Beside her Corky admired her profile, the clean lines of her face bones, chiseled, not too sharp, just well defined. She was staring fixedly straight ahead and very gradually he came to realize that she had not yet admitted his presence. He regarded her more warily. How could she explain their written communication without admitting he was there? Or someone was there? And this muttering, with an occasional curse thrown in, what was that all about?

The morning newscast was giving details concerning a car bomb, calling it a suicide mission in which seven people had been killed, and countless injured. The driver was among the dead, the voice intoned.

"That's a lie," Corky said.

Lauren swerved, caught the wheel harder than ever, and continued to drive. A muscle worked in her jaw.

Corky let out a soft breath and relaxed his own strange muscle a bit, became less coherent, with bits circling in wider orbits, but he kept the center in the front seat of her car. But what they said about the car bomb was a lie, he said to himself. He had seen what happened, the woman watching, the car without a driver, the men— He stopped the line of thought. How had he seen any of that? When? On television, he said doubtfully. It had to have been on television. He remembered seeing it all, even the name incised in black on white marble: World Television Corporation.

Now that he had relaxed, he knew he was treading the dangerous margin where it was easier to fly apart than to maintain a center. But if he kept a tighter center, he might spook her again, and next time she might not be able to keep control of the car. They needed time alone, he thought almost desperately, time without interruptions, without traffic, without followers. With the thought of followers, he realized that he had been monitoring a car-to-car conversation between two men who were at that moment following Lauren. One car was a dark gray Impala, the other a green Dodge. Two men were in the gray car, one in the Dodge. He looked over the Impala, traced the wire from the phone one of the men spoke into, examined the electronic gear without understanding what any of it was, and then did the same with the Dodge. It was two car lengths behind Lauren's Toyota, keeping that distance easily. The driver spoke in a terse monotone to the other men. The Impala was in the middle lane, several car lengths back.

Lauren was unaware of them both, Corky was certain. He did not dare let go enough to be able to enter any of their thoughts, and at the moment it did not occur to him that he could do such a thing. He concentrated on keeping a center as close to Lauren as he could, and that left him very little to work with away from her.

Traffic was slowing as a long line of cars was funneled onto Interstate 5. Lauren and the Dodge had no choice; they were in the turn lane. The Impala was in a lane that allowed a turn or not. The driver flicked on his turn signal, and Corky made up his mind. He had to get rid of them both, and he might as well try now, he decided. He left Lauren and gathered shape in the back seat of the Impala. He reached past the driver and turned off the signal.

The driver turned it on again, frowning slightly in annoyance. His partner was speaking to the agent in the Dodge, paying no attention to him. Corky turned off the signal again.

"What the hell," the driver muttered. "Damn thing's broken." He pushed the button to roll down his window. Corky pushed it, and the window stopped going down, shot up instead.

"What's wrong?" the other man asked, putting his hand over the mouthpiece of the phone.

"Electrical systems fucked up. I thought this baby was in the garage last week."

"Christ! It was. Just don't lose her. Okay?" He sounded disgusted and turned his attention back to the phone.

Corky depressed all the window buttons and the wind flowed through the car. The driver slowed down; behind them other drivers began to lean on their horns.

Corky closed the windows. He reached past the driver, who was sweating, and looked wild, and began to push buttons, turn knobs randomly. The windshield wipers came on; the radio blared, the airconditioner blasted frigid air, the vents opened wide, a tape player came on full volume playing "Wyoming

Blues," and now both agents were swatting as if the car were full of hornets. Corky turned off the phone.

"I'm pulling over!" the driver cried, and cut in front of a Chevy, crossed to the side of the busy street, made a sudden right turn onto a second street.

"The colonel will kill us," the other agent said over the wail of the tape before he could get it turned off.

"The colonel can go fuck himself!" The driver switched off the ignition and held up his hand; it was shaking. "My God," he said in a near whimper. "Holy Christ, what was going on?" The car was quiet; everything off that should have been off, the motor stilled. Corky streaked back to Lauren, who was gazing straight ahead with her fixed, nearly blind stare.

At that moment the colonel was in a speechless rage, standing at the open door of the vault. The Corky commie's papers were scattered again. The light was on.

"Soon's I saw it, I backed off," the security guard said at his side. "No one's gone in yet. We'll lift prints if there are any."

Ponderously the colonel turned and glared at him. "I want a list of everyone who has the combination and the keys and whatever else it takes to open the goddamn thing. Right now! And the man on duty through the night! Right now!" The whole damn company, Trigger Happy realized, the whole goddamn company was suspect! This security turkey, the president, down to the janitors. The whole bunch of them! This turkey had said just a little too smugly that, of course, they had all had a complete security check. He'd find out that he didn't know what a real security check was! "Where's the sergeant who was supposed to be watching the vault door last night?"

"In the outer office, sir. Sergeant Mattingly."

Trigger Happy jerked around and marched to the door. Without looking back at the security guard, he grunted, "I'll see him with McWilliams. You stay out."

Lieutenant McWilliams was waiting for him, escorted him to the right office and opened the door. Sergeant Mattingly sprang to attention. He told the only story he could: he had seen nothing, heard nothing. He had been awake and alert all night, and had passed the time doing a crossword puzzle. Trigger Happy confiscated it.

In his own office again, he stood at the window and studied the landscape: too many trees for real security. A man could duck behind a tree, make a dash to the next one, all the way from the parking lot to the main building. It was raining. He knew McWilliams was standing on the opposite side of the room, not quite at attention, that was not required, but neither was he at ease. Mattingly was McWilliams's man; they had worked together many times before, he had said. Trigger Happy nodded now. That figured. One more thing, he thought darkly, just one more thing and he would bring in a whole new crew, his own men, handpicked, trusted. These bastards were all amateurs, every last one of them. So West Coast laid back, elephants could stampede and they wouldn't notice a thing. He had not yet moved from the window when the report came in that one of the surveillance cars had malfunctioned and dropped out, leaving only one agent following the Steele girl.

McWilliams made the report, and now his face had a pallor that had not been noticeable before. He had few details yet, only that the electrical system had failed in the chase car. Trigger Happy listened without expression, then made a dismissing gesture, unable to speak. He had turned to ice.

He sat down heavily at his desk. His gaze happened to rest on the crossword puzzle, done except for a small section in the lower right-hand quadrant. A four-letter word for a volcanic lake. MAAR? He did not believe in any such word. He did not believe anyone could do a puzzle like that with a ball-point pen. Not a goddamn sergeant in his fucking army. He nodded, his eyes narrow and cold. That figured. The sergeant, Morris Pitts and his failures to get to her, maybe McWilliams, security at the plant, probably everyone at Waycross Clinic . . . What had the paper called this area? The gateway to the Orient. Stories about trade delegations going to China, to Japan, Korea, other delegations coming from them all. Go up the coast, cross over Alaska, and where would you come out? Russia. That close. That easy. Gateway to the commies, that's what it was. Gateway, getaway. There wasn't a single goddamn son of a bitch in the Northwest he could trust! He thought of the silver-haired agent and repeated the words. Where had he been when we lost China? he wondered, and made a mental note to check. And the area FBI director? Those were his stooges letting Steele go where she wanted when she wanted without a tail. Where had that turkey been? Who did he report to?

He thought of the scarecrow, Bill Bentson, denying anything happened. *They* had got to him, he knew now. And probably to Mallory Akins too. Sure they would deny anything happened.

Slowly, painfully, he worked it all out. No one was to be trusted for now. That was number one. The Corky commie's papers had something in them that they wanted, and had not been able to get yet. The papers were not safe anywhere unless he took charge of them personally. And the puzzle, he decided, belonged with the Corky commie's papers. That puzzle was too pat, too phony. No one did the *New York Times* crossword in ink. He knew that in the same way, just part of the vast body of knowledge that guided him day after day without question. And he could not let even a hint of his suspicions reach *them*. He had to pretend to trust McWilliams, for instance, and watch everything, everyone. Enough rope, that was first, and when he had the goods, he would fly back to Washington and present his case, bring the roof down on the whole city, if that's what it would take. He saw himself as the white man, wearing the white hat, on the white horse surrounded by *them*. He called McWilliams back and ordered up the Corky commie's papers, all of them, and when they were brought to him, deliberately stuffed everything into his briefcase and turned the key in the lock. He already had put the puzzle in it. He would study it in his hotel suite that night, and study the Corky commie's papers until he had their secret, and meanwhile they were in the only really safe place there was.

*　　*　　*

Lauren pulled off the interstate at the first gas station complex. After filling her tank, she parked and looked for a telephone. She had to call Peter, tell him she would be back in a few days. Ask for help again? She almost snorted aloud at the thought.

The green Dodge pulled in and the agent waited until it was clear that she was going to make a call. Then he parked also, and started to walk toward the phones. He had to report in, complain about being alone on such a difficult case.

As soon as the agent left his car, Corky floated inside it, where he solidified enough to put the car in reverse and release the emergency brake.

"Look, Peter," Lauren was saying, "I have to have a few days off. I . . . I'm not well. It was too much of a shock, having that man vanish in front of me. Just tell my clients to sit alone in my office for their fifty minutes. They'll get as much benefit as they would from me!" Her voice grew shriller as she talked, not letting Peter get in a word until she finished.

"Lauren, Lauren! My God, a stroke of genius! My dear Lauren, you are a genius! I never thought of doing that, never, never. And you—"

She hung up, glared at the telephone, then left the booth. She heard but paid no attention to a shout from the other side of the gas pumps: "Hey, mister, your car's rolling!" She took no notice at all of the minicrash and the commotion that followed. She got back behind her wheel, started her engine, and pulled out of the station.

"The government's good for the insurance," Corky muttered, thinking of the way the Dodge had run ever so gently into a very large truck with a very large and angry driver.

Lauren clamped her lips on the sob she refused to allow at the sound of his voice. She looked straight ahead, both hands tight and hard on the steering wheel.

"Lauren, it's all right," he said softly. "Both cars are gone. No one's following us. We can talk. Okay?"

She drove faster and he leaned back uneasily. Suicidal? He had not thought so before, now he was less certain. After a minute had passed she slowed a little and he relaxed also. But he had to talk to her, he knew, had to make her admit he was there, make plans on where they were going. He cleared his throat. "Are you all right?"

"Oh, sure," she said in a shrill voice. "I'm having a breakdown. Peter won't take it seriously. Agents are after me. I don't know why. I don't know where I'm going. And I'm talking to my own hallucination. I'm fine, really fine."

"I'm real enough," he muttered. "I'd make myself visible to prove it, but I don't seem to have any clothes. You didn't bring your beach robe, you know." She was doing eighty again. "You're going to get a ticket, if you don't kill both of us first," he said reasonably.

Tears blurred her vision and she hit the brake hard. A truck behind her blasted its air horn, then pulled out to pass.

"Don't you know where we're going, really?" Corky asked. "I know this area. Pull off at the next exit. There's a shopping center a mile or two off the road, and we'll need a few things."

"Oh, God," she moaned. But, since that was what she had intended from the start, she began to watch for the exit.

"My conscience," she said aloud. "Or my superego. My unconscious. The right hemisphere."

"What are you talking about?"

"The voice of God. The devil. The manifestation of a long-repressed split personality. Schizophrenia, delusions of persecution."

"Oh," he said, understanding finally. "None of the above. There's the turn. At the road, make a left for the shopping center."

She obeyed without demur. She had noticed these turns on the map, she told herself, and simply had not thought about them all again.

The store he guided her to was a K Mart, where she struggled with her shopping basket for only a second or two, then let it take her where it would. The men's department—jeans, sweatshirt, socks, sneakers, a robe. The women's department with similar clothes for her, some of them even the right size. Toothbrushes, toothpaste. The stationery section. A sketchbook floated to her basket, pencils, a notebook. She started to turn toward the checkout counter; the basket was jerked the other way. She tugged for a moment, then gave up and followed it. A woman holding a small boy by the hand moved quickly out of the way, staring hard at her. The little boy was smiling broadly.

"We'll need a bag to keep our things in," Corky said close to her ear. She shuddered. "I hope you have enough money for all this stuff." A zippered bag rose from a display, floated to her cart.

When she started to drive again, it was away from the interstate on a small, winding road. She saw a sign for the ferry to Whidbey Island. Of course, she thought.

"Now that I have some clothes," Corky said, "if you want to stop someplace, I could come in all the way and get dressed."

"No! It's bad enough that I hear voices. I don't want to see hallucinations. Never again!" Could she control it? It had not occurred to her to try to control her own madness before.

"Lauren," he said reasonably. She hated it when he sounded reasonable. "I'm real. Honest. I don't know how I got into this condition, but I am real. Why is it easier for you to believe in hallucinations than to believe I'm real? One seems as unlikely as the other to me."

She eased the car into a line waiting for the ferry. There were only four other cars. The boat was drawing near with a cloud of gulls in eddying motion over it, the wide wake brilliantly white against the dark-gray water, the sky only fractionally paler gray. Here at the docking area the odor of fuel overwhelmed the ocean smells.

Staring ahead, Lauren said, "I'm neurotic. I don't sleep well. I'm fearful of the future. I don't trust my own ability as a therapist. I hate making up tests and administering them. I despise telling people to stay in jobs that aren't good for them, and I do it every day. I know Peter is a phony, our office is a cheat, Warren Foley volunteered his head for football too many years, and Rich Steinman is a wimp. I wouldn't trust any of them with my real feelings or fears. I'm too tall and my hair is awful because I don't know what to do with it. My feet are too big. I was too smart in school and I never made any friends because I couldn't talk to anyone and they didn't like me because I was so big and ugly."

Suddenly the air was filled with the noises of engines being started. The ferry had arrived; the cars were awakening, her line coming to life. A stream of arriving automobiles snaked off the ferry, passed slowly. Lauren realized that she could say these things, things she never had even thought through. She could say them all. She had not gone into psychoanalysis because she had been afraid to be analyzed; she had decided there was no point in that because overt behavior was all that mattered, not what bleak landscape filled the terrain of the psyche. She had denied the psyche altogether. Statistics and averages and norms and patterns of behavior mattered, nothing else. And she had not talked. But now she could. She would.

"What I'm going to do," she told her hallucination grimly, "is find a grocery and buy some food, get an isolated beach cabin, and do my own analysis, for as long as it takes." She drove onto the ferry and continued to sit in her car as other drivers left theirs to take up positions at the rail, watching the departure.

"I'm lonely," she whispered. "Why is that? Why should a healthy young woman in this day of liberation be lonely? And you," she finished with fierce satisfaction, "will stay there and listen, and when you finally vanish and don't come back, I'll know I'm cured."

"When you buy food, will you please get enough for two?" Corky asked meekly.

"Hallucinations don't eat!" she snapped, and yanked open her door, got out, and went to the rail and watched the swirling gulls, the dwindling dock, and then the growing island.

The cars ticked as they cooled down; doors slammed; people talked, shouted, laughed; the workhorse engines of the ferry grumbled and roared in her ears, entered as vibrations through the metal deck beneath her feet. She faced the island, into the wind, and blamed it for the burning in her eyes. The wind smelled of ocean now, and it was very good.

# Chapter Thirteen

YEAH, Corky wanted to say to Lauren. Lonely, that's right! That's exactly how it is! He was overcome with a feeling of solemnity, an unexpected upwelling of sadness. Lonely, by God! Yeah, lonely. He could go talk to the guys, kid around, smoke a joint, drink a beer, and each one of them would sink deeper and deeper into himself. Or he could go somewhere with Joan, talk about the movie they had just watched and say, really good, wasn't it, or, what a stinker, and that was the end of that. He always returned to his drawings, a painting he was working on, something that let him be alone, not because he especially wanted to be alone, but because it was easier that way. He could say what he thought to the drawings and they didn't laugh at him, or look puzzled, or worse, look blank. Lonely. She had put a name on what had been bugging him for years even when he was surrounded by people, or maybe especially when he was surrounded.

He watched her lean her elbows on the rail and gaze out over the water and he knew her eyes would be bright with tears that she could blame on the wind in her face, just as he could blame the wind for his own burning eyes. He wished he could comfort her, and he knew that his presence was not only not a comfort, but actually a threat to her well-being. He sighed and eased himself from the car and stood by a nearer rail to watch the circling gulls. At least they knew what the hell they were up to, what life meant. Garbage, he thought; to a gull garbage meant a good life.

They left the ferry and she started to drive on the island, no destination in mind, no rush now. She was so deep in her own brooding thoughts that she saw little of the scenery she passed: farms, sheep, goats, cattle, and always the mountains. Sometimes the road was high enough to catch a glimpse of the sea or the pass that separated the island from the mainland. On the east side of the island no wind was apparent; as soon as she drove over a crest, made a curving turn, the wind blew with a steady force. The land narrowed, and at the waist both the pass and the ocean were visible; Lauren began to come back from the abyss her thoughts had carried her to. She nodded at the landscape in approval; this was what she had been looking for, fresh wind, sea air, few people, no noise. She marveled now at the size of the ferns on the steep hills. Deep forests and ferns, a primeval scene, a healing scene. At Oak Harbor she stopped in a grocery and bought food enough for the next day or two, and again held back her wail of protest when things she had not chosen appeared in the grocery cart, when she lost control of it and followed where it went.

She found a store that seemed to specialize in limited selections of everything and picked out a tape recorder and six hours' worth of tapes. She added a notebook also, remembered she already had bought one and started to put the new one down. Very clearly she thought, but the other one is for him, and she bit her cheek to keep from crying out. At the counter she asked about cabins, cottages, anything except a motel. Kirby's Cottages, she was told, and listened carefully to the directions, and then was on her way again. She knew exactly what she intended to do.

The narrow lane that left the highway wound about the foot of a steep hill that looked like a fern farm. A meadow sloped down to the ocean front, where a deep rocky beach gleamed under a receding tide. The waves were high and noisy, just what she needed, she thought with satisfaction. She could climb, walk, hike, meditate, drown herself, throw herself off a cliff, whatever seemed appropriate. Mr. Kirby accepted that she wanted a cottage with an ocean view, and that she was alone, with bland disapproval.

"Never been out here in the winter, I expect," he said, taking her credit card. "Move you tomorrow, tonight, whenever you get ready. Wood's on the stoop, power's on. Number six. Restaurant's down the road a mile, Smiler's Fish House. Good food. Number six's equipped, though, if you want to cook."

He was a bent brown man with gnarly hands, a corduroy face, and very blue eyes. Now he smiled at her. "You want anything, miss, you yell. I'll be right here."

"Thanks," she said. "I just want to be alone and get some work done. I'll be fine."

A gravel-topped track led her to number six, which was as isolated as Mr. Kirby had said. Behind it the fern-clad hill rose steeply; dense evergreen trees cut off the view from both sides, and in front the hillside dropped down to the sea. The ferns rippled and waved, darkened, lightened in a dance with the constant wind. Perfect. She stood on the protected little stoop, taking one very deep breath after another, drinking in the sea air, welcoming the wind songs, the ocean sounds, the noises that were not manmade, not horns, traffic, not telephones. Finally she entered the cabin.

The living room had a large fireplace, windows that overlooked the ocean, with a kitchen area at the end. It was paneled in a glowing red-hued wood; there was a braided rug on the floor, a red and yellow afghan on a couch, a coffee table before the couch, several wooden chairs with red cushions. Cheerful. Warm. Inviting. The bedroom also had windows facing the ocean. Perfect, she said again silently. She went out to the car to unload.

She picked up the groceries; Corky lifted the bag from K Mart and carried it in. She moved out of the way, wide-eyed.

"How do you explain that?" he demanded, putting the bag down on a heavy table.

She moved backward, too pale, too stiff. "It happens," she said in a low voice. "The patient does things and forgets, blames the delusional system she has worked out. It happens."

He rummaged through the bag, looking for the robe, pulled it out and yanked off the price tags, tossed them down, started to put on the robe.

"You can't be here," Lauren said through tight lips. "You can't. I saw you die. If you're here, you have to be a ghost, and I don't believe in ghosts!"

He had started to form a more solid self when she spoke, had become almost visible. Now the robe fluttered to the floor; he was gone.

Lauren sank into a chair at the table, shaking. After a moment she got up and finished unpacking, then made coffee. When the coffee was ready, she took it to the window and held the hot cup with both hands, trying to warm herself with it. The ocean swells became waves that crashed into the shoreline with the rumble of constant thunder. Mountains of scudding foam raced before the wind. Puffs were carried aloft to be shattered, to scatter and vanish. Just like him, she thought. Tomorrow she would walk the beach, she told herself distantly, and hike the hill, and . . . Tomorrow seemed a long time away.

The shock of her words had dispersed Corky, and he fought desperately to hold enough to let him think of what the words meant. Dead? Was that his problem? He did not feel dead, but, he had to admit worriedly, neither did he feel anything like he had felt for all of his life until recently. He was in the office with Mr. Kirby, reading a horoscope magazine. He was on the beach with two small children dashing here and there. He was in a car poking along on the highway, with an elderly couple. All wrong, he thought, the center whirling out over the Juan de Fuca Strait, landing on a cargo ship heading north. He spun out of it again, and was in a store in Oak Harbor. Here, then there, without transition, without willing it, without moving or thinking. Here, then there. Was that being dead? Where were the others? No, damn it! he cried soundlessly. He was not yet through with living! He spun back to the cabin, where Lauren was at the window talking. The tape recorder was on the windowsill, turned on.

"When I was little," she was saying, "we had a large globe of the world, and one day I realized that if I started to walk south, I would end up at the South Pole. From anywhere on earth I would end up there if I kept going long enough. But at the South Pole there was no way to get back home without help, without instruments. A difference of a fingernail width would take me to Moscow or to Madras, or somewhere else. That made me realize that the world is mysterious and dangerous. You can go out alone, but you need help to get back. That's why you can't go home again, not because of family or other problems. You can't find it." She paused.

Corky was not all the way back yet; he could see that she was shivering. The cottage was frigid. He went to the door. "Keep talking," he said. "I'll bring in some wood, and make a fire."

She bowed her head. Her coffee had grown cold. She set it down. "If you need to be haunted," she said softly, "it's best to have a ghost who is willing to work." She heard the door open and close and she turned the tape player to rewind a little, then played it back. When she heard his voice on it, she nodded. She had expected that. She was being very thorough in her madness.

She watched a few logs float into the cottage and drop to the hearth, watched kindling appear, then paper. She did not move from the window. She doubted that she could move. Actually, she thought, she admired her creation more than she was willing to admit on the tape.

"After I get some heat in here," he said, "I'm going in the other room and make myself a real body and put some clothes on it, and then we have to talk."

She nodded. That was what she had come here for, to talk it through, to make a record, and then analyze it, cure herself. Soon the fire was blazing and he was getting his clothes out of the bag, ripping off price tags, tossing them down. She had the impression of anger, of jerky movements. The clothes vanished into the bedroom and the door slammed. Now she could move. She went to the groceries and drew out a bottle of wine, a round of cheese, bread and butter, and took everything to a table by the couch before the fire. She brought the tape recorder to the table and turned it on again.

Corky stalked into the room, red hair out like dandelion fuzz, round blue eyes indignant and angry. "How do you account for the fire?" he demanded. "Your hands aren't even dirty. You don't even know where the woodpile is."

"In psychotic breaks," she said, looking in a brooding way at the flames, "patients are capable of deceiving themselves about their actions to the point of denying them altogether, and rightly so, since they have no memory of them."

"That's crazy!"

"Exactly."

The rumble of the surf and the cracking of the fire were the only sounds. Lauren slipped off her boots and socks, stretched her feet out toward the fire. She had planned nothing, had worn warm clothing, and it was too warm now with the cabin heating up rapidly. Corky sat on the floor and leaned against the couch, also gazing into the fire. Very soon it would be too hot here; they would have to push the couch back a little. He reached past her and got a piece of bread, buttered it, added cheese. "No onions?"

"I don't like onions on cheese."

"Well, I do." She had brought only one glass for the wine. He got up and brought a second one, poured for them both. He began to eat, then said, with his mouth full, "What if I hit you where you can't reach, left a bruise that others could see?"

"Psychotics often do terrible damage to themselves in ways that appear impossible. Stigmata, rashes, even fevers." She took a long drink of her wine.

"What if I made love to you?"

"Autoeroticism," she said with a shrug. "Another well-known symptom."

"And if I got you pregnant?" he demanded, his anger surfacing again. He felt baffled. There seemed no way he could prove to her that he existed; she had answers for everything.

"The literature if full of cases of false pregnancies. Sometimes the women even deliver, babies no one else can see, of course."

He poured more wine for her. "You should eat something," he said, buttering another piece of bread.

"I am eating," she said wearily.

He looked at her sharply, then gave up for the moment. There had to be a way to get through, but he could not find it. "You don't have to worry about me," he said. "I won't hit you, or make love to you either."

"I'm not worried about that," she snapped. "I'm not having that kind of breakdown. Eroticism isn't one of my problems."

"Mine neither," he said happily. He touched her toes, very pink and warm now. "Warming up?"

She shook her head, then nodded vigorously. "Yes, I mean. The fire's very nice."

"And the floor's very hard," he said, and stood up, then sat on the couch, not quite touching her. He had to lean across her to reach the cheese.

She watched his hand move toward her, past her body, and she thought, here she was with a man, an apparent man, talking about things like eroticism. She never had been able to talk about sex with anyone except in her professional role, or the pseudosophisticated empty chatter that college students could not resist. Neither of those counted. She thought of the time when her sister had slapped her and threatened to tell on her for talking dirty. She had been twelve, her sister fourteen. And she had not talked dirty, not really, since then. But it was all right, she realized; she could say anything, do anything. She was alone. The windows overlooked the sea; the door was locked. And she had the tape recorder on, to make everything therapeutic, she added almost guiltily. If sex was not her problem in reality, why had she brought it up now? Her unconscious was taking visible form, even if she didn't believe in her unconscious. It was providing a waking dream in which she could control things. She could find out who she was, what she was, and she needed no outside help for the process. No one would ever know anything about it, and later . . . Nothing followed, but even that was all right. Later she would know what to do with the material, how to interpret it, reconcile it. She knew the process even if she had never used it or believed in it.

She drank down her wine and put the glass on the table. He was just drawing back his hand with more cheese.

"Why did you say you wouldn't make love to me?"

"Not fair to you. I mean, you don't actually believe in me yet, do you? It would be taking terrible advantage of you."

She shook her head. "That's not why. You think I'm too tall, not very pretty, not sexually attractive."

"You're attractive enough, but not for me, Lauren. You're not my type. But I know you wouldn't consider me either. Why not?"

"Nothing about you is an acceptable sexual fantasy. You're not my idea of a phantom lover. You're too short, and your hair is awful. I bet it feels like copper wire. That's what it looks like." She reached over and felt it; to her surprise it was crisp but strangely soft and thick. "And your eyes are funny," she said, keeping her hand on his hair. It was like petting a warm animal. "Too round, like a doll's eyes that snap open and shut."

"Your eyes are strange too," he said. "Sloe eyes, dark and pointed, like an Egyptian cat's eyes." He touched her hair and nodded. "A sleek, unpredictable cat."

"You probably don't even know how to make love to a woman. Wham bam, thank you ma'am."

She was playing with the buttons on his shirt; almost magically, it seemed, they came undone.

"It's too hot in here," he said, lifting her arm, pulling her sweater off. "I'd be afraid to make love to you in your state, as confused as you are. You wouldn't even know if it was good, if you liked it."

"I'll tell you if I like it," she whispered.

He ran his hands over her small, very firm breasts, and closed his eyes and took a deep breath. "It wouldn't be fair," he said. "You're not the type for casual sex. I can tell." He leaned over and kissed her breast above the nipple, ran his tongue over the nipple and took it into his mouth. She shuddered.

When he drew away, she opened her eyes and said, "It isn't casual sex. It's therapy." He kissed the other breast and she began to pull his clothes off frantically. He was just as frantic as he undressed her.

"That awful red hair on your belly!"

"I can't find the end of your legs. It must take you forever to get pants on and off."

"My dream lover should be taller than I am and strong enough to pick me up and carry me for miles."

"You're almost bare. As hairless as a snake, and damn near as long."

"And you're an orangutan!"

"Ah, but you've got the magic button!"

"Oh, God! Dear God!"

"You're supposed to tell me if you like what I do."

"Dear God, don't stop! Please don't stop! I like it! I love it! There! Here! What a magnificent prick I've given you. Oh, put it in now. Now!"

She erupted with a scalding orgasm as soon as he entered her. It was so unexpected, so total, he stopped his movements and held her; she clutched him hard and cried out. When he moved again, they both climaxed and she screamed. Corky groaned as if fatally wounded. Then she was weeping convulsively.

Suddenly he was gone. She screamed again, this time in anguish. "I don't want to be cured now! Not yet! Come back! Please come back!"

Then he was back, holding her tightly, and she wrapped her legs around him. "I was afraid you were gone for good."

"I thought it might work," he said with satisfaction. "It was worth a try. Now we can go for some variations."

She realized that he had come back, renewed, refreshed, if panting a bit. She did not even try to stifle her joyous laughter.

# Chapter Fourteen

SHE stretched and yawned, realized she was in bed with a blanket over her, snuggled down, and closed her eyes tighter. This time she did not drift back into sleep. There was a vague memory of staggering to the bedroom, half supported by his arm, of bumping into the doorframe, giggling— She shook her head. She never giggled, and she did not stagger, and certainly did not rely on anyone's arm to help her to bed. She turned over and abruptly woke up all the way, sat up. Her head was whirling, the room spinning dizzily, the bed tilting. She lay down again, closed her eyes.

Corky came in and sat on the side of the bed, touched her cheek tenderly. "Hi. I thought I heard you waking up. You okay?"

She moaned and pulled the blanket over her ears.

"Look, Lauren, you haven't had a bite to eat all day, and it's going on seven now. Not eating, the wine, everything hit you pretty hard. Why don't you shower and I'll make us some dinner. Okay?"

She moaned again. "I thought you'd be gone."

"Where? Now, up and at it, kiddo. Shower." He continued to stroke her hair gently, the little bit of it that showed from under the blanket.

"Go away," she begged. "Please. I know what's wrong with me now. I don't need you anymore. Please go away."

He kissed the top of her head. "We need each other, Lauren. Come on, get up. I'm cooking. Ten minutes."

She listened to his receding footsteps; when the room was silent, she uncovered her head and looked around. Corky, that was what he said his name was, she remembered. That was just right. Bottled up, corked, stoppered, uptight, that was her. Corky was just right. She sat up and clamped her lips against a moan. She felt sore all over. Good and sore, she corrected herself. Mostly good. She touched her nipple in wonderment at its sensitivity, then the other one. Her cheeks burned with the memory of his hands all over her, his mouth all over her; and her hands and mouth all over him. There was a responsive throbbing in the pit of her belly, and she got up and nearly ran to the bathroom and shower, where she stood with her hands clenched, her arms stiff at her sides under the driving water.

Corky hummed as he checked the potatoes he had started baking; he began to prepare two steaks. He had already made a salad, and only wished he had caviar and pâté and champagne to offer her. Rose petals to strew before her, and orchids to place at her breast. A bower of carnations and lilies, a bed of cool soft hummingbird down. Harp music and a chorus of children's voices far in the distance, and a perpetual sunset, and moonrise all together.

She entered the living room, did not even glance in his direction, but went to the table by the couch and turned on the tape recorder.

"Part of my problem probably stems from repressed sexuality, after all," she said.

He stared at her, speechless.

"I will stop delaying sexual satisfaction with Morris as soon as possible on my return to the city."

"You won't get any satisfaction out of that bum," Corky yelled at her. He turned the steaks, sputtering with anger.

"He understands my needs perhaps even better than I have

understood them," she continued, ignoring Corky. "It was apparent at our first meeting that he desired me, and that, no doubt, is what precipitated this little crisis. I have no experience with men who show openly that they desire me. I feared him in a way that I haven't feared other men. For the first time I have met a man who may be my equal intellectually as well as physically. I have to accept that and welcome it."

"Come and eat," Corky yelled, and slammed the potatoes onto the plates, forked the steaks out of the skillet. He was muttering under his breath when she joined him at the table. She had the tape recorder with her.

"You can explain all this, I guess," he snarled. "And fucking all afternoon. You've never looked prettier in your life, you know." She started to cut her steak, watching her knife and fork, not him. "Yeah, psychotic break, you forget things. Yeah."

He started to eat his food and neither spoke for several seconds. They were both ravenous.

"You never had so many orgasms in one day in your life, I bet," he said at last.

"Sometimes not even one. I thought it was because I didn't need it. I know some women don't. I accepted that. I thought it was because I was too nervous, too afraid of what they were thinking about me, my size, how big my feet are. I froze. Now, after criticizing myself out loud, I realize I don't have to be afraid of criticism."

"Jesus! I'm here, Lauren! Look at me! I'm here too!"

She looked past him, through him, over him, not at him, and she spoke into the tape recorder, enunciating her words clearly.

"I understand," she said between bites, "that this is just the beginning, but it is such a profound insight that I have hopes that the rest will proceed rapidly now."

Corky banged his fork on the table. "Look at me! Pretend you see me, at least. What would it take to make you believe in me?"

She gazed at him finally, and her look was kind. "If I believed in you, I would try to help you. You have a more severe problem than I do. Your behavior is absolutely unacceptable. You can't pop in and out the way you do, at a whim, not let people see you one minute, and be here completely naked the next. That is not normative behavior, I'm afraid."

"I can't help it!"

"Why do you think you can't help it?"

His look was bitter now. "You know as much about what happened to me as I do."

"I thought we were going to talk about you," she said pleasantly, "not about me."

"Why me?" he demanded. "I'm not a threat to anyone."

A threat? Did people see her as a threat? She listened to herself more intently, glad she had turned on the tape recorder. "Go on," she said. "Why do you say you're not a threat to anyone?"

"Because I'm a nobody! I don't have money, or position, or power. I'm not a physical threat. I'm a coward and I'm lazy."

"I've never been called lazy in my life!" she exclaimed then. "The way I've always worked! I got my Ph.D. at twenty-seven! Held a job all through school, found my job within months of graduating. I've never had time to be lazy."

"Me!" he yelled. "I'm talking about me!"

"A coward?" she asked. "You said coward. Why?"

"I always walked away from things instead of facing them. I didn't want trouble. My brother Timmy fought all the time, bloody nose three days a week, and I decided early that it was dumb. I was a coward. They'll all tell you so."

She nodded. "If I'd been Joan, I never would have dared go to war. I would have been afraid to mention hearing the voices."

"Yeah, I know. Every time Joan wanted to talk, it meant she wanted to tell me what was wrong with me. I had to listen. That's what talking meant, and I was afraid to say no."

"First they might laugh at you if you mention voices or anything not considered normal, but if you keep it up, they put you under a doctor's care and start the tranquilizers and talk sessions until you deny anything not completely normal. And they decide what's normal."

"Yeah. They laughed at me plenty. It was worse when they called me cute. A teenage boy doesn't want a beautiful girl to say he's cute, but no thanks. That hurts, you know?"

"They never called me cute. No one in my life has ever called me cute. Grotesque maybe, not to my face, but I knew what they were thinking."

"And then they remembered an errand, or a phone call or that the dog had to go poop or something. Sometimes they let me sleep with them. You know the difference between someone who lets you and someone who wants you? There's a difference, believe me. Joan wasn't like that. That's why I liked her."

Lauren shook her head. "Loved. Adored. Worhsipped. She was immaculate to the end."

"I wouldn't go that far. I mean, I knew from the start that she thought I might be her ticket out."

"She was my ideal, my role model, and I failed her," Lauren said with great regret. "Cowardly, that's true, and I never realized it until now."

"Lauren," Corky asked cautiously, "what are we talking about?"

She had been gazing past him, a rapt expression on her face. Now she focused on him again. "I was explaining why, if you were real, I would feel compelled to help you."

"Well, I'm not sick, so forget it."

"Of course not," she agreed. "You're dead." She picked up her knife and began to cut her steak again.

He attacked his own steak viciously. "Some choices," he grumbled. "I'm your hallucination, or I'm sick, or I'm dead!"

"You see my problem concerning you," she said, eating again. "If you are real, the question is, a real what? Ghost? Then the question is why are you haunting me? I never did anything to you. I didn't even know you."

"I'm not haunting you!"

"Then go away."

"That's not how you talked a while ago."

She felt her cheeks burn, but she said gravely, "I may undergo many personality changes during my therapy. That's only to be expected, and none of the altered states is to be regarded as final or as indicative of my true nature or feelings." She looked about the cheerful little cottage; the fire was burning quietly; beyond the occasional snap there was the reassuring rumble of the ocean, and the sound of rain on the roof. Inside, it was snug and secure and warm. "I can put aside my inhibitions for the time being," she continued into the tape recorder, "examine the various repressions that have resulted in a temporary break in my routine behavioral pattern, and perhaps map out a new behavioral pattern that will be more suitable for my present professional role in life. Perhaps I have carried a juvenile pattern into adulthood, and this is my method of communicating that fact to myself."

Corky was watching her in awe. "Like I said," he muttered, getting up to make coffee, "you're not my type. Answers for anything, everything, and the answers are all baloney."

He banged the coffeepot, splashed water, made a mess, muttering. She ignored him and continued to speak into the tape recorder. "A more probable causative agent," she said calmly, "is a brain tumor in the right hemisphere, affecting the visual cortex to a certain extent, and certainly affecting the neocortex—"

"Lauren, knock it off!" He sat down again and took her hand. "Let's talk about that night I first saw you. Remember? I was in a little restaurant with . . . a friend, and you came in. I wanted to draw you and followed you to your office. Remember? What happened then?"

She nodded agreeably. "Yes, that night precipitated the crisis, which, however, must have been building for a long time."

"What happened?" he pleaded, pressing her hand.

"A man got on the elevator with me. He looked very much like you, of course. Exactly like you, I should say. He followed me off at my floor and when I frowned at him, he made a gesture like"—she disengaged her hand and made the palms-up gesture—"this, and he headed for the window at the end of the corridor. At the turn of the corridor I looked back to see if he was still there, and he vanished in a blue cloud of smoke."

She frowned and squinted thoughtfully. "No, that's not right. There wasn't any smoke. That's what the policeman said later. What I saw was a man glowing blue and then he vanished, without taking his clothes with him. They were on the floor." She nodded at her story; it was complete. She added, "And ever since then I've been seeing him in hallucinations."

"Jesus!" he said helplessly.

"Then the fat policeman said I planned the whole thing with the missing man. For insurance or something like that."

"He's not a policeman," Corky said. He got up for the coffee and brought it back, poured for them both. "He's in the army, a colonel. Toler Harris Musselman. Trigger Happy. He wants to be a general."

"How . . . ?" She had thought he looked military, she remembered; she simply had not consciously made the next assumption. But it was obvious now to her.

"That doesn't explain much," Corky said, "but so far it's all we have. Trigger Happy's after you because he thinks you know something about what happened, and that you're part of a spy ring. He thinks I'm a commie spy. I got rid of the tails today, but they probably already traced you to this cottage. You've been using credit cards all over the place, and you had to give the license number when you registered us in here. So they'll find you when they want you."

She had gone very pale. Now she gulped the too-hot coffee; her hands were trembling. "The whole delusional system," she said, and moaned. "Classic paranoia, persecution, conspiracy, the works. Oh, God!"

In exasperation Corky cried, "I'm real, damn it! They did something to me. I black out and apparently I disappear, and then I come back, only sometimes not all the way, and when I'm invisible I seem able to go anywhere instantly. I don't know how, or why, but that's what it's all about."

She closed her eyes, nodding.

"It's like they activated a muscle I always had but couldn't find," he went on in a wondering voice. "I can use that muscle and make myself vanish, and I can stop at a certain point that lets me go through walls, or be anywhere I want, but past it, I black out. I don't know what happens to me then."

"Why do you come back to me? I didn't even know you!"

"I don't know why. You seemed to be calling me. I looked in on other people, but they didn't want me and you seemed to. I thought you could help anchor me, maybe. I don't know. I would be floating around somewhere and remember you. I called you Minerva, my goddess—"

She made a hoarse, strangled noise and he stopped in consternation. "Even that," she whispered, "calling myself a goddess. Even that!"

He could think of nothing to say. He went to her and held her and they clung to each other.

She washed dishes while he brought in more firewood, and then they sat in the living room. Now and then she made a comment into the tape recorder, but they were brief and without real content. He sat on the side of the fireplace where he could look at her, and he sketched her over and over.

She picked up a pen and made a note in the notebook: *Trigger Happy Musselman—Toler Harris Musselman.* It meant nothing to her. She put the pen down and stared moodily into the fire. After a moment she turned on the tape recorder again.

"Father was disappointed that I was a girl," she said. "He never told me so, but he didn't have to. I was the third girl, and I should have been a boy. We all knew that. I'm taller than my father is." She glanced at Corky, who was turning a page in the sketchbook. "Since you're here, you might as well fill in your background. I draw a blank for you."

His hand flew as he sketched. "Dad was Jack Corcoran?" She shook her head and he shrugged. "You don't follow the horses, I bet. Anyway, he was a jockey up until ten years ago. Good jockey. Won the Kentucky Derby, took the Triple Crown one year." She looked blank and he sighed. "That's fame. The biggest three races in the country, that's all. Made him a mint. Then he was hurt, and now he trains horses and doesn't ride anymore. I was too big to be a jockey, and not big enough for anything else. My brother Timmy rides."

He talked and drew and he told her things he never had told anyone before. About his father's four wives, each one younger and more beautiful than the last. Each one more avaricious than the last. His father had made a fortune several times over and the wives walked out with it each time. There was no bitterness in him; that was how it had been, that's all. He told her about never finishing a year in any one school. New York State, Kentucky, Virginia, Maryland, Texas, Miami. Hialeah was one of the prettiest tracks, he said, but the Kentucky Derby was the one to win, the one that got you mentioned in the almanac.

"Where's your mother?" Lauren asked.

"Don't know. She got the dough, he got the kids."

She shut her eyes. Insane. It was truly insane. Her family was so staid, so proper, so stable, this was ridiculous. A fantasy family?

"Anyway, I put in a year at Texas A and M, and didn't much care for it. I put in a year at Berkeley and dropped out. Then half a year at the Rhode Island School of Art, a few months at City College in New York, and then headed west."

"Why?" she asked faintly.

"I never stopped to wonder. It just seemed a good thing at the time. No horses, I guess."

She made a note. A girl's first adolescent sexual fantasy, to control a horse, tame it, master it. Had she come west to escape horses? Sex? Love? She shook her head. She had come west because it was where she could get a job. She thought of Joan of Arc in her armor, riding her white horse to battle, leading armies in a holy cause, and shook her head harder. Nonsense.

"What's the matter?" Corky asked, putting aside his sketchbook at last.

"Nothing. May I see what you've been doing?"

He handed it over and she stared in amazement at the top

page. He had drawn her feet! She turned the page, her feet again. And her hands. She burst into tears.

"What have I done? Lauren, please, what's wrong? Don't cry. Please."

She remembered that she had promised to tell the tape recorder everything that came to mind, everything that could have a possible bearing on her breakdown. Gasping and choking, she started: "Mother and both my sisters wear five and a half. All of them. When I was nine I couldn't wear my sister's shoes anymore. I tried to bind my feet, the way Chinese women did, but I had to take off the rags every morning and it didn't help. They just kept growing and growing." She wept harder. "Frankenstein feet!" Then she jerked, tried to sit up. "What are you doing?"

He was stroking her foot. He kissed the sole and ran his cheek over the instep. "This is the most elegant foot on earth," he said softly. "The most beautiful foot I've ever seen. Such fine bones, and a wonderful arch. Each toe is perfection. And the little pinkie. I want to keep it in my pocket and take it out to pet from time to time." He kissed each toe.

She moaned with pleasure and suddenly she knew she had to have him, it, the hallucination, whatever he was, now. She opened her legs and drew him to herself.

# Chapter Fifteen

DURING the night Corky got up to put another log on the fire. The wind had come up hard; it rattled the windows, forced entrance to the cottage, made little eddies here and there. He sat on the couch, gazing at the flames, and tried to make sense of what had happened to him. Lauren was sleeping.

He knew he could not abandon her, no matter what else happened. If he had not followed her last week— Last week! It seemed an eternity ago. If he had not followed her, she would not be implicated. In what? he demanded, and the answer came swiftly. Trigger Happy Musselman believed there was a spy ring and that she was part of it. And he believed that Corky had been killed by . . . something from CaCo laboratories. Corky stared at the fire, hunched as if he were cold although the room was quite warm. How did he know any of that? He knew it the way he knew the houses he had lived in as a child, the way he knew the apartment he had lived in at Berkeley, the way he knew his brother Timmy. He had a memory of Trigger Happy talking, thinking even, exactly the way he had other memories.

Morris Pitts worked for Trigger Happy, another memory. Maybe Lauren was right and he, Corky, was dead. His grandfather thought so, she did, Trigger Happy did, the tall, thin scientist. He himself was the only holdout. And he no longer could be certain. How could anyone tell if this was what being dead was like? Why didn't someone come collect him, take him to where dead people were supposed to go? He should call his grandfather, reassure him that he was not dead. But how could he do that if he couldn't even convince himself? He gnawed his lip and glowered at the fire. He could use the strange new muscle and instantly go anywhere, listen to people, watch them, even touch them, but he remembered what Trigger Happy had thought, what was in his mind. And that was impossible.

He concentrated on the night it started, and tried to make sense day by day of what had happened to him. He could remember seeing his grandfather, who had assumed he was dead. How had he gotten there? Nothing came. He remembered going to lunch with Lauren and Morris, causing a scene. He remembered going to Morris's apartment and the giant microwave oven there. Being in the elevator with Lauren and a crowd of people. Routing her followers on their way to the island. He remembered finding his own sketches and notebooks at least twice, once in a hotel room, the next time in a vault. Joan with a new man, his own apartment ransacked, Morris and another guy snooping in Lauren's apartment. He was fast running out of memories of the week, and he knew they did not account for much of it. And Musselman? When had he seen him? And where? How did he know he was a colonel and wanted to be a general? He did not question the knowledge; he knew it.

There were stages to his . . . condition, he realized. Like now, he thought, as he held out his hand, turned it over examining it, he was as normal as he ever had been. He located what he had come to think of as the muscle and flexed it, watching his hand. It vanished; he could still feel it exactly the same as before, but it had disappeared. Stop, he told himself. He felt his body from his head down his legs. It felt normal. There was a stage where he could not hold anything, he remembered, where his clothes just melted away from him. He looked about, then picked up a pencil and held it up. It floated before him. He flexed the muscle a little more, and now he could see Lauren on her side, one arm under her head, a soft smile on her face, sound asleep. And so he experimented. At a certain point that he came to recognize, the pencil dropped, and his K Mart robe fell to the couch. He saw the honeymooning couple. Inept, he decided; he and Lauren could teach them a thing or two. He saw the family in number three. All sleeping. Mr. Kirby was in front of his television, working on a horoscope, paying no attention to the box. A barge was moving in the strait, rocked by the waves under a high wind.

The center was here, there, and getting weaker as he continued his experiments. He felt the urge to let go, felt the tugging of the whole world, the need to fly apart, and abruptly he was back in the cottage, breathing heavily. That was where it led, he knew. The next stage led to the blackouts, the loss of memory, time unaccounted for. And the next stage led to memories he had no other way of acquiring. He pulled on his robe again, chilled, and afraid.

Maybe he was dead, and he was refusing to let go. That pull was strong, almost irresistible, and the pull could be toward oblivion, except he was holding on, he kept coming back. He had days missing, long periods he could not account for, and if he went again, maybe he would stay in limbo next time. She would decide the hallucinations were over, that she was cured, and she would end up in Morris Pitts's bed pretty damn fast. And Morris Pitts was bad news, worse than a snake oil salesman. They at least gave something to the sucker; Pitts would just take and take, and then how would she feel about herself when he wrung her dry and walked out? Corky suspected that Pitts would be very good with her in bed, especially now that she had found her own magic muscle. They might even frame her for something or other, he thought indignantly; Musselman was convinced that she was part of a spy ring. Musselman believed any means to whatever end he had in mind was justified.

And how the hell did he know that? He shook his head, and knew it was true. Then he admitted that although what he had been thinking was all true, he had not verbalized yet the real reason he had to stick with Lauren. For the first time in his life there was someone he couldn't walk away from.

His entire life had been a series of moving on—childhood, adolescence, college, up to a week ago. Moving on had been the only way of life. Like an army brat, he thought. Churchill Downs was home during the spring season. Then Belmont. Hialeah for the winter, always moving on. When Joan got that appointment for him down in L.A. he had been willing to move on again. He would have gone down there, interviewed for the job, come back to clean out his apartment, if he got the job—moving on. It never had mattered much where he was; he was building up a nice cast of characters for the cartoon strip he planned to peddle. Here, California, with Joan, alone, it had not mattered. Moving on. And now he was going to stick as close as it took to get Lauren out of the mess he had got her into. And then they would see. There had to be a way of convincing her that he was real, not a hallucination, not dead.

Even that was dangerous, he understood. She was exactly right; he was totally unsuitable for her—too short, funny-looking, terrible hair, doll eyes, no real future, ignorant, uneducated, broke all the time. She deserved a prince, a guy who could carry her forever while he, Corky, might be able to drag her a few yards on a good day. And none of that mattered, he told himself, and wished he could make himself believe it.

He began to gnaw his lip again, wondering if he was really dead, if this was what being dead was like for someone not willing to let go.

At eight-thirty the next morning Trigger Happy was studying the map of Whidbey Island, scowling darkly. Just a hop away from Canada, and those canucks were little better than commies themselves with their socialized medicine, always the first step. Finally he had men he could trust, men he had picked, and they were on their way up to Whidbey. The state cops and a federal marshal were all that stood between him and defeat. He had ordered them to stay the hell away from her unless she made a

move toward a boat of any kind. Or unless she made contact
with someone from a boat. Just watch, he had growled, and for
chrissake, don't lose her!

It was clever of her to pretend she wasn't on the run, using
credit cards all over the state, giving her right license number
and all. Clever. He hated clever girls. He still did not know how
she had disabled two chase cars, or even if she had, not yet. But
he would soon. His boys were on the job, Captain Leonard
Drissac and Sergeant Dave Carroll. Beauty and the beast, they
had been called more than once; he thought of them as the brain
and the bulk. He had taken Drissac into his confidence as much
as he was able to confide in anyone. Stay the hell out of sight.
Don't use visual scanning at all, rely on the locator, and the
screen all the way. We want to know where she goes, where she
stops, if she makes contact, picks up anyone or anything. Can
do? Yessir. And he could, Trigger Happy knew. He could deliver.

And Trigger Happy could trust him because Leonard Drissac
understood the threat every bit as much as he did, and believed
in the cause as fervently as he did. They had worked together off
and on for fifteen years; they got along.

On the island, Corky was looking down at the beach where two
little kids were already busy hunting for shells or sharks or
something. Lauren was dressed to go out and he had his sweatshirt over his arm.

"Look, if we go to the beach, I have to go invisible, and I don't
want to. I want to talk to you, not have a crowd watching the
lady talking to herself. Let's go up the hill to the fern forest
instead. Besides, it won't be as windy up there."

She shrugged. All morning she had pretended not to see him.
And she was not talking to him. She had decided to stop
indulging herself and the first step was to deny the existence of
Corky. But she did not want to share the beach with the two
little boys and their parents either. She picked up the key,
glanced around, then went out and locked the door, stuck the
key into her pocket, and started up the gravel road to where the

trail began. Corky was at her side, pulling on his sweatshirt. In the cottage was a brochure that listed the available recreational activities. Shelling on the beach, half a dozen trails up the hills, fishing from the other side of the island, where boats were available, golf. The shortest trail, the brochure had stated, was to the fern forest and waterfall, a one-hour hike. The longest wound in and out of the hills for five hours. She made the turn to the one-hour hike. It would take her to the crest of the hill, where she could see Canada to the northwest, and the Olympic Mountains to the southwest. She started to climb the first part of the trail.

The wind was sharp and biting that morning; the sun was brilliant, the sky a deep blue, and everything was dripping, the trees, the Scotch broom that filled the understory here, the tough grasses that grew waist-high. The trail made a turn and the wind was cut off by the trees; the forest grew denser. The trail was groomed, steep but easy. Lauren had no breath for talking, or, it seemed, for thinking. She felt curiously blank as she climbed.

Corky finally had a plan to demonstrate to her satisfaction that he was actually there with her, and that he could be other places at the same time. First they had to reach the crest.

Silently they continued on the trail, now level, and they began to see the first ferns. They were four feet high, six feet or more across, each frond gleaming with raindrops. The ferns increased in size with each step. Six feet tall, eight feet. Lauren caught her breath and stopped to gaze at the alien landscape. Like a million years ago, she thought, fifty million. The fronds responded delicately to the breeze that forced its way through the cover of the forest, all of them in ceaseless motion, dipping, swaying, agleam with recent rain. They stretched out all around her. Corky was as awed as she was by the view.

"Like being in a fairy tale," he whispered.

She nodded in perfect understanding. They walked on. They came to a narrowing of the trail, where it skirted a chasm that was filled with ferns, like a soft green cloud. And now they could hear the roar of the waterfall ahead. The next turn brought it into sight, a brilliant white ribbon of water falling forever straight down to crash in a fernlike geyser among rocks.

"Fairyland," Lauren said, and could not hear the words over the roar. Corky held her hand and smiled, nodding.

The trail became steeper once more after they left the waterfall, and at the crest of the hill the wind blew hard. Up here there was a flat gray expanse of rock with a fence all around.

Slowly, blinking against the wind, they walked around the perimeter. There were other higher mountains on the island that cut off the view of the mainland to the east, but down fifteen hundred feet they could see ships navigating the Juan de Fuca Strait, and beyond in the mist there was Vancouver Island, with its own mountains climbing into the sky. Due west was what appeared to be open water, the curve of the strait lost in ocean mist. Then the snow-topped Olympic Mountains.

Corky pointed almost straight down, to the beach that the boys had been playing on, empty now. "Look," he shouted over the wind. "That log rolling back and forth in the surf." She nodded. "Just in from it on the beach, see that shiny thing? A can, Coke can or beer can. See it?"

The sun flashed on the can, magnified the brilliance, made it painful to look at. She nodded again.

"Lauren, I know you don't believe a thing I've said. But if I can appear down there and toss that can into the surf before you can count to five, you'll have to believe me just a little, won't you?"

The look she gave him was scathing. Silently she hunched her shoulders against the cold wind.

"One thing," he said. "Pick up my clothes, will you? The wind will blow them away if you don't. I'll be back in a second or two."

For a moment the sweatshirt hung empty before it fell. The jeans crumpled to the ground. She stared at the clothes, then swiveled to focus on the can on the beach, and watched it rise from the sand, make an arc, and vanish into the waves.

"Dear God," she whispered. Almost instantly she denied what she had seen. If she could hallucinate a phantom lover, a ghost who ate her food, a companion on a hike, then hallucinating the toss of the can was nothing. But she did not believe it. The two little boys had appeared from behind a basalt stack; they were standing at the edge of the water looking out. Unless she was hallucinating them, too, she realized, there had been witnesses to the can's mysterious toss into the surf.

Corky had been concentrating on making hands solid enough to pick up the can, but as soon as he launched it, he realized that two men were entering the cottage. He streaked into it ahead of them. One was lean and very suntanned, muscular and hard, good-looking in a rugged man's-magazine-ad way. The other was over six feet and nearly as wide as the door. His nose had been broken and rebroken apparently; his eyes were hidden by mirror sunglasses. Neither made a sound. The tapes, Corky thought wildly.

The recorder and tapes were still on the table at the end of the couch. The big man moved on into the bedroom silently, the other one examined the living room. The fire was sputtering, burning low. The lean man had seen the tapes, was moving toward the table, when the other appeared in the doorway to the bedroom holding Corky's robe.

"She's not alone," he said in a low voice.

As soon as they were both turned toward the bedroom, Corky snatched up the tapes. He couldn't tell which tapes she had recorded on, could not risk leaving the wrong ones; he tried to pick all six up together. One slipped through his hand, clattered when it hit the table, and both men spun around. Corky tossed five tapes onto the smoldering logs. Sergeant Carroll darted to the fireplace and grabbed the poker, yanked the firescreen out of the way and started to poke at the tapes. Corky pushed him off balance and turned to retrieve the dropped tape. Drissac already had it in his hand. There was a soft explosive *plop* from the fire as the first of the tapes burst into flames; the air smelled of burning plastic. Corky grabbed for the tape that Drissac was holding and had just closed his hand on it when the sergeant swung the poker at where his chest should have been. The poker met no resistance. Corky had dispersed. The tape fell to the floor.

Drissac snatched up the tape again, and Sergeant Carroll was already back at the fire, scrabbling the flaming tapes to the hearth. They were all blazing fiercely.

"Let's get out of here," Drissac said. Sergeant Carroll pushed the burning mass back into the coals, replaced the fire screen, and they left the cottage, taking the tape, Lauren's notebook, and Corky's sketchbook.

Lauren stood on the crest of the hill, holding Corky's clothes against her chest, watching the two little boys throw things into the water. The waves brought the can to them and one threw it back. Finally, shaking with cold, she turned and started back down to the cottage, frozen, bitterly disappointed, frustrated, holding the clothes. Had she carried them up? she wondered, and knew there was no point in pursuing it any further. She could not tell if her shaking was due to the penetrating chill of the wind, or to the effects of her fear. For she was more terrified than she had ever been. For a moment she had believed in him, actually accepted him as a real man, doing real things, and she knew she was lost if she came to believe in her own hallucinations. As long as she knew they were tricks of her mind, there was hope for a reasonably fast cure, but if she started to believe her delusional system was reality, that meant she would have to be institutionalized. She would not be able to function in the real world if her private world became real. She shook her head in despair because more than anything she wanted to live in the private world of her mind, the world that included Corky and making love repeatedly and talking about things forbidden for so many years.

She came to the waterfall again, this time opposite the place where they had stood and gazed at it together. She remembered how warm his hand had been. And she knew she had to reject every thought of him just as soon as it surfaced. She must not visualize him, remember any of the things he had said, any of the things he had done to her, with her. Every time she started to remember, she had to think of something else instead, something compelling that required great mental effort, all her attention. Like what? she asked herself, looking at the ribbon of water. Clients, she answered, turning away from the scene. Work, she continued. Peter was right, after all, damn him.

She stumbled and trudged down the mountain. The ferns had shed their burden of rain and no longer sparkled and glittered. Fairyland was gone.

# Chapter Sixteen

LAUREN entered the cottage with slumping shoulders, exhausted. She dropped the clothes on the couch and went into the kitchen to make coffee. She put water in the pot and sat down at the table. For a long time she sat without motion, until the cold chilled her again, and then she went to the fireplace and put the last log on the fire. It was true, she thought bleakly, she didn't know where the wood was stacked. She had forgotten already.

She sat on the couch and watched the fire take hold, waited for the warmth to penetrate her chill. Then she moved again, remembered to finish making coffee, remembered she wanted to pack up, go home, go to work. She went on in this way for the next hour, starting one thing, then another, forgetting to finish, sitting to gaze at the flames instead. She sat for a long time on the side of the bed with her hand on his pillow. She had awakened entwined with him, his body warm against hers, his hands warm on her, his breath warm on her. Now the cottage just felt cold. The red cushions were tawdry and worn; the gaiety of the funky paintings of ships and gulls had turned into dime-store art. She started to pack finally, and when she got to the tape recorder without tapes, she did not even sigh, simply added it to the bag along with the sneakers and sweatshirt and jeans, the robe, everything she had bought for him.

When she started to drive at last, she did not even see the battered dark car that passed her on the state road. It turned off and was in line before her car at the ferry landing. Today the water was brilliantly blue and choppy, the gulls almost fluorescent white against the blue water, bluer sky. She stood at the rail and stared at the receding island and tried to think of the tests she had to devise, the two thousand employees she would be responsible for, the overtime, the long weekends it would mean, and she welcomed it all. Damn Peter, she muttered. Damn him to hell for being right. If anything was going to save her, it would be work, and he had known that, the bastard.

Trigger Happy listened to Leonard Drissac's report, asked the sergeant a few questions, and sent him away for food and sleep. As soon as the sergeant was gone, Trigger Happy asked Drissac, "You confirm what he says?"

"Yes, sir. We could have stayed a little longer, as it turned out, made a sweep, but at the time it seemed prudent to leave, keep out of sight ourselves."

Trigger Happy nodded absently. "Go on to bed, Leonard. Join me for dinner here, around eight."

He sat in the nice deep leather chair in his hotel office without moving after Drissac had left. Then he looked again at the Steele girl's notebook, the note with his name, his full name, and his nickname, and he felt a chill creep up his spine. Damn few people knew his full name, he reflected, damn few. But the real chill had come when he listened to Sergeant Carroll.

"Something or someone took those tapes off the table, sir, and tossed them on the fire. And that same something or someone tried to pick up the tape the captain was holding. I figured if there was a hand, even if I couldn't see it, there had to be an arm, even if I couldn't see that, and if there was an arm, there had to be a shoulder, and so on, sir. I swung the poker at where there had to be a gut."

He could not fault the sergeant for not connecting with the someone or something. After all, he had seen nothing. In less than a day, he thought grimly, his handpicked men had gone to the heart of the problem unerringly and had reported exactly what happened, no more, no less, while the local stumblebums were still falling over shadows. Neither could he fault them for recovering a blank tape. They had brought back information more precious than anything that might have been recorded.

Item, he thought then: Someone had gotten into his rooms, these very rooms, without being seen, trying to get at the Corky commie's stuff.

Item: Someone had gotten into the vault, unseen, trying for them.

Item: Someone had tampered with two chase cars. All three men swore the Steele girl could not have done it.

Item: Someone, unseen, had been waiting for the Steele girl to get back from her rendezvous—walk, wherever the hell she had been. But why had she been carrying clothes? They missed connections? He was waiting in the cottage and she expected him to be somewhere else? He shook his head over it.

Drissac said she had spent the night with a man. And Drissac was never wrong about things like that. An unseen man? An invisible lover? He snorted in disbelief. Another man then. The Corky commie had been there waiting. The lover had gotten away; she had brought his clothes back. By sea? In a wetsuit? In disguise? Wetsuit, he decided. Nothing else made much sense. He had to strip and put on the thing, and she had to get rid of his clothes, and the Corky commie was waiting for her to finish the mission when Drissac and Carroll walked in on him.

He sat there all afternoon working with it; he made phone calls, and he made many notes. Lining up his pigeons, he called it to himself. Just lining up his pigeons.

Shortly before seven that Thursday evening Lauren left her apartment on foot, walked the six blocks to the professional building, and entered. Four agents watched her all the way.

She found the others already in the conference room for the weekly staff meeting. Peter jumped up and ran to her at the door.

He put his hands on her shoulders and kissed one cheek, then the other, then clasped her to him.

"Peter, about yesterday and today—"

"Absolute genius, Lauren darling. The most astonishing stroke of genius. I simply can't tell you how utterly speechless I am that you devised such a brilliant strategem. Did you anticipate such fabulous success? I must examine your notes, follow your amazing line of reasoning to plan this magnificent coup. Have you come up with a name for it? I toyed with several, I must confess, but no, I yield with all the good grace I can summon. The spotlight is yours, darling Lauren, my most darling Lauren!"

He kept one arm around her shoulders and walked her to the bleached-teak conference table. "I should have planned an entrance for you, darling Lauren. A band, flowers, small children throwing rose petals, a fatted calf. Gentlemen, our own Lauren, returning in triumph, our own dear, dear Lauren."

"Good going, Lauren," Warren Foley said heartily, sincerely. "You played it so tight, we didn't even know you had the ball until the scoreboard lighted up. Beautiful run. Beautiful."

"I agree absolutely," Rich Steinman said, squirming in his starched underwear. "That is, it was so unexpected; I mean, not that I ever doubted your ability, ah, but to have done such a, ah, novel thing, that is so new, without consultation or anything, that is, ah, I always thought we should at least mention, if it wouldn't interfere, I mean—"

"All we need is a dormouse," Lauren cried. "What are you all talking about?"

"Not a tea party," Peter said, waving her to her usual seat. "But a bottle of champagne, the one we were cheated out of by fate last week, only now with an even more moving celebration." He brought an ice bucket with the bottle from the sideboard and Warren helped by bringing glasses, beaming at Lauren all the while.

Peter opened the champagne. "I have a little confession, Lauren dear. Please forgive me. Don't judge me too harshly for my moment of doubt, my weakness in your moment of triumph. I had carpenters drill a little tiny peephole so I could watch now and then. I couldn't help it, dear, dear Lauren. I should have trusted, I know, but even admitting my perfidy, I am so glad I did. So glad. It was incredible. Mrs. Blackman, the little lady with the violet hair and the funny nose? She was first. She sat with a frightened look and I felt my heart sink, fearing a failure of unimaginable magnitude. But then, after ten of fifteen minutes, she rose and looked at the plants very closely, and looked around for water. Then she went to your desk, your very own desk, my dear Lauren, and she studied the buttons on the telephone and finally touched one. She was startled by Gloria's answer, of course, but she held her ground and asked for a glass of water. Gloria, of course, delivered it instantly, and Mrs. Blackman dismissed her. Dismissed her, Lauren! Our timid little Mrs. Blackman! Then she watered your plants!" He beamed at Lauren and poured the wine.

Warren held up his glass for a toast. "That was the crowning play, Lauren, adding a couple of sick plants. That was what won the game, I bet."

Lauren was staring wide-eyed first at one, then another. She gulped down her champagne and Peter refilled her glass.

"Mr. Chapman was the deciding factor," he said, smiling gaily at her. "He sat down for less than a minute, then he went behind your desk and sat down there, even put his feet up on it, and played chairman of the board or something. I caught him on his way out and he was swaggering, Lauren dear, literally swaggering with a feeling of importance, probably for the first time in his life, a genuine feeling of being a real somebody."

She downed the second glass and Peter wagged his finger at her, but poured again. "When you reveal your own name for this ingenious plan, you must tell me if I am close when I guess it will be something like primary exclusion therapy. You, of course, are the primary, and by positioning your clients in the place of your power and then excluding yourself, you return power to them to control their own lives once more, to actually deal with their own problems in a meaningful manner, to regain the feeling of self-importance which they have relinquished however slightly by the act of seeking help."

Lauren gulped the third glass of champagne and then started to giggle. "Excuse me," she said, and jumped up, fled to the bathroom, where she stood leaning against the door, shaking with helpless laughter.

When she was composed enough to rejoin them, they were discussing the main topic of interest, the plans for the Caldwell Corporation. Her mind kept drifting off, and she knew she would fall asleep if she stayed. After only a few minutes she yawned and stood up and said she was going home now. Peter's eyes glowed; Warren looked worried about her, and Rich nodded in secret agreement with himself. She was drunk, he thought, near to passing out.

"I'll work up the Schwindler-Latham tests at home," she said, putting on her coat, picking up her purse. "When I'm done, I'll be in touch."

"Peter!" Rich screeched. "I mean, she's, ah, just leaving, that is—"

"Isn't she wonderful?" Peter said soothingly. "I knew that when the cocoon opened, something quite incredible would emerge, something magnificent and lovely and brave. She walks in beauty—"

She walked out of the anteroom and had to stop in the hallway outside because she was overcome by giggles again. Big girls don't giggle, she told herself severely, and wiped her eyes, laughing harder than ever.

At dinner, Drissac had gone over the list of people Trigger Happy had working for him and put a check mark by those names he could vouch for, either because he had worked with the men himself, or he knew and trusted agents who had. The approved list was very short; it included Morris Pitts.

Now six men sat in Trigger Happy's parlor, most of them already acquainted. There was Morris Pitts, who had nodded briefly at Drissac and Sergeant Carroll. There was Joe Krueger, who was a lieutenant in the army sometimes, working out of army publications offices here and there. He looked like a nervous accountant, with oversized glasses and a little tic. And there was Stan Harlow who, like Morris Pitts, was on special assignment from the FBI, under the direction of Musselman. Harlow was in his fifties and looked soft, too pale, and tired. But Drissac had approved him with a curt nod. "I want him on my side at all times," he had said. That was enough for Trigger Happy.

He had provided whiskey, brandy, even peanuts, and they were all comfortable, waiting for him to begin.

He briefed them and concluded by saying, "There's a nest of them right here in River City, boys. And we can't see one of them!"

"That explains it," Morris Pitts said softly. "At lunch she was just going to unload when things starting getting knocked over. I didn't know what the hell was happening. That explains it!" he said vehemently.

Sergeant Carroll and Captain Drissac exchanged glances and nodded. The sergeant leaned forward and lowered his voice. "How do we know he isn't here now?"

"I haven't left these rooms since morning," Trigger Happy said. "And I have been pretty damn careful about who came in."

Drissac summed it up for them all, very coolly, efficiently. "Let me give you a working scenario, gentlemen. We don't have enough facts yet to know if this is accurate, and we won't know until we lay our hands on Corcoran. But we can put together a picture with what we do know at this point in time. This man Corcoran has a method of making himself invisible. Using it, he was able to get into CaCo and sabotage the laser. We doubt that he had any intention of leaving town the day of the test. It seems more likely that he would have found an excuse to arrive in that restaurant one way or another to make contact with Steele. Then he heard the fog reports, not that he had been fogged in, gentlemen, but that arrivals had been delayed. The test was due to have gone off by five at the latest, as you recall. He had gotten to the computer, sabotaged the laser in whatever fashion their side demanded, and now he realized that it had not gone off as scheduled, and he had no way of knowing if it would take place that night, the next day, or when. He had to get to the Steele woman and warn her, alert their allies. They talked in the elevator; they must have had an abort device with them. They went to the one location in the city where they were in a direct line with the laser, and they set off their remote control. It backfired. Instead of destroying the laser, their device caused it to fire; it reached across the two miles in a straight line, homed in on the device itself, and destroyed that. That accounts for the blue glow Steele reported. Corcoran knew the area would be swarming with investigators very fast, and he used the invisibility trick to get out, leaving Steele to take the fire. The colonel, obviously, believed the laser killed him, disintegrated him, and the scientists went along with that. God alone knows what they really believe. The Steele woman played along, too, or maybe she even believed it that night. By all reports she was in shock. Maybe she thought her confederate had been blown to hell and gone. But ever since then, she's been in continuous touch with him, carrying out his orders, meeting others, making deliveries, or doing whatever they require of her."

Harlow shook his head doubtfully. "Nobody's going to buy it."

"We aren't selling," Colonel Trigger Happy Musselman said in a low voice. "Do you understand what this means? Think what's in this one damn area! Nuclear subs, the Stealth bomber, companies like CaCo, the Caldwell Corporation. Hell, Boeing owns half the state. Think of the Stealth bomber, gentlemen: invisible to radar, right? Why not a man invisible to human eyes? That's what we've got here! Think, an agent who can slip in with others anywhere he wants, see what he wants, slip out again, taking what he wants. He's still a man, just like you and me. He eats and sleeps and shaves, just like you and me. He puts his pants on one leg at a time. And he leaves fingerprints, just like you and me. In my office here, in the vault at CaCo, in Steele's apartment, the cabin on the island. By the time we got through explaining, proving what Drissac and Sergeant Carroll and I know damn well is true, he'd be in Russia. No, gentlemen, we're not explaining a damn thing yet. We're on a manhunt, and I want that goddamn Corky commie! And no one is to know a damn thing until we have him, or his body! Preferably his body. If they can't see it, they can damn well feel it!" He took a deep breath and drank down a brandy. "Besides, we sure don't want to give the Russians a clue that we believe it for a goddamn second. Got that? They think they've got the perfect agent. Let them think it for now!"

Harlow listened patiently, his pale face impassive, not convinced. "If he's invisible, why doesn't he just take off, report in?"

"Because I've got something he wants," Trigger Happy said. "Twice he's tried to get his notebooks and drawings. He got someone to open the vault at CaCo, God alone knows how, but he messed up and left his prints, and he tried to get those papers from this apartment even earlier. We didn't know what we were dealing with then. Now we do. I don't think he's going anywhere without those papers. Maybe the secret of his invisible act is in them and he knows damn well we'll crack his code eventually. Some of the best people in this country are working on them right now. Maybe he's waiting for reinforcements, or orders. Could be that's what it was all about at the island, they sent a message out through the guy who got away. We don't know enough. But we do know he's still hanging around, still sticking close to Steele. And they don't know we're onto their secret. So we have the edge for now."

Deliberately Harlow turned to Morris. He had worked with Morris Pitts many times, trusted him thoroughly. "Tell me again about the evidence you found in her apartment."

Morris went through it all once more. "His hairs were in her razor, still wet. Too many wet towels. His prints on her mirror, the counter, all over the kitchen, everywhere. Hot fresh coffee. I planted the bug myself on the back edge of an old textbook on the top shelf. He must have been watching," he said coldly. Inwardly he was seething with rage. She had let that creep sleep on her couch, had slept with someone on the island, and was playing with him, Morris Pitts! His voice revealed nothing of his inner turmoil. "As soon as she entered, she yelled at someone to get out and stay. Then she threw the bug out the window. No time for her to have found it, no matter how good she is. We've had that apartment building sewed too tight for anyone to get in and out without our seeing them. We've been over every inch of it looking for him in another apartment. No dice. Now we know why. He was there all the time."

Harlow scowled at the floor and finally shrugged. "It's the damnedest thing I ever heard of, but I give. What next?"

Trigger Happy grunted his satisfaction and poured more brandy. Now they could get down to business.

# Chapter Seventeen

---

IT always confused Trigger Happy when people said the world was complex. There had been a time, when he was very young, of course, when he had thought so himself, but to hear mature people say it now made him wonder how their heads were screwed on with some of the threads missing. The world had become simpler year by year and he hated people who tried to mix things up again, people like scientists and economists and shrinks.

He was sitting alone musing about this after his little army left, good men all of them. That was another thing, there were good people and bad, simple as that. You could trust the good people and had to keep an eye on the bad eggs. Simple. The only safe way to go was to assume everyone was in the bad camp until time proved otherwise. Cover your ass, that was the only safe way. Them and us, another good motto. Commies and not commies. No fence hangers, no middle ground, just them and us. He nodded and poured himself one last nightcap. Tomorrow they would bring in the infrared scanners, get them set up, and then let that little commie come sneaking in. He nodded. Let him try.

No talking outside this room, he had ordered, even after they had the scanners in place. CaCo was crawling with commies. Hell, all Seattle was crawling with the vermin. He could tell. He nodded again. He always had been able to tell, just by sniffing, by instinct, some secret gift that a few fortunate ones had. Hell, he thought then, he didn't need a special gift; they gave themselves away every time they opened their mouths. Mental health, socialized medicine, day care, sex education, fluoridation, demonstrations—all that naturally gave them away, but those were the big signals that anyone could see. There were other signals that only trained eyes could spot. Like the Steele girl drinking Scotch in public that night he saw her. A little thing, but revealing. Letting a stranger—Morris Pitts—pick her up, even more revealing. Leaving home without being married, living alone. He grunted in disbelief that there were so many clues that no one else had noticed, added up. Going off to college, out of state even, then moving clear across the country. Letting the Corky commie draw her naked feet! He narrowed his eyes, remembering the sketches, the dirtiest yet by that little snake. If there hadn't been anything but that one set of drawings of her naked feet, he would have known, he said to himself. That was enough right there. Real perversions, not like looking at pictures of good healthy tits, nothing understandable like that, no sir, that little creep drew feet! He finished his drink in a single gulp, got up, and prepared for bed. And she let him, he kept thinking. She let him!

Morris Pitts was stalking around his own apartment at that time, not even muttering, just thinking hard about Lauren. His apartment had been done by Juanita and Juan, the best decorators in town. The carpet was thick velvety forest green with a mellow glow when the light was right. The wood was all cherry and rosewood; the metals chrome and silver, with copper touches on ashtrays, in the fireplace equipment. The paintings were by local artists, one a subdued misty Japanese-like Mount Rainier; one was a bold abstract nude in yellows and oranges and purples. He thought it hideous, but other people were impressed when they saw the signature. One was an impressionistic waterfront, more Renoir than Renoir could have done personally. Morris rarely saw any of them. There were two Chinese vases, deep blood red with a beautiful patina; one held pampas grass, the other three cattails. The walls had a nubby paper the color of pale wheat; the couches, two of them, were covered with the same wheat color, this time a canvaslike cotton. A black lacquered coffee table was so brilliant, so deep, the eyes were led ever inward, searching for a surface that was not revealed.

The entire apartment was like that, furnished with the biggest, or the best, or the shiniest, or the newest, and always the most expensive. He suspected it must be beautiful; he had paid enough for it to be the most beautiful setting in the state.

Now he walked soundlessly through the deep forest floor of his carpet and saw nothing, thought only of Lauren Steele. He very rarely had worked in his own district, as he was doing this time. Usually he made a little business trip—to Cannes, to Singapore, Brussels, once to Cleveland, for God's sake! He did what he had to do, had a little vacation, then came home again, always accomplishing his mission with no missteps, no delays, efficient every time. Each little job inevitably involved a young woman; he was on that list, a specialist among specialists. And he never failed. Never. *They* had approached him back in college, and he had said, sure, why not? If he had been in East Berlin in school and the other side had approached him, he would have said the same thing. It wasn't for the money. His family had had money for generations. It wasn't for any ideology; he had none. It was playing a game with the entire world for a gameboard. International chicken. International Risk. One time a year, twice, even three times a year he rolled the dice and moved, then his turn was over. That was enough. He thought addicted gamblers were a bore; he would play for the highest stakes just often enough to keep it interesting, amusing, to keep an edge. He would not be engaged more than that, he had said in the beginning, and that had been acceptable. Some men were needed now and then who weren't known, not identifiable.

He did not like working in his own territory. He was one of the most eligible bachelors in Seattle and he liked that fine. His social life was full and for a week now he had put people off, turned down invitations, begged off engagements already planned. And all the time that stringbean of a woman had been playing with him. His only advantage, he decided, pacing angrily, was that he knew what her game was and she did not realize yet that he was a player too. When he thought of her on the island with Corcoran and another guy, the one she slept with, the one they smuggled out by sea, he felt his fury turn to hot ice inside him, burning and scalding and freezing him all at once. He had told Lauren that his father had worked in a munitions plant, and that was true, but he had not told her that his father owned the damned plant. He remembered one blistering afternoon that he had spent lighting matches and tossing them in one of the warehouses, out of boredom, betting each time with himself that it would not ignite anything dangerous. He had been fourteen. He remembered how he had felt that day—more alive than he had ever felt before, more alert, more complete, ready to die, ready to kill others. The feeling had returned several times for him; he welcomed it when it did. That was what he worked for, to force it awake now and then. In the beginning, this assignment had not seemed likely to stimulate it, and he had been wrong. This weekend, he promised himself. This weekend.

Drissac and Sergeant Carroll were in a suite exactly like Musselman's, across the hall from his. Drissac had copies of every report that had been made to date, including the one that said Steele had left the meeting earlier that night, crying. Drissac had one room, the middle room was the joint command office, and the sergeant had the last room in the line. Only Drissac was to read the reports. The one thing they had accomplished that night in the staff meeting was to set up a hierarchy. Musselman was in charge, naturally, and Drissac was his aide with access to everything Musselman received. No one else was to be told any more than necessary. No one had questioned that. Drissac read through the reports until nearly two, called room service for sandwiches and coffee, and continued reading and thinking for another hour or more. In the distant room he could hear Carroll snoring.

Musselman had jotted a note: can we chill him out, make him reveal himself that way? Maybe, the captain thought, images of footprints in the snow appearing before his eyes. Tear-gas him? Smoke him out? Use the girlfriend as leverage? He found the reports about Joan, skimmed through them again, and discarded that idea. Joan was like a soft, cuddly teddy bear to be taken to bed and put aside afterward. A pro like Corcoran wouldn't give her a second thought after he was finished with her. Steele? Could she be a lever? He doubted it. They were coworkers at most. Corcoran had spent too much time with the other one to have had time to make out with Steele too. But, more important, agents knew other agents were expendable. That was how they played their games.

He was naked as a newborn, Musselman had insisted, and Drissac agreed. Mist a room with paint? Use spy dust on him? He looked again at the pictures of Corcoran's clothes left behind in the hall that first night he had vanished, and he frowned. The guy could make himself invisible, but not his clothes, it seemed. Did that mean it wasn't a real device that did it? A pill or something like that instead? Or an implant? He nodded at that idea. They had to have his body, find an implant, or whatever it was. Fantasizing about becoming invisible, the things he could do if no one could see, he ate the last of his sandwich and finished his coffee, and brooded about the pictures of Corcoran's clothes. How the hell had he gotten out of his shoes without untying them? His jeans were zipped, belt buckled. How the devil had he done that?

Lauren had gone straight home from the office. The agent had reported that she had been crying, and that was wrong. She had been shaking with laughter.

In her apartment she had started to giggle again, and periodically, as she made scrambled eggs and toast and coffee, she laughed out loud. After she cleaned up her kitchen, she wandered aimlessly for a few minutes, found herself remember-ing, and very quickly went to the small utility room where she had put boxes of papers. She looked until she found the tests she would modify for the two thousand Caldwell Corporation employees, took them to the table, and sat down to start making notes.

The print seemed to dance before her eyes; letters ran together, blurred, drifted apart. Lines went up and down erratically. Even the words she could make out were nonsense, she realized. She flipped through pages, squinted, and read a line chosen at random: *Number in ascending order your expectations for your job with 1 being lowest and 10 your highest expectation.* She nodded gravely, that made sense, now, didn't it? One lowest, ten highest. *Fulfillment, self-respect, respect of others, chance to be creative, socializing, large salary . . .* She thought, a chance to put a gidget in a gadget all day, but found no place among the possible answers to number it. She turned a page. *What is the primary responsibility of an employer to his employees?* Not to be a woman, she thought, but that was not among the answers either. Primary responsibility, she said under her breath, then aloud, "Primary exclusion therapy!" She put her head down on her arms on the table, but strangely her giggles turned to sobs and she could not stop.

At length she stumbled to the bathroom and washed her face, eyed herself in the mirror with disgust, and went back to the papers. She tried to concentrate the way she had promised herself she would, but it appeared that her hand was not getting the message. She watched herself write: Kentucky Derby, Churchill Downs, Louisville, Kentucky. Preakness, Pimlico, Baltimore. Belmont Stakes, Elmont, New York. Johnny Corco-ran. Hialeah, Miami. Then she got up and went to the bookcase to find her three-year-old almanac; there was an entry under horse racing that included a list of Derby winners. She ran her finger down and stopped at *Sea Wrack.* She was shivering when she put the book away again and sat back on her heels on the floor before the bookcase.

"There is no such thing as mind," one of her psychology teachers, Geraldine Buxton, had lectured forcibly. "There is the brain, as concrete an organ as the liver or the spleen. Physiologically we know what happens when the lungs perform their function, and we know what happens when the brain performs."

Dutifully Lauren had written in her notes: *Concrete brain.*

"No one attaches any mystical significance when we prick a finger and the damaged nerves send a chemico-electrical signal to the brain to tell it of the injury. What we think of as reflex is the brain performing its function. But when it performs equally fast with other kinds of activities, mystics attach metaphysical meanings. What they call intuition, memory, dreams, are all as explainable as the pin prick and the reaction to it."

She had written: *Prick.*

She moistened her lips. At some time she must have read about *Sea Wrack.* A memory trace had been established, a pathway through the neurons that facilitated that particular memory when the proper stimulus was provided. And Johnny Corcoran, she went on, nodding a little too hard. He had been one of the top jockeys twenty years ago. She had read about him too. And the Triple Crown, the racetracks, where they were. All that had been in the newspapers enough times for most people to know about it. No mystery there. The brain was filled with memory traces that were not activated for years. She nodded again. Right.

And Toler Harris Musselman? Same thing, she said under her breath. People like that made the newspapers, a police officer making an arrest. Or even if he really was an army colonel, that was more likely to result in his picture being in the papers. Decorated for something or other. A Senate witness. There were many reasons for someone like that to have his picture taken, for her to have seen it, remembered. She was no longer nodding her head.

No, she told herself weakly. No more. She had promised not to think of all that again, never again. Stiffly she got up and realized how truly exhausted she was. She went to the medicine cabinet, got out the sleeping pills, and took two with a glass of milk. Then she went to bed.

They played hide-and-seek in and out of the giant ferns that were festooned with diamonds. They were as small as humming-birds in the deep, fragrant shade, and they flew like fairies, darting here and there, calling to each other, their laughter silver music. He gathered diamonds and made her a necklace, and when he placed it around her neck, his hands were like fire, his mouth tender on her neck, her breast, then hotter and hotter. The ribbon of water flowed over and around them, sang to them and they fell into the green pillow of the chasm, but she could not stop her fall; she plunged through into a deep dreamless sleep.

Corky drifted. Across a black desert, at sea, in cities and the countryside. Sometimes a bit tried to drift the wrong way and was rebuffed, but never enough to force a center to gather. He experienced birth and death and loving and hating. Actor, acted upon, drifting in an infinitely interesting universe that was also timeless. Just drifting.

# Chapter Eighteen

LAUREN woke up with a dull, sleeping-pill headache. She dragged herself to the kitchen to make coffee and regarded the tests on the table with loathing. Later, she thought; she would settle down and start. Later. The coffee helped marginally; the shower helped a little more. It was only nine and already she knew this was not going to be a good day.

She looked around the apartment bleakly, turned on the television, turned it off, turned on the radio, turned it off. She picked up magazines that had been accumulating unread and went to the couch with them, but failed to open even one. Toler Harris Musselman, she thought, there had to be a way to check. Her sister Cara was an article editor for a fashion magazine in New York; she would know how to check something like that. She glanced at the telephone, but did not touch it. Bugged, she thought clearly, and found herself shivering.

She stood at the window with her arms crossed, glaring out at the world. A fine mist was hanging in the air. Fall, damn you, she willed it. But it hung there. That was how Seattle weather was; when it wasn't raining, it might as well be. One sunny day, six of rain or mist or fog. Four different times she had gone up to the top of the Space Needle, and each time the mist and fog had closed in, had hidden the surrounding mountains, the lakes, the world. She could get into the car and drive for hours, she thought, and knew she would not do that. To where? For what? Go to the library and see if there was a way to check on an army colonel? She shook her head. Go for a walk, walk until lunchtime, have lunch, buy a book or two, then come home and work and read. She glanced at her watch and was dismayed to find that it was only ten minutes after nine. It felt as if she had been up for many hours already. Finally she turned from the window to put on her boots, her raincoat, find the big black umbrella she had bought. She remembered swinging it at *him,* and deliberately summoned the tests to her mind, tried to consider what she might be able to do with them. She dressed and left her apartment.

As soon as she was on the sidewalk, two men in gray business suits left a newsstand across the street and sauntered to her building. They entered, went straight to the elevator without a glance at the security guard, who, in fact, averted his gaze. He knew Dr. Steele was undergoing a tough security clearance check because of some big contract her company had landed. It made him feel secure, knowing the thoroughness of the check.

The men did not speak in the elevator, or in her apartment when they let themselves in. Immediately one opened his briefcase and withdrew a wandlike apparatus. He pointed it toward the room and slowly swept the entire visible apartment. He watched a tiny screen set into the lid of his briefcase. Then he checked the entire apartment with his instrument. He nodded.

At his signal the other man took down one of a pair of wall lamps. He placed a light bulb with a scanner inside it in the fixture, made a new connection with the wires, and put it back. The man with the portable scanner lifted the phone and dialed. He motioned to his partner and waited until he had moved across the room, listened, hung up. He inclined his head toward the door, and they left. It had taken less than two minutes. The scanner would detect anyone in the living room, the dining space, the kitchen, part of the hall. Across the street in a third-floor hotel room Sergeant Carroll watched the radarlike image, the two blips, and then nothing. Operational, he noted in his records book.

Lauren walked in the opposite direction from the way she usually went to her office. She did not want to think about Peter Waycross, about her clients sitting in her office alone, about the peephole. Monday, she told herself firmly; she would go back to work on Monday, stop all this nonsense and pull herself together. Where had it gone sour? she suddenly wondered. She had wanted to become a psychologist at one time. She remembered very clearly how much she had wanted her degree, her own office, people she could help. Of course, she had anticipated a better salary, prestige, respect, but it would all come, she had been certain. She really had wanted to help people. And the most help she could give, she went on without mercy, was by staying the hell away from them. She could lead two lives; keep an office for people to go sit in, and have a real job on the side. Like . . . She glanced around her. She had never walked in this section before; she had left the smart boutiques and toy stores, the computer shops and menswear shops. Here was a marina with a showroom of boats. Across the street was an electrical supply house. Maybe she could sell boats, or light bulbs. She reached the next intersection and paused. Straight ahead was the CaCo complex, still several blocks away, but looming over everything here. Slowly she turned and looked back. And there was the professional building. The two ends of a dumbbell, glaring at each other through the mists.

Abruptly she made a right turn and walked more briskly along the side street until she reached the next corner, where she turned right again, heading back to her apartment. The mist was penetrating now, almost a rain. She opened her umbrella and strode without looking at the commercial establishments, the dealerships and hardware stores. Ahead of her the professional building dominated the skyline.

A bookstore, she remembered. Maybe three or four mysteries, something diverting without being demanding. It seemed impossible for her to keep her attention on anything, even her own past. Her mind kept skittering away, back to the things *he* had said; the totally insane things he had said, she added, the things they had done, the incredible, magical things they had done. There is no such thing as mind, she told herself. Only a brain, a concrete organ. Organ set in concrete. Ossified organ. She stifled a giggle and tightened her lips, walked even faster. You made your bed, she told herself, and now you have to lie. . . . She frowned, but at the moment did not know how else to complete the homily. She had to tell them it was for their own good to put the gidget in the gadget, to be steady and reliable, to get there on time. The late starter never wins. Early birds are like worms. A penny saved is a stitch in time. The brain in concrete. Everything she knew she had learned at one time or another. Memory traces. Memory tracks. Racetracks. If Toler Harris Musselman was in town, he had to be in a hotel.

She came to a complete stop, and was bumped by someone who didn't. She paid no attention. A hotel. Of course. If he really was a policeman, he would have his own home; if he was a traveling colonel on tour for the Pentagon or anything like it, he would have a hotel room. Now she looked around, trying to orient herself, locate herself. There was a coffee shop on the other side of the street; there would be a telephone, a phone book, hot coffee, a doughnut. She started to cross; horns blared, and she stopped in confusion, remembered traffic, and went to the corner, waited for the light to change, and then headed for the coffee shop.

The telephone was outside the women's room. On her fifth try the answering operator gave her the room number for Mr. T. H. Musselman. Lauren hung up quietly and went to a booth, frightened and bewildered.

In his hotel command post Trigger Happy got the verbal report that she had lighted in the coffee shop. He traced her path on a large wall map.

"Look," he said to Drissac. "She got here and put up that damn umbrella. A man's big, black umbrella, not the sort of thing for a girl. A signal. Exactly ten minutes later she's on the phone to someone. A signal to someone at CaCo, where else?"

At his side, Drissac studied the map also. Straight line to CaCo from that corner, and a big black umbrella would be visible from any upper-level room on the north side. Slowly he nodded.

"Where the hell is Pitts?" Trigger Happy grumbled.

"He'll connect," Drissac said reassuringly. "He's on line, waiting. Relax, sir. We've got her hemmed in this time."

"Wish to hell we knew who she was calling. See if you can get anything on that from CaCo. Did she go through a switchboard, or direct? Goddamn her, why didn't she use her own phone? She knows, that's why. She's smart, Drissac. Too smart. I don't like it." He swung around sharply, away from the map. "And why are they covering for her at the clinic? Pretending she's there working, seeing patients! Hah!" His face was somber when he looked at his aide. "CaCo, the clinic, who else, Drissac? How many more? My God, what've we stumbled on here?"

"She gave a signal, and maybe she received one too," Drissac said, equally somber. "Maybe she wasn't calling CaCo at all, maybe she was calling *him.*"

Trigger Happy nodded. "Start the boys checking out her entire route this morning, everyone along the way. In the coffee shop. Every damn one she saw! You handle her tail. I want to know every place she stopped, even hesitated, every person in the shops she might have signaled to. Find out if any trucks slowed down alongside her. They like to use trucks, goddamn them all!"

From time to time as they talked and planned, one or the other glanced at the little monitor with its radar sweep. The room remained clean.

Lauren drank coffee and tore a doughnut apart; she got out her notebook and made three columns, three if-then sets. If Corky was dead, then he was a ghost haunting her. Why her? Because she was the last one with him. He wanted someone to avenge his untimely death. He had unfinished business that someone had to take care of. He hated her. She smiled slightly at the last statement, but did not discard it as a possibility. He wanted someone to notify his family, his lover, other people. He wanted to expose his killers, through her. She wrote notes slower as she exhausted the reasons she could think of. Sheer malevolence? Ineptitude? He had intended to haunt someone else and landed on her doorstep instead?

She went on to the next proposition: he was not dead, just in pieces most of the time. Immediately she drew a blank with this one. In pieces meant dead. The waitress refilled her cup; the restaurant began to fill with luncheon customers. She continued to stare at nothing and make a note now and again.

The third proposition: she really was having a breakdown and he was part of a grandiose delusional system. There was no way she could discount this. It was possible that she had remembered the racetracks, the horse, the jockey's name. It was possible that one of the policemen had mentioned Musselman by name. Why was he registered in a hotel? She shook her head. But the fact that he was there did not mean Corky had been right about him. A visiting policeman. His house had burned down and he had temporary housing. A real colonel, but not from the army, from a . . . an FBI police training school or something like that. A different man altogether.

Gradually she realized that no one could prove herself sane, not really. Sanity by consensus, by mutual agreement, by public polls, television-talk-show opinions. What else? Sanity was behaving within the norms tacitly established by society; outward behavior was all that mattered. Inner devils could roar and sear and torment; as long as outward behavior continued in an acceptable manner, who would know?

Sanity was accumulating debt and paying it off and accumulating more. Sanity was wearing a green apron and support hose and working in a diner for three thirty-five an hour and smiling at the customers. Sanity was pretending things would get better tomorrow, next week, next year. Sanity was pretending there was no beast inside roaring and searing, tormented and tormenting. Sanity was being firm with clients and telling them there was self-esteem in standing on an assembly line all day putting a gidget in a gadget; and it was putting the damn gidget in the damn gadget and asking someone else to confirm that it was all right to do that. Sanity was training to be able to help people deny the existence of the beast, and it was training to learn how to ignore its cries and bellows of outrage and hurt.

It was accepting rush-hour traffic and too many horns and poisoned food and too many wars and deaths and killings and armed people shooting other armed people and unarmed people alike and terrorists and more terrorists to fight the terrorists and politicians lying and lying and the war machine rolling forever onward and hunger in the shadow of wealth and too many children and too many people and too many fat religious leaders telling everyone else what their duty was and making everyone hate feeling too fat or too thin or too blond or too dark or too tall or too short or too old or too young and people being divided into trainers and trainables and pretending it meant the good life and good health and mental well-being and teaching guilt and shame to those who faltered and having courts—

"Miss, are you finished?" The waitress in her green apron slapped the check down on the table, smiling, then walked away.

Lauren looked around guiltily. People were lined up waiting for tables. Hurriedly she found money to pay for her coffee and doughnut, now reduced to crumbs. And a tip, she thought then, oh, God, a tip, and she felt more guilty than before.

She walked slowly when she left the coffee shop, in no hurry to return to her apartment, nowhere else to go at this time of day. She had decided nothing, absolutely nothing, had chased herself in circles, in fact, and had returned to the starting gate. She recognized that as a racing term, one *he* had used, and she bit her cheek. The mist was more rainlike now, still gentle, not very cold. She kept her head lowered and saw nothing.

She heard her name called and felt a hand on her arm simultaneously, looked up to see Morris Pitts smiling broadly at her.

"I knew I wasn't mistaken," he said. He backed her up a step or two so that she was under an overhang, shielded from the slight rain. "Don't move," he said. "Please, don't move. I'll be back in a second." He looked into her eyes with his happy dark-blue eyes and then turned and nearly trotted away, across the street, skipping in between cars packed thick with the noonday rush.

On the opposite side she could see him talking earnestly with a heavyset man in a gray raincoat. The man was shaking his head, Morris spreading his hands, backing away. He turned and left the man, dashed back across the street, and rejoined her. Now he took her hand.

"I told him my colleague sent you with a message that my grandmother just died," he said, grinning at her. "Did you see him? Pig face, snout and all. Let's play hooky, you and me. Have lunch with me, spend the afternoon with me."

She tried to disengage her hand, shook her head, and he held her tighter, the light gone from his face now, his eyes shadowed.

"Lauren, please. I have to talk to someone. People like him, pig face, my partners, this whole scene . . . I think it's killing me. I know that sounds pretty melodramatic, and God knows I wouldn't say it to anyone else. But you . . . please, Lauren. I need help desperately."

An hour later they sat in the restaurant at the Yacht Club overlooking Washington Lake. Sailboats bobbed in the distance, brilliant sails looked like gaudy birds against the dull water, the duller sky. Everyone had treated him deferentially here; his table was ready, the waiter had said. Lauren had looked at him suspiciously at that and he shrugged. "It's always ready," he had said, almost as an apology.

And now that they were here, she felt that he regretted asking her, that already he had changed his mind about talking. Anything on the menu was excellent, he had said, and lapsed into a long, troubled silence while she looked over the many pages of offerings. Finally she put it down.

"Something light," she said.

The waiter had appeared magically. Morris didn't glance at him. "Poached trout, fiddleheads in garlic butter. Tell Eddie to see to the wine."

The waiter bowed slightly and left and finally Morris looked at Lauren, his eyes still troubled. "I hope you're not a wine fancier, know all the best labels, that sort of nonsense." She shook her head. "Good. Waste of time. It keeps changing. That's what you pay a wine steward to keep tabs on." He reached across the table and took her hand. "I'm sorry, I didn't think when I said I wanted to talk about my job, my life, the universe, everything. That's what you do all day professionally, listen to poor souls complain."

She withdrew her hand, but gently, and she said, also gently, "Most people who come to see me don't have membership in the Yacht Club and pretty boats. Is one of them yours?" She glanced out the wide windows at the moored boats.

He nodded. "Show you later. *Prissy Lady.* When I first got her, I spent every spare hour fancying her up, painting, polishing, putting in shiny brass, all that junk. Prissy. It seemed appropriate. I haven't been out on her in six months."

"Well, unlike my clients, you could turn your back on everything, do exactly what you want. Why don't you?"

"Do what?" he asked bleakly. "You'll laugh, but I really went to law school thinking I might be able to help people in trouble. Knight-in-shining-armor dreams. Boy-type dreams."

He saw her eyes widen, knew she was startled enough to lose her guardedness at least for the moment.

"Oh, no!" she said very quickly. "Not just boy-type dreams."

The waiter brought the ice stand and their wine and fussed over opening it, letting them sample it. That was all right, Morris Pitts knew. They had all afternoon, all night, all weekend, and he had one foot in the door whether she realized it or not.

# Chapter Nineteen

SQUATTING with a boy on the side of a black river, waiting for the boat that also would be black. Hearing a soft whistle, answering with a clay whistle shaped like a grotesque bird. On the boat, in the clearing where many boys and men waited in darkness, a thousand tons of coca also waiting. Fear and excitement and weariness, itching from many mosquito bites, hungry. Running with a small girl to greet her father, laughing, and being the father hurting from love for her. Being a drunk man raising an arm feebly to ward off a blow with a bottle. Feeling the bottle hit, hearing the soft oath when something splashed on the attacker, being the attacker. Shooting off with the bit that had been the fatally wounded man. Slammed back.

A bottler saying, "We don't want to buy out the bastard. We're going to smash him." Being the frightened secretary who was also a spy for the one to be ruined. Knowing what it was to face financial ruin, personal ruin. Being with a man carefully wiring a bomb, concentrating with him. Working on a bicycle, concentrating. Swimming laps, skiing, huddled under an airplane wing, fire smoldering in the distance, wreckage everywhere. Pain, twisted back, pain. Feeling another bit, flying with it, Slammed back.

Boistrous singing, being married, sacred, holy love and passion and lust so scrambled together there was no start and stopping.

Being the bride, shy, fearful, remembering the stories of pain and pregnancy and blood. On patrol on a snowfield wishing for warmth, an end to winter, an end to patrols, home. An old woman staggering, falling. Feeling the bit that was the woman, weaving in and out with the bit, rising. Slammed back.

Singing, dancing, acting, watching the singers and dancers and actors. All at once, everywhere. Now and then following a bit somewhere else. Always being slammed back.

Then nothing. Most of what Corky experienced was wordless. He was the people he met, felt with them, knew with them what they knew, loved, laughed, died with them. When nothing was there instead of the whole human tapestry, for a timeless period he shared the nothingness also, but gradually there was something again. And this time it was entirely wordless. He was enveloped in the thought that was the thought of the world, and for a time he knew what the thought knew, and it was without words.

He knew: he should not be here; he had penetrated the other place that always slammed him back; there were many others, all others, beyond reach but aware of him; they would not or could not harm him, not directly; they were going to send him back and wait for people to kill him, soon now; as long as he was discorporated he would be free to come and go, and they had to be watchful; if he came back, they would keep him in the kind of limbo he had just experienced. He knew most of all that he had been warned.

"I don't know," Morris Pitts said over loganberry crepes. "It seemed that every step of the way someone nudged me and I wasn't even aware of being touched. And one day I woke up and found that I had a luncheon date with pig face. How does that happen, Lauren? It's not what I planned, what I wanted or expected."

Lauren gazed past him at the bright boats rising and falling with the choppy gray water. "If someone had said to me that one day I would tell Wanda Torrance that all she was good for was to put a gidget in a gadget day in, day out, I would have gone into something else. Sales, or advertising, something rotten and crooked that everyone knows is rotten and crooked. They think I'm here to help them. Hah!"

"He wants me to help him save seven, eight thousand dollars on his income tax this year. And I don't seem to be able to work up much enthusiasm for the whole thing. Lauren, I don't seem to give a shit if he saves tax dollars or not!"

"I used to think that people would come to me in distress, suicidal even, and with a few words I would get to the heart of their problem, straighten them out, and they would adore me." She finished her wine and did not notice that he refilled it instantly. The waiter brought another bottle.

"I saw widows falsely accused of cheating on welfare, and I saved them," Morris said. "I made wonderful grandstand addresses to the juries and got them off, and got them increases in their payments, saved the kids from dying of malnutrition, stuff like that."

She nodded. "I saved them too. From drugs, from accepting physical abuse, from becoming prostitutes." She drank. "Oh, what's the use? Let's go look at your boat."

He held up the bottle, still half full, and nodded. "In a minute. I think I need coffee. You?"

"I suppose."

He emptied the bottle, giving most to her, and held up a finger for the waiter, who appeared again as if by magic. Morris ordered a pot of coffee, and two brandies.

"It's the lousy system," he said moodily, gazing at the waterfront. "It lets people like pig face save thousands on taxes, and makes widows with small children go hungry." He picked up his glass but did not drink. "The money he keeps would make the difference between poverty and a decent life for her." He put the glass down again.

"It's sanity versus insanity," Lauren muttered. Then abruptly she said, "Excuse me." She got up and walked through the emptying restaurant, spotted the women's room, and went inside. She stood still, just inside the door, almost as if afraid someone had followed her.

Now what, she asked herself. And she did not know now what, only that something was not right, something about this whole luncheon with Morris, the wine, too much wine for lunch, his championing widows and orphans. She studied herself in the mirror, blurred around the edges, almost wild-eyed, and suddenly she said softly, "He's seducing me!" The image in the mirror looked surprised, then thoughtful, then nodded. Why? she asked the mirror reflection, and it did not know any more than she did. Another notch in his gun? she asked herself. A new kind of conquest, not a celebrity, or a society woman, or a debutante, or a beautiful model, just a working woman? Was that prize enough? Because she had refused to see him all week? She was a challenge? Finally she asked the question she was most afraid to answer: he liked her? He did not find her awkward and uncommonly large and big-footed, but actually liked her? Her lips had gone dry, her throat was parched; she felt feverish.

Without looking away from her own image, disbelieving, fearful, hopeful, pale now and cold, she reached for her purse and took out a lipstick, her hairbrush.

At the table Morris told the waiter to take away the rest of the wine, the glasses, everything except a lovely silver coffeepot and two bone china cups and saucers. No cream, no sugar. He had the brandy taken away also, untouched. If he had overplayed his hand, he thought, gazing at the boats at the marina, he would back up a few steps and advance again more slowly. If she came out with her hair neatly combed and her lipstick fresh and inviting, then on to the next step.

If you go fly-fishing, he thought, you get the best equipment money can buy, the best flies experts can tie, and you find the best spot in the stream. You let the fly touch the water, just touch it, and you take it away again, let it touch again, maybe again. You don't hurry it, don't spook the trout, don't splash around and make the waters muddy. You play with it, tease it a little, and in time you pull in a nice, shiny, fat rainbow trout.

And the funny thing is, he thought, the trout's had a good time too.

She returned with fresh lipstick, hair nice and neat. He stood up and held her chair. Before she could resume her seat, he took her hand and kissed the palm.

"I missed you," he said softly.

They went out to the boat, *Prissy Lady*, and he showed her the latest in navigational aids, none of which she understood. The master stateroom was as big as her bedroom, the galley better equipped than her kitchen, everything beautifully decorated and furnished. The lounge was big enough to hold a dance in. He showed her his charts, the islands he had visited, the ones he intended to visit, someday, he had added almost regretfully, when it got exciting again. The San Juan Islands, he said, had their own microclimate, almost tropical at times, in the rainshadow of Vancouver Island. He pointed them out to her, and did not touch her. He seemed, she thought, as nervous as she felt, with a new tension between them, one that made her move away if he got too close, that made him move just as fast if she came too near him.

The boat would sleep twelve, and needed a crew of two, including him. It could go to Hawaii, he said, or Japan, anywhere. She believed him.

Late in the afternoon the sun came out and he rushed her into a cab and they went to the Space Needle, where he pointed out the mountains, the lakes, the boat canals, the bays. This was his world, she thought, gazing at the city with lights starting to shine here and there. Above the noise, the confusion, the horns and dirt and hurrying crowds eager to be home and have dinner and see the news, or something. He was used to so much money, with things eased before him, the path cleared, no barriers. What did he know actually about sanity and insanity? He had said it was the system at fault. What did he know about the system, about anything except a life of ease and plenty?

"What is it?" he asked, studying her face intently.

The light had failed; the last elevator was on its way back up and they had to leave the top of the lookout, rejoin humanity below.

She shook her head. "Everything looks so easy from up here. You can forget the hurts and the questions and the problems, just pretend they don't exist."

"They don't have to exist if you don't want them to," he said. He was drawing close to her, his expression intent, when the elevator arrived and the attendant called: "Last car!"

For a moment he held her gaze, then he grinned slightly and took her by the arm. "I demand a raincheck," he said in a low voice.

What few people understood, he thought, riding down with her, his hand firmly on her arm, was that it was enjoyable to land the trout, to have it in one's grasp briefly before handing it over. He had wanted to kiss her as much as she had wanted it. He wanted her in his bed as much as she wanted that, too, he thought, and unconsciously his grip on her arm tightened.

They had left the elevator and started to walk to the street, when he suddenly stopped. "Lauren, hold it a second, okay. There's something . . ." Quickly he strode several yards away from her and reached out to grab a man by the shoulder, jerk him around. She could not hear what they said. Morris had his fists clenched and the other man backed off a step or two, then showed something to Morris. His clenched hands opened. For another moment neither man moved, then Morris came back to her. He looked strained.

"Let's walk," he said in a tight voice, his lawyer's voice, she thought.

She glanced over her shoulder. The other man was coming. "Who is that? He's following us, isn't he?"

"You," Morris said in that unfamiliar voice. "He's FBI, and he's following you. This is the third time I've noticed him today." He stopped again and faced her, took her by the shoulders and studied her with an intensity that was disturbing. "Are you in trouble? All afternoon I've been unburdening myself. I never thought . . . Lauren, are you in trouble? I am an attorney, you know. Let me help."

She gazed at him, then at the FBI man, who had stopped and was looking every way but at her. She turned back to Morris and slowly she nodded.

She paced his luxurious apartment without seeing it. Beyond the windows the lights of Seattle sparkled and glowed. A jet passed over the city with red and green lights like a Christmas tree in the sky. She swung away from the window and finally sank down onto the soft couch. Morris put a drink in front of her.

"Drink it," he said. "You need something."

She shook her head. "I'm going crazy, I think."

He sat down in one of the pale chairs with a drink in his hand, his expression neutral, his gaze fixed on her. "I proclaim myself your attorney," he said. "I'll have a formal agreement drawn up Monday. As your attorney, I can make them stop harassing you, if they are, but only if I know what's going on. Tell me, Lauren. What's going on?"

"I don't even know what they want!" she cried, and now she picked up her glass and took a long drink. Scotch and water. She hated Scotch and water. She gulped another drink. "Last week a man followed me to work, Thursday night, and he disappeared in the hallway on the seventh floor. And they say we conspired to make him disappear, for insurance, the policeman said." She took another drink.

Morris shook his head at her, mournfully, she thought. "That's police business, not FBI. What else?"

"Nothing else! He's dead, and I didn't do anything. I've seen him a few times. Hallucinations. He's haunting me!" She drank down the rest of the Scotch and banged the glass down too hard. "That's all! I'm going out of my mind!"

He had hardly touched his own drink. He regarded her over the rim of his glass and said reflectively, "If they accuse you of subversion—FBI jurisdiction, you understand—an insanity plea might work." He put his glass down and steepled his fingers, his gaze distant and thoughtful; he tapped his fingers over and over. Then he shook his head. "Nope, I don't think so. Not with your background. They could convince a jury that you have the knowledge to fake it. You say you've seen him? Actually seen him?"

She nodded numbly. "Not really. Hallucinations."

"Tell me about it. When, under what circumstances, how often."

She moistened her lips. "What do you mean, subversion?"

"I don't know. FBI business anyway. When did you see him again?"

Her face went so blank that he was afraid she was passing out with her long dark eyes wide open. The Scotch and water had been mostly water, he thought aggrievedly with some impatience.

"They don't think he's dead, then," she whispered finally. "That must be it. They think he's alive."

"Lauren, just tell me about it. I can help you, but I have to know what we're facing."

She came back from her retreat and considered him for a moment, then shook her head. "I told you," she said. He knew she was lying, she thought, and there was nothing she could do about that. If she started to tell him anything, she would tell it all, and there was no way she could ever tell anyone that Corky had brought her to the peak of orgasm by caressing her feet. She stood up unsteadily. "I have to think," she said. "I don't know what happened any longer. I thought he died in a blue glow and they said he planned it himself and that I helped. That's all."

"But you said you saw him. Actually saw him, not just that you heard him, or felt him, anything else? You saw him, flesh and blood like other men?"

She turned scarlet and nodded. Peter would tell them, she thought, and she added, "He just appeared, naked, and then went away again. I thought I was haunted. I have to go home, Morris. I don't feel well."

She wanted to take a cab home, but he refused to allow it. He drove her back to her apartment and she did not say anything else on the way. She sat stiffly, staring straight ahead. At her building he tried to go in with her and she shook her head, was unyielding when he finally embraced her and kissed her.

"I'll call you in the morning," he said. "I know a few people I can get in touch with and find out what they're after. Don't worry about it, okay? I'll take care of you, Lauren. You've very precious to me."

He watched soberly until the elevator doors closed and she was out of view. Then he returned to his Porsche and allowed himself a grin. The fish was nosing the fly, he knew, and expert fisherman that he was, a fish at the fly was as good as a fish in the creel. He drove to Musselman's hotel to make his report.

Musselman nodded and sent him away again, then said to Drissac, "She'll either try to run, or try to get in touch with the Corky commie. We tighten the screws one more time and she yells for Pitts. Is that how you read it?"

Drissac agreed that he foresaw the same scenario, and he went to his own rooms, where he had a telephone network in operation. Steele was covered so tight, there was no place for her to go. It was like driving game, he thought, you make enough loud noise and frighten it thoroughly and drive it right into the pit. Pitts, he corrected himself, and got ready for bed.

As soon as Lauren had gotten inside her apartment and pulled off her coat, she made a pot of coffee. She was light-headed from so much alcohol that day, and she had to think.

They thought Corky was alive. They must have reasons for believing it, and that meant that she was not mad. Her cheeks burned when she thought of spending the night with him, the things she had said, the things they had done. She paced, waiting for the coffee. Why were they watching her? He had said they thought she was part of a spy network. Why?

She poured coffee and sat at the table with it. No notes,

nothing in writing, she decided, and remembered the notes she had made in the coffee shop earlier. She hurried to her purse and brought out the notebook, tore out the page, and then burned it in the ashtray. The infrared scanner picked up the heat flare, and the watching man made a note: subject burned papers.

It seemed clear to her that they expected to get to Corky through her somehow. Why else watch her every movement? And if they found him, then what? She poured more coffee, and now she began to feel hungry. Lunch had been a long time ago. She made a cheese sandwich.

They didn't know it all, she decided. They knew Corky was alive, but how much more? She frowned, trying to remember everything he had said. He could go through walls, be in one place, then another, instantly. She saw the can fly out into the surf again, saw his clothes melt away from him, saw the listening device hanging in air. She went to the utility room and stood for several minutes gazing at his sneakers, still tied. She remembered holding him, feeling him dissolve, then reappear bigger than ever. She closed her eyes as a rush of pain and pleasure swept her. They couldn't know any of that, or they wouldn't be trying to catch him with the methods they were using. Guards couldn't keep him out, or keep him in either. Suddenly she felt icy. If they caught him, they would have to kill him. With someone like him loose there could be no secrets. They would kill him.

What if they had a plan to make him come forward? They would use her, she knew, and could not think how. She gnawed her knuckle. Morris, she thought, he would know how to help, what to do. He might not believe a word of it, but he would help any way possible. At least he would make them leave her alone so that if Corky came back she could tell him to run, to hide, never to come near her again. She nodded, and tears blurred her vision. She had to tell him that. Or better, let Morris tell him. She hurried to the phone to call Morris. She dialed, then hung up before the first ring, remembering that she couldn't use this telephone.

Joe Krueger, who was monitoring her phone, called Morris

and told him to expect a call. "She dialed and hung up," Joe said. "Bet she goes to a pay phone. Stay on tap for it."

Morris Pitts smiled and whistled as he turned the steak he was broiling.

Lauren put her coat on again, left her sandwich untasted, and went out.

# Chapter Twenty

IT was not raining, but the streets and sidewalks were still glistening. Myriad lights shattered, reformed, elongated, shriveled to points. The caution light of the traffic signal cut a golden swath and vanished. Lauren walked slowly, her head lowered. How much could she tell Morris, how much would he accept without deciding she was insane? She could prove nothing, she knew, and it sounded as crazy as she had thought it was from the start. Maybe it was still that crazy and she was being swallowed by her own delusional system at last, no longer capable of stepping out of the frame. There were many people on the sidewalks, going to dinner, returning, frequenting the shops that kept late hours on Fridays. Right now, she knew, someone was following her, someone she could not spot, maybe that woman in the long white coat, pretending to be window-shopping. Or that man in the jeans and faded jacket—a scientist, if not a spy. Maybe both. Or that heavy man in a black suit, scowling ferociously. She ducked her head again; she couldn't tell. Morris was trained in such things; that was how he had seen the last one.

She hesitated at a pay telephone. She had not decided how much to tell Morris, exactly what she would say to him. It was too confusing to decide while she was walking. There was Hilda's Café, where Corky had said he first saw her that night that now seemed ages ago, lifetime ago, when her only problem was how to make Peter Waycross give her more meaningful work at the clinic. And that problem was still hanging in there, she thought bitterly then. It seemed that she could solve none of her problems. Resolutely she turned and entered the café and headed for one of the booths, a dim one this time. She did not want to read, she wanted to think. And to eat, she thought, sniffing hungrily.

Corky saw Musselman watching television, and studied the sweeping arm of the little monitor, mystifed about what it was doing. He found the sergeant across the street from Lauren's apartment with another screen, heard the sergeant tell someone on the phone that she was moving. He found Lauren again, and four others he felt certain were watching her, at least four others. Cautiously he circled the area, not forming a more solid body yet. A passing car caught his attention and he entered it, saw another of the little screens, a man watching it intently. This one kept showing blips, a confusion of blips. Then Lauren was alone on a corner for a moment and there was only one blip. Several people joined her; the screen filled with their blips. He streaked away.

They knew, he thought, fighting the panic that threatened to send him off again; he swirled high above the traffic, pedestrians, a police car, two kids on bikes. They knew and accepted it even if she was still resisting the idea. He pulled enough of a center together to approach her again, and he watched the car park just past where she turned to go into the café. One of the men got out and entered the café; the other sat in the car watching the screen. The one with the wandlike thing walked back past her booth, then left to rejoin his companion in the car to wait. Corky streamed into Hilda's Café.

He flowed into the space between her and the wall and cautiously flexed his muscles. "Hi," he said in a whisper. "I'm here. Can you move over just a little?"

She went rigid. Her throat felt paralyzed, her tongue numb.

She managed to turn her head enough to look, and saw nothing. "Don't you dare show yourself naked!" she whispered.

"Don't worry. I just need an inch or two. This is as far as I'll go, promise."

She scooted over a little and picked up the menu to hide behind. "Where the hell have you been? People are watching my every move. They'll get you!"

"Shh," he said softly. "Order me a pocket bread sandwich with Chinese roast pork. And a glass of milk. Please."

The waitress was standing at the table, looking at her curiously. Lauren pretended to be concentrating on the menu. She couldn't very well order two sandwiches, she thought, and said without looking up again, "Crab Louis and coffee and a pocket bread with Chinese roast pork and a glass of milk."

"Are you expecting someone?" the waitress asked then. "You want me to set another place?"

"No. I'm . . . it's for me."

"Okay. You want the coffee later?"

"Now," Lauren said, near desperation. "While I'm waiting for the rest."

The waitress nodded and left, and Lauren said angrily, in an undertone, "You're making me look like a fool. Why did you come back? Why don't you just go away, somewhere far away, and stay there?"

"I don't know why," he said. Even lower, he added, "They have a gadget that lets them see people on a screen. Like a radar screen. They're following you with it. That means they know about me."

"If you haven't done anything, why don't you just go to the police, or a doctor, or someone to get help? Maybe they, the FBI, can help."

"They'll want to cut me into little pieces to see what makes me turn on and off."

The waitress brought coffee and put it down, then leaned over to ask, "Miss, are you all right?"

"Fine!" Lauren said quickly. "Fine. I'm—I'm rehearsing lines for a play. Opening tomorrow, you know." She knew she was too bright, too cheerful. "Nervous, I guess. I'm fine. Thanks."

The waitress looked her over doubtfully, shrugged, and went away again. Lauren sagged against the back of the booth. She saw her coffee move very slowly and she made a lunge for it, shoved it to where he could reach it. She could feel him next to her; he was shivering. She put her elbows on the table, folded her hands before her, and leaned her face against them to screen him as much as possible while he drank the hot coffee. He moved closer to her and she shut her eyes and drew in a deep breath.

"You have to leave," she said very softly. "You don't have to let them catch you. After a few weeks they'll get tired of this game and they'll leave too."

"Can't," he said just as softly. The cup was lifted, tilted, returned to the table. "If they think they've lost me, they'll pick you up for interrogation."

"But that's just it. I haven't done anything. Ever. Even if they ask me questions, what can I say? They can't really do anything to me."

He touched her hair, then her cheek. What they could do, he thought, was break her, using Morris Pitts if possible. If she became too suspicious of him, they could put her away and treat her for a breakdown that would be fairly easy to document. Talking to naked invisible men was the road to the hospital and drugs and God knew what all. He said none of this. The waitress brought their food and refilled the coffee cup. When she had gone again, he said, "I want us to be together, Lauren. And I have to have a safe place where I won't be freezing, where I can think. Any ideas?"

She took a bite of her salad, considering it. Not her apartment. They must have another of the scanners there, or they could install one. Not his apartment, for the same reasons. She did not watch his sandwich rise and get eaten. That was too much.

He was thinking furiously as he ate. She was too striking to escape notice, that was one problem. No airplane, no train, bus, taxi. People would see her and remember. Not her car; a bright yellow Toyota! He didn't even own a car; his bicycle had been enough. He stopped chewing. His bicycle. Okay, but to where? For the first time he almost wished she was shorter, less memorable. Even on a bike she would attract notice. More notice than on foot maybe. People looked at women on bikes. If she were a guy—he found himself nodding. That was it. She had to get out as a guy. That opened a whole new chain of thoughts for him, and he visualized a fishing shack on an island he had gone to with Joan once. Her father owned it. There were a thousand islands out there; this one was only a dot on a map. No one would be out there in February, he was certain.

"Hi," a small voice said close to Lauren's ear. She turned to see a little boy, obviously standing in the booth behind her. "You got a dog?"

"No."

"I feed my dog under the table. His name is Big Mouth. What's your dog's name?"

"I don't have one. Shouldn't you sit down and eat?"

"I give him stuff I don't like and he eats it all."

His hair was like corn silk, his eyes big and dark, his nose peppered with freckles, and he knew she was feeding her dog under the table. He was looking at Corky's plate, the sandwich gone, the glass of milk poised two or three inches above the tabletop. Slowly it settled to rest on the table. The little boy grinned. "My dog does tricks too. He can stand on his back feet and walk."

Corky growled and the boy laughed. A man's face appeared next to the boy's. He was blond and freckled too. "Sorry," he said, glancing at Lauren, her table. "Come on, Skip, leave the lady alone. You want ice cream?"

Skip sank out of sight. Lauren could hear him telling his father that the lady was feeding her dog under the table, just like he did. The man chuckled and ordered ice cream.

Then Corky whispered into her ear, "Order coffee and sit tight until I come back. Okay?"

She nodded and he was gone again. The booth had become very cold and lonely. She was trying to think where they could go and be safe for a few days. Peter had a cabin in the mountains, but she didn't even know exactly where. She had a few acquaintances here, no real friends, no one she could turn to and ask a favor of, not one of this sort at least. By the way, I'm sheltering a fugitive, may I borrow your house? It was her fault. She was to blame; it was her responsibility to set things right again, she added almost virtuously.

It was nearly half an hour before Corky returned, slightly out of breath. "Back to your place," he said, shivering at her side. "Do you trust me?"

Her nod was immediate. "Okay. I want to take you with me for a few days. Pack warm clothes, mine, too, and toothbrushes." She thought there was laughter in his voice and she smiled faintly, remembering the other time. "I'll call you. I'll let the phone ring three times, hang up and call back instantly. You get it on the first ring. I'll just say something like everything's okay and hang up. I want them to think you're getting a signal. Then you go down, get in your car, and start north on I Five. I'll be with you as soon as I can. Got all that?"

She nodded again, and this time the waitress took it for a sign that she wanted her check. She brought it, looking at Lauren suspiciously; she waited until Lauren pulled on her coat and left the booth before she turned away.

Lauren walked back fast, not paying any attention to anyone on the streets. She had to strain to keep from smiling, and she felt prickly with excitement, like a schoolgirl planning to elope. The rain had started again in a fine, steady drizzle. There were very few people out in it. She thought she could feel him now and then at her side, but she was not sure.

No bicycle, he had realized at his apartment; someone had ripped it off. Instead, he had streaked out to locate the island he remembered, and then he found an outboard motorboat. He had checked out Musselman, who was nervous because Lauren was moving; he looked in on Morris, who was pacing, scowling at the telephone. The sergeant was alert, watching his monitor. A second man with him was bored, leaning back in a chair with his eyes closed; he was wearing earphones.

Corky had examined Lauren's car thoroughly and had found the device they had planted, but he did not know exactly what it was. He would find out as soon as they were on the road. If it was a bug, he would get rid of it; if it was a homing device of some sort, he would leave it alone.

He kept a tight hold on his center as he looked in here and there, watching the various players take up positions. He gave Lauren half an hour to get packed, and then he was in Bellingham, eight-five miles away, inside a condo. He called her number, let it ring three times, hung up. He dialed again and gave her his brief message, "It's okay," and hung up again, and then streaked back to the apartment across the street from hers. The man with the earphones was wide awake now, listening. He looked at the sergeant and said, "Bellingham. That's all."

Sergeant Carroll nodded and called Drissac, who reported to Trigger Happy; many new wheels were set in motion. When the colonel was told a few minutes later that she had left her apartment in her car alone, he nodded his satisfaction, as did Drissac. Just as they had planned, Trigger Happy thought. Morris had spooked her enough to put her on edge; and now the Corky commie creep was calling her in. Bellingham, he mused, almost on the Canada border, and that, too, was what he had thought; they would make a run for it. Drissac made his call to McChord Air Force Base and ordered the two helicopters that were standing by, and then they waited to make certain she was actually heading north on I Five. The reports came at five-minute intervals; they were all the same: Driving fast, heading north, alone.

When Drissac left, the colonel sat by himself, taking the reports as they came. He wondered if the Corky commie would become visible after he died. He hoped not, not until they pumped him full of dye or something. He had a pleasant little fantasy in which he stood at a long metal table covered by a white sheet that bulged with what had to be a body, then pulling off the sheet triumphantly to reveal nothing. He could see the expressions on their faces, the Joint Chiefs, the Secretary of Defense, the Surgeon General, all of them. The President? First he shook his head, then he muttered, "Why the hell not?" and he put him in the picture too.

Lauren drove with fierce concentration, denying over and over that she was very frightened. She wondered if Joan had been frightened when she led her forces against the English, or had her voices sustained her without fear?

She found herself speeding again and again, slowed down with great effort, only to race once more. She wanted to drive faster and faster until she was flying.

"Relax, Lauren," he said suddenly from the other seat. "I'm here."

She gasped and slowed down again, and was now just at the speed limit. "Are you all right?"

"Hard to say," he said after a moment's thought. "I'd have to come more into focus to tell, but I think so. They have a homing device on the car, but no bug, so we can talk. They'll give you some room to maneuver because they think you're leading them to me."

"What are we doing?" she said in a near wail. She felt his lips brush her cheek and she reached out to feel him. He was shivering again. "Are you cold when you're . . . not so solid?"

He laughed and turned up the heat. "Nope. Don't feel my body at all then. Now, what we're doing—"

"Then you should stay . . . the other way. You'll catch cold."

"Shh. Listen."

She drove north to Burlington, where she left the interstate and bought gas; she walked back and forth under the lights as if stretching her legs. She carried her black umbrella and kept her head ducked as she exercised briefly. Then she drove out and turned onto Highway 11, which ran parallel to the interstate all the way into Bellingham. After a mile she slowed down again, this time to pull into a roadside rest stop. She parked as close as she could to the rest rooms, and angled her car in in such a way that it would screen her from the car following. Again she opened the black umbrella and shielded herself with it as she hurried to the women's side of the small building. She carried the zipper bag with the warm clothing and toothbrushes, half under her coat, not as if to hide it, but to keep it dry. Corky was there, waiting for her. He was naked, of course.

Wordlessly she pulled off her coat and he wrapped himself in it, then put on her hat. "Okay?" he asked anxiously.

She nodded, then shook her head violently. "You won't fool anyone for a minute!"

"I'd better," he said with a touch of grimness. He kissed her lightly and opened the door, stuck the umbrella out and opened it, and then ran to the car, hoping no one would notice that Lauren had lost her shoes somewhere. The car should hide his feet, he thought, sliding in behind the wheel, closing the umbrella at the last minute. He drove off fast and in a second the chase car took up its position in the rear.

The two men inside the chase car relaxed minimally when the one with the scanner nodded. The report to Trigger Happy was the same as before. Driving north alone.

Corky was humming under his breath when he led the chase car into Bellingham. He was not surprised that traffic had increased quite a bit, in fact, that the traffic at two in the morning was almost heavy. He led them in and out of side streets, past residential areas, through the waterfront section, and then he headed east, through town, into the wooded hills beyond, up a narrow dirt road to a lookout point that he was surprised to find. He took out the keys and tossed them into the woods below, and streaked away, back to the rest stop where he had left Lauren.

If he had stayed, if he had followed Drissac to a phone and listened to his conversation with Trigger Happy, he would have been more worried than he was when he joined her and they started their walk to the boat he was planning to borrow.

"She gave us the slip," Drissac said in a low, very controlled voice that was so emotionless that it sounded like a computer voice. "She can do it too," he said. "He must have taught her how, or maybe they all know how by this time."

# Chapter Twenty-One

SOMETIMES he was with her, his hand holding hers, guiding her; then he was gone, but always to return quickly, to change her course, or just to be there, holding her hand. They stopped at a ramshackle wooden dock that had pools of pale light at regular intervals along its length. The boats moored here would have been as out of place at the Yacht Club as Corky himself. Fishing boats, a houseboat or two, sailboats with makeshift rigging, makeshift sails no doubt stowed away, ready to go at the whim of an impoverished sailor; there were inboard motor boats to navigate quiet waters, from the bay to the islands in the Sound.

The boat he had chosen looked impossibly small to her, dangerous, but he led her aboard silently, and pushed off from the dock, dipped an oar into the water, steered it out farther and farther. The lights of the dock had been dim; no one had been in sight. Only the soft slap of waves against the boat, the less soft splash of rain everywhere could be heard now. She could see nothing before them; behind them the lights vanished fast, hidden by rain and mist.

Corky waited until they were well away from the dock before he started the engine. It sounded like cannon fire. He throttled it down; they tilted a little, and headed into the blackness.

She was terrified of the black water, of the dangerous little boat, the rain, a storm that would come up unexpectedly, sweep them for miles before capsizing them, sharks, killer octopi, pirates, Trigger Happy and his men.

"I need you," Corky said after a few minutes. She could not even see him. The rain had soaked her to the skin; she was shaking with cold. She started to creep toward his voice through the darkness. "Good," he said, and his hand was on hers, guiding it to the rudder. "Hold this exactly how it is. Right back." He was gone.

She nearly screamed her terror, but she was afraid to, afraid to take a deep breath, afraid to move. She closed her eyes and held the rudder steady.

"Okay," he said, back again. He made an adjustment and rested his hand on hers. "I'll check again in a minute," he said, ridiculously cheerful, considering that he was naked, a fugitive with the United States Army after him, the FBI, God only knew who else, in the middle of the Sound in pitch-black night with rain everywhere. He felt happier than he had felt in his life, he was thinking, holding her hand, her body next to him.

He checked their location twice more, each time melting away from her, leaving her alone a moment, then making a minor adjustment in their course. At last he slowed them to a near stop, and he said, "You'll have to steer us in. I'll lead the way, but I can't do both."

She shook her head violently. But already he was gone. Straight ahead until he changed directions, she thought grimly. She might plow into rocks, another boat at anchor, a submarine, a whale, but she would steer straight ahead until he told her otherwise. She was biting her lip, straining to see. He was there a second, turned the rudder, was gone. They crept onward and suddenly she felt the boat scraping bottom.

The engine stopped. "Help me pull her in a little more," he said, and she climbed over the side, into the frigid water that was no higher than her knees, tugged on the boat with him. They pulled it high enough to keep it from floating away immediately, then his hand was on her elbow and he was guiding her again.

"Our clothes," he said, hefting the little bag she had packed. He was no longer whispering, or shouting over the boat noise. "Your purse." He handed it to her. "You don't have a flashlight, I suppose."

She remembered a keychain light and rummaged in her purse until she found it. The light was feeble, but enough to see his laughing face. His hair was plastered to his forehead; rain ran down his nose. She knew she looked much the same, except that she had on clothes that were plastered to her body.

"Almost there," he said, grinning happily. He pointed upward and she turned the tiny light in that direction. It did not penetrate the darkness and rain more than a foot. He took her hand and they started to walk.

Stumbling, banging into rocks, sliding, they made their way to the rocky cliff and found a rock, log, and sand trail up it. At the top, set back from the edge, was a shack. Corky opened the door and they entered. Her light showed only that it was a crude, unfinished shack with a table and several chairs.

"There are candles," Corky said. "Get dry and try to warm up a little. I'll be back as soon as I can." Then he wrapped his wet arms about her and kissed her.

She stood shaking in the little house on an island somewhere in the ocean and listened to the rain on the tin roof and waves crashing into rocks somewhere far below. She had to have light, a fire, dry clothes. She stood, afraid to move, afraid of the blackness of the shadows all around her. The tiny flashlight was so feeble, ready to give up at any moment. She thought of being here without any light, and in panic she swung around and probed the shadows for candles, a fireplace, stove.

Going back was faster. The lights onshore guided Corky more or less to where he had launched the boat, and he found himself easing into the sheltered cove in less than an hour since leaving Lauren. He spotted the right dock and cut the engine, drifted in with only a nudge or two of the paddle. He was tying up, when a watchman tramped by without a glance. Then he was done, and he streaked back to the island and Lauren.

Trigger Happy knew she could not have escaped the network already in place by three that morning. More scanners had been flown in to Bellingham, more men. The border had been closed until scanners were available; every car, everything that rolled was undergoing examination. So far they had found three cats and two dogs, all breaking quarantine, or trying to. Highways had been closed, roadblocks installed, manned by scanner-equipped personnel. Drissac was staying up in Bellingham, in charge of the operation. And he knew he could trust Drissac, and Sergeant Carroll; he did not have any trust at all in any other person connected with the whole operation. Had someone let her slip through? How? A mistake, or because the other side wanted it that way? That was how this affair had been from the start, bungled, mistake-filled, excuse-ridden.

He cursed the weather, and the mountains, the deep woods that would let anyone hide for days, slipping from tree to tree. They were making a tight ring, a scanner to every dozen men; outside its perimeter, another ring, more scanners. She might hide behind the damn trees for a while, but eventually she would have to make a run, and then they would have her. He knew it, and yet he cursed and paced and drank Scotch and smoked cigars, and snatched up the phone on the first ring throughout the night. Beginning early in the morning, they would start a house-to-house, again armed with scanners. No way could she keep hiding. No goddamn way! He snatched up the phone again.

The scanners located seven privates, four sergeants, two lieutenants, uncounted coyotes, uncounted deer, dogs, rabbits, even a goddamn bear, but no tall, ungainly girl. No red-haired Corky commie.

Lauren woke up to see fog pressed against the window; she turned over, molded herself closer to Corky, and drifted to sleep again. He was drifting pleasantly in a state of mental fog that allowed fantasies to play themselves out in his mind. They would go away to a tropical island and sleep in hammocks on a beach, eat pineapples and bananas, drink exotic drinks with strange fruits floating in them. He would draw and paint and she would read and write wonderful learned books.

They would skin-dive for shells and float in emerald water as warm as their bodies and watch red and golden fish. They would ride elephants in India and camels across the deserts of Africa, sail the fjords of Sweden, stroll the boulevards of Paris. And every morning he would wake up to find her in his arms, her breath warm on his neck, her fragrance in his nostrils.

She stirred again and this time she yawned and mumbled something unintelligible, then sat up, pulling the cover off him. He grabbed it back.

"It's all right," he said soothingly. "We're safe here."

She turned to look at him; she was wide-eyed and sleep-mussed and the most beautiful woman he had ever seen. She shook her head.

"Were you dreaming? It's okay, remember?"

She shook her head again. The dream, she remembered then, had been terrible. Not quite a nightmare, but close. She had been on a string, like a bead at the end of a string being swung around in a circle. Bull roarer, she thought, remembering the way Australian aborigines made them, a weight on a line that they whirled to make a terrible noise that frightened away the women and children from the men's secret ceremonies. But Corky had come in closer, not frightened by the noise she made. He had tried to grab her again and again, always moving in closer. And she had come wide awake.

"We'll never be safe," she said then in a low voice. "I'll put on coffee if there is any."

The shack had three rooms, the one they had slept in that would have slept six more people on cots and the floor, the kitchen, and a large living room that also had two cots in it. It was all paneled with rough redwood. The floors were bare, smooth boards. No curtains, no drapes, nothing decorative. A fishing shack, he had said the night before, a place to come to and dry out and rest, then go out after the big one again. There was a wood-burning cookstove in the kitchen, and overnight the fire had gone out. She had spread all their clothes on chairs to dry; everything had been soaked, what she had worn as well as everything in the little bag. Now she picked the driest of her things and dressed hurriedly, chilled already. Corky passed her, wrapped in a blanket, and went to the stove, added paper and wood, and stood huddled over it until the fire was blazing.

She investigated the cabinets while he dressed. There was a good supply of food, just not much variety, she decided. Oatmeal, rice, beans in jars tightly closed. Tins of cornmeal and flour, instant cocoa and instant coffee . . . It would do.

Set back from the house, under an enormous fir tree, was a privy. She went out to use it first, and stopped just outside the door to gaze at the world below, all around her. The fog had lifted to a uniform level that truncated surrounding hills and mountains. All the slopes were solid green, and the water below was just as green. The hills were fringed with color—violet, gold, pale green. She turned to examine the rest of the landscape. A series of islands? A chain? They seemed to go on forever, all surrounded by channels, some wide, some narrow; then she saw a much wider body of water; behind her a steeply rising hill cut off the rest. The hill was covered with immense fir trees with wide clearings between the trees that cast deep shade. On the edges of the woods were masses of ferns, and heather in bloom, mauve and deeper violet, and Scotch broom in vivid yellows. The air was fragrant with heather and ocean smells that were fresh and clean, winy.

After breakfast they explored the tiny island. Their shack was on the southwestern edge, two hundred feet above the sea. They had come ashore at a minuscule beach, where Corky had had a clambake on his last visit here. He pointed out where the huge bonfire had been, where they dug the clams, boiled seawater. . . . They climbed the hill, a precipitous rocky mountaintop covered with trees that had found enough soil to sprout seeds and then created enough soil to support roots. The hill was four hundred feet higher than the cabin, six hundred feet over the narrow channel that separated this island from its nearest neighbor to the west. At the southern end the next island was several hundred feet away. A channel narrowed until at the northernmost point it was less than fifty feet across. The water, funneled through the channel, roared here, pouring south with the rising tide, thundering north with the ebb. From the crest of the hill there was a sheer drop of hundreds of feet along a black, weathered basalt cliff down to the cascading water. The channel on the eastern side was wider and more placid, dark green smooth water, three hundred feet across. That side had a long, narrow beach of golden sand. The other two cabins were above the north end of the beach, the boat docks empty, no one else on the island.

They had climbed the steep hill, had walked the northern end of the island, had walked the length of the docks and gazed at the water below, and now they were strolling on the beach. The sun had come out; the sky was pale blue. They could see a bank of clouds hanging over the mainland to the east.

"Look," Corky was saying, "what I'll do is go back to shore and call the newspapers, not the FBI or the cops. I'll say I saw a man with red hair leaving here in a boat, heading toward Victoria, that he shot at me, and was in a hell of a hurry. When they come, I'll tie you up and vanish. Not tight, or enough to hurt you," he added quickly. "Just to make it look like I kidnapped you and left you here to perish of exposure or starvation."

She held his hand harder and shook her head. "Kidnapping, spying, a fugitive. They'd shoot you on sight. They'd take me to a hospital, you know, and in the examination, they'd find out . . . they can tell if you've had sex recently."

"Tell them I raped you."

She smiled softly, looking at the sand. "Let's find a different way out of this mess. They'd never believe that."

They walked silently for a few minutes, then she said, "You can escape anytime you want, and they'll never find you. That's what you have to do, just go somewhere else, far away, start a new life, and never come near me again. They might watch me for a few months, or even longer, but it can't go beyond that. I'll get a lawyer right away to look out for my rights. Morris Pitts offered—"

He snorted angrily. "He's one of them."

She stopped. "How do you know that?"

He tried to think how he knew, and failed. He just knew it. And he knew Morris Pitts was one of *them*. He spread his hands helplessly.

"You believe me, don't you?"

She nodded, then said bitterly, "The first tall man with money who ever gave me a second look. I should have known."

"He sees you as a target, a job," Corky said. "Lauren, I see you as the most beautiful woman on earth. Everything about you is beautiful! Everything! Maybe if I eat more meat I'll grow a little taller. Some people don't reach their full size until they're older than I am, you know."

"It doesn't matter," she said. "You're going away. Where? That's the problem. Not anywhere on the West Coast; maybe altogether out of the country would be best. Do you speak any foreign language?"

"No. A few words of Spanish and French and a little German. You pick up stuff like that hanging out at racetracks. I won't leave you, Lauren. They want you as much as they want me now. It's my fault. I should have stayed away from you before, and now it's too late. They think you're part of it all."

"You've said that before," she said. "Exactly what does it mean? Corky, you know things you shouldn't know. How did you learn them? When? How do you know what they think?"

He looked at her helplessly.

"Let's go back to the cabin. Let's try to piece together this entire last week or more. Where are you when you black out? Can you control it? You always come back; maybe it's something you can use."

He felt a wrench of fear tighten his stomach and chest. "I

can't," he said too fast. "I can't go there again. They warned me."

"What do you mean?" She regarded him with troubled eyes.

He shook his head. "You're right about all this," he said reluctantly. "It's what I wanted peace and quiet for, to try to make sense of what's been happening. Let's go make notes."

Hand in hand they turned away from the beach, climbed the hill that was not so high at this end, and went down the other side to the cabin.

He told himself positively that there was nothing to worry about, nothing to fear. He was only going to talk about it, not do it again, whatever it was. His stomach did not seem to believe any of that.

# Chapter Twenty-Two

"ALL right," Lauren said back in the cabin at the table. She had her notebook out. "Let's start with the first day, Thursday. You followed me and you were standing by the window; when I turned to see you, you glowed blue and vanished. That was the first time. Right?"

He shook his head. "We need two sheets of paper, one for what you saw, one for what I thought was happening?"

She ripped out extra sheets of notebook paper and put them in the middle of the table, then waited until he scribbled on his.

"What do you have?" she asked then in a low, worried voice.

"It runs together. That night, and then you dropped a pot and screamed."

She swallowed hard and wrote down what he had said. She kept her gaze on the paper. "That was three days later, Sunday."

"I don't seem to have any first, second, third sequences," Corky said. "Let's just write down what I remember and then try to sort it out by days. How's that sound?"

"Okay. But . . . there are phases, aren't there? I mean, right now you look solid and all here, but in the boat, in the car, other times, you sort of come and go."

He nodded. "It's like a muscle somewhere in here." He felt his solar plexus. "I can tense it or relax or just forget the whole thing."

"You can control it?"

"Not all the way. Sometimes I lose it." She was gazing past him, her eyes narrowed. "What is it, Lauren?"

She blinked, and then drew two lines that started out parallel; they narrowed to make a funnel that finally closed. At the wide end she drew in an oval that filled the space. "This is how you are now, solid, visible, normal. But somewhere along in here, you disappear, still solid enough, but invisible. Along the lines somewhere you aren't solid any longer, and you can go here and there instantly, like back in the car and the boat. But you still remember what you do; you still have a mind working. Then nothing. That's scary. Where do you go then? Why can't you remember?"

"That's what I intend to find out," he said grimly. "First we have to try to find some parameters. The next thing I remember is seeing my grandfather on his farm in Arkansas. I don't know when." Gradually he filled in all the pieces he could remember— seeing his papers in the hotel room one time, in a vault another time, seeing Joan, friends. He remembered sleeping in Lauren's apartment, shaving, watching Morris and another man there. She shook her head in disbelief that he had slept in the apartment without her awareness. He shrugged and went on jotting down the memories he was certain of. When he was done, up to the day he and Lauren had gone to Whidbey Island, there were fewer than eight hours for which he could say with confidence that he knew where he had been.

They stopped writing at the same time and she was smiling slightly. "You wrecked our lunch that day? Knocked things over on the table?"

He took her hand. "I was afraid you'd accept him at face value, and that would have been pretty bad."

"You decided to be my protector," she murmured. "My Superman."

"Some Superman! If I'd stayed away from you, you'd be safe now, not out on an island wondering if they'll charge you with subversion or something."

"You're Superman enough," she said softly, and felt her cheeks flush.

They both stood up, still holding hands. "Too much thinking and walking," Corky said. "I think we need to rest now."

She laughed and they went to the bedroom.

He lay watching her sleep, his head propped up on his hand, until his arm started to go numb. Then, moving carefully in order not to wake her up, he rolled away, out of the bed. Still he hesitated, watching her, the most beautiful women he had ever seen; he loved her lanky, coltish boy-walk, her elegant, bony feet and hands, the way she ducked her head when her cheeks flamed. And he knew he was the last man on earth for her. The worst possible thing that could have happened to her was tangling up with him.

He picked up his clothes from the floor and softly went into the other room to dress and think. The roar of the water rushing through the narrow channel was soothing at this distance; outside, it was almost too loud to talk over when the tide was changing. It was like a giant inhaling water, exhaling it in mighty torrents.

The sun was getting low, casting long streaks of dust-dancing motes; the windows were so sea-misted that the light coming through was tinted pale yellow, the dust motes almost silver. He knew he should build up the fire before the cabin got any colder, but he stood without moving. The light shafts were filled with the dust, yet the dust was everywhere, just lighted up in that column, the dance involuntary, at the whim of the air currents.

Abruptly he sat at the table and reached for the paper. Something, something, he thought; the dust reminded him of something. He began to sketch.

He redrew the parallel lines and put a stick figure between them. That was normal space occupancy, he thought; he began to draw the lines converging, and added the same stick figure, with parts poking out above and below them. That was when he was still fairly solid, but invisible. As he regarded the narrowing lines, he put the pencil down and leaned back. Where did the leftover pieces go? Where did memory fail him? He realized then that he would have to experiment, and the idea filled him with dread.

He sensed Lauren, and turned to find her in the doorway watching him. She was wrapped in the thin blanket they had dug out of a cedar box. Hurriedly he got up and went to the stove to build up the fire. Before any experimenting, he had to take her back to the mainland, he decided, poking at the wood. He could not risk abandoning her out here alone, and he never seemed to know when, or even if, he would be back.

"After dark," he said, not looking at her, "I'll get another boat, and at dawn we'll go back. I'll get one that will take us down to Seattle this time. Okay?"

"Good. I was going to suggest that myself."

"Yeah, the best thing to do is split up. You can tell them I forced you at gunpoint to submit to me."

"All right." She went to the window, facing away from him.

"It's for the best," he said. "We're no good for each other. I mean, I've got under a hundred in my checking account and I can't touch it. I'll be on the run. You know that."

"I know. They can't catch you and if they did catch you, they can't hold you and if they could hold you, they can't touch you, can they?"

"I don't know." He was holding the poker and suddenly remembered the agent who had swung a poker at him in the cabin at Whidbey Island. That had sent him flying apart. And the time that Lauren had tried to hit him with her umbrella; that had sent him flying. Maybe she was right. He put the poker down and closed the stove door.

"I think Buenos Aires would be good," she said. "I've read that there is a big European community there."

"Fascists."

"Some probably, but there are other people too." She leaned her forehead against the glass. "Can you move that far all at once?"

"I could do it in hops if I had to. And when I get there I can steal food and sleep wherever I find myself. No problem."

"I thought there wouldn't be any. You mustn't write or call or get in touch in any way, of course."

"Right."

"Good," she said, and moved from the window with a brusque motion. "I'll get dressed. Want to go for a walk before it gets dark?" She stopped at the doorway. "Oh, you should get a boat before dark. You can't scout out the way and steer too."

"Let's walk now," he said.

Still she paused. "This is what you want, isn't it? To go away and hide yourself."

He nodded. "The only thing to do. It isn't as if we have anything real going for us. I mean, we've just known each other for a few hours actually."

"That's what I was thinking too. And we both agreed the first time that we're not at all right for each other. You are pretty short."

"And it doesn't make a guy feel too great to have a woman taller than he is either. But aside from that, you've got a career, a profession. You should get out of the clinic though. Find a different job."

"Why?"

"One of your colleagues, the little wimpy one, is thinking of ways to get rid of his wife, and he's probably going to crack wide open and cause a scandal. Wouldn't do you any good to be around."

"How do you know that?" she demanded from the doorway.

"He's sure his wife starches his shorts. He's got a champion case of jock itch. She doesn't, but she does use a strong detergent and bleach because she thinks he's dirty. She doesn't rinse it all out either." Corky stopped and shook his head. "You didn't know any of that, did you?"

"No." She hurried to him. "And you know all kinds of things you shouldn't know. Like the colonel wanting to be a general for the bigger pension, stuff like that."

"Not for the pension alone," he said. "He wants to get a consultant's job when he retires. Colonels are a dime a dozen; generals make the big bucks. That's what he's after. He hates the army and thinks they've slighted him because he didn't go to West Point."

She stared at him, horrified. "My God, don't ever let anyone else know you can do that," she whispered. "Corky, they'll find a way to kill you just for knowing too much!"

He nodded, his blue eyes very round and nearly blank suddenly. "That's it!" he exclaimed. "I get scattered just like the dust! That's what it reminded me of!" Like the dust, he was everywhere at those times, and each mote was aware.

She reached for his arm, shook him, and the blanket fell away from her shoulders. He caught her to him in a tight embrace, then released her and picked up the blanket, wrapped it around her. "Two choices," he said. "Rest some more, or take a walk."

"It's going to be too dark for you to go steal a boat," she said. "It would be dangerous to do it alone. I mean, you'd probably lose the boat and have to do it again. So, we could take a walk now, and then later go to bed again, for one last time before we separate." She searched his face and he nodded. "What did you think of just now?"

"I'll show you." He went to the table and showed her the sketches he had made. "Here, where the guy fills his space, it's like right here and now. Then invisible, but solid. On down the line until there's just a little bit inside, most of him outside. Somewhere along there, I seem to get inside people, just like the dust gets inside you with every breath. And then I seem to know whatever they are thinking and feeling, not just what they're saying and doing. That's how I know about the colonel and the President and Peter Waycross and Rich what's-his-name. And you."

"The President? Me?"

"I think maybe everybody," he said in wonder. "People I don't even know who they are, or what they're doing or the language they speak. But I know what they think and feel."

She looked again at the sketch. "What's beyond here?" she asked, pointing to the end of the funnel. "What happens if you go all the way to the end?"

He shook his head. "I don't know. It looks like a flytrap, open one way. I just don't know." At her sudden gasp, he added, "But remember that I've always come back. That's just a drawing, a map."

"The map is not the territory," she said just as positively. "This is like drawing time and space. Any squiggle could mean anything in a drawing, and mean nothing in real life." She turned from the table with a quick movement and hurried out. "I'll get dressed. Right back."

She had to hurry so that he would not see that her eyes had filled with tears. Rock and hard place, she thought. Devil and deep blue sea. Pinnacle and peak. If they caught him and he had to escape to that place, he might never come back. He didn't know how to got there, how he stayed, how he left again, and one time he might not leave again. She had to send him away from her, someplace safe, someplace she didn't know about, where they couldn't find him through her. If they thought he cared for her, they might use that knowledge. If they thought she cared for him, they might find a way to use that. She had to persuade him to leave, convince him that she was through, that it had been a game. She had to stay out of bed with him because in bed there was no pretense possible. A long walk, then dinner, then . . . Gin, or hearts, or Scrabble, or something. There were cards, games in the shack, things to do. They would play until it was time for him to go get the boat. She blinked back tears as she pulled on her clothes, already feeling abandoned and bereft.

"What do you think?" Trigger Happy asked Drissac.

The captain looked exhausted that afternoon. He had not slept all night. "She got out," he said wearily. "Don't ask how because I don't know, but if she's still up there, I'll eat her."

"They both got away," Trigger Happy said murderously. Now

he was eyeing his old comrade with suspicion, along with everyone else in the state.

"There's something fishy," Drissac muttered, pacing. He could not sit still when he was this tired. "Why go up that particular road? It's a dead-end road up to a park. Steep hills and woods all around. It doesn't make any sense. Why go up there knowing she'd have to go out on foot?"

"Maybe she didn't go out on foot," Trigger Happy suggested darkly. "Keep our guys chasing their tails up there while she's skipping across the border. After she got a lift down the hill again. You check on who all went down?"

"They thought of that," Drissac said tiredly. "They checked every moving object with the scanners. She was on foot. If she actually went up at all."

Trigger Happy watched him through narrowed eyes, itching for someone to hit, something to throw, someone to shoot. Anything to relieve his tension. Earlier, Naval Intelligence had visited him. Two of them, cool, superior, aloof, asking questions, answering nothing, giving nothing. They would be back, they had said. They wanted this one, this whole operation, he knew; they wanted him out. If there was glory, they wanted that. They would see that if there was blame, he would get it. That was the way they worked, they had made that very clear, and they wanted no help from amateurs, from out-of-shape army colonels who were supposed to be observing kooks with kooky discoveries. They had the resources, the experience, the trained personnel, links with street people, drug pushers, whatever it took to get information. He chewed his cigar and glowered at Drissac, who was pacing steadily.

"Well?" he finally prompted.

"It's the sequence," Drissac said, and now he went to the table where he had spread out maps to show Trigger Happy what the problem was with the area Steele had chosen to hide in. "Look," he said, pointing to Interstate Five. "She stopped for gas here, and walked up and down under the lights for a few minutes. In the rain. Making sure they saw her, knew it was her. Back on the road, on Highway Eleven this time. She stops again here, to use the toilet. It's a rest stop, not used much that time of night. No one else was there. They saw a raincoat and umbrella go in, and they saw an umbrella and raincoat come out, get in the car, and start driving again. Scanner showed one person, not who it was."

Trigger Happy looked blank.

"I don't think she's the one who gave us the slip in Bellingham," Drissac said. "They changed places at that rest stop and he got away, but she's still hiding. And if we have her, we'll get him. One way or another."

"Then she's not invisible too?"

"I'd be willing to bet on it. That was one of the oldest switcheroos in the business, and our guys fell for it."

Trigger Happy peered at the map. There was the goddamn Sound right there, all those islands, and Seattle within walking distance practically. But she was a distinctive-looking girl, he reflected, not one that could hide easily. He nodded then.

"I think you've hit on it," he said softly. "Run a check on those two guys following her." It still left them with the problem of explaining how the Corky commie had given them all the slip, but that was something he could handle. The Corky commie was an old hand at stuff like that, an experienced agent, for God alone knew how long and with what kind of training. But the girl had presented a real dilemma. They had not been able to find a long enough blank in her life for her to acquire real training. School, summer jobs, the job here, all time accounted for as far back as they could check.

That night, when Naval Intelligence returned, Drissac was with Trigger Happy and they both listened grimly as their whole operation was dismissed as one bungle after another. Both the Intelligence men wore bluejeans and turtlenecks. One even had an earring, for chrissake!

They had a substance to spray on the floor of her apartment, and his, they said. Anyone who walked on it would leave prints. And they had a small cannister of a special gas that would go off with radio control, cause nearly instant unconsciousness within a radius of one hundred feet. This was to become a coordinated venture, army-navy cooperation all the way. Their men would join the watchers and listeners. They would replace the homing device on her car with something a little more sophisticated, one said, and did not explain what it was or what it would do. Trigger Happy and Drissac remained mute.

"We're checking the waterfront now to see if she took a boat, or if anyone took her out in a boat. We don't think she left the area, just from what you've told us. That rest stop is half an hour from the docks at Blanchard. It looks like a case of being lured away to give her time to get a boat and leave. We'll know in a couple of hours."

They exchanged glances and stood up. They looked like a couple of waterfront rats, ready for anything that came along—a job, a drug haul, a mugging, anything.

"You'll share your reports, of course," Trigger Happy said. "I assure you of our full cooperation."

The one with the earring said, "Our orders are to give you reports as they accrue, sir." The "sir" was not quite mocking.

Trigger Happy went to the door with them, shook hands, and locked the door after them. When he turned to face Drissac he was livid. The captain handed him a glass half full of Scotch and he drank deeply.

"Those bastards! Those goddamn fucking bastards! Why are they poking their noses in it? What's in it for them? How did they get word? Who's the whistle-blower this time? Oh, those bastards!"

"It's their turf," Drissac said thoughtfully. "They probably get to scan most reports regarding this whole area. And they do have a nuclear sub coming home soon. I guess they're antsy after all those demonstrations last month."

"They told you all that?" Trigger Happy demanded, his suspicions flaring again.

"It was in the papers," the captain said dryly. "And the demonstrations were on every newscast on television. Over at Bangor, remember? Last time they launched one of those babies the protesters filled the Sound with little boats trying to stop the whole thing. I bet the navy will fill the Sound this time with their own boats."

Trigger Happy went back to the map and regarded it bitterly. The navy was taking over in the name of national security; he could feel it in his bones. And they didn't believe in an invisible spy. They would treat this business like attempted sabotage, and the Corky commie would escape again. He could feel that in his bones too. He knew with a vast certainty that the Corky commie and the Steele girl and God alone knew how many others were holed up on one of those islands just waiting for the nuclear sub to put into port. The one with the earring had smiled at the list of proofs he had accumulated about the invisibility; they would let him slip right through.

His face was mottled with fury at the thought of the navy making an Anzio-type landing, blasting away, missing the main one, the Corky commie. But they had the contacts, the charts of the islands, the boats. Suddenly he turned to Drissac. There was something he had after all, he decided.

"Get Morris Pitts over here," he snapped.

# Chapter Twenty-Three

"THE problem," Corky said that night after they had eaten canned stew and canned peaches with great appetite, "is that people don't automatically give station identification. You just think and feel and accept who you are, where you are, and that's the end of it. So I don't know exactly who thinks he wants to commit murder, or to whom it's going to be done, or when or how. Sometimes I remember something, like a view, or a sign, something that acts as a marker. Like the Oval Office. Or Grampa's farm. Places I've been or I've seen in photographs or television or something."

"But it's terrible to feel everything!"

"It's not like that exactly," he said, and he was not certain what it was like exactly, just not terrible. "There's so much that none of it seems overwhelming," he said after a moment. "That sounds awful, doesn't it? But that's how it seems."

"And you don't know how you get to that phase," she murmured. "Or how you get out of it."

"It just happens," he said. "Zap, I'm there. Zap, I'm back looking for a place to light. Usually wherever you are."

"That's what's so frightening. It's like having a whole different universe suddenly, where you don't know what the rules are, what's dangerous, what's to your advantage, anything about it."

He knew more today than he had known a week ago, he

thought. He knew how to use the muscle to vanish, to evaporate enough to pass through solids, and come back. He knew there was the area where he might just as easily go the other way as back to the real world, and he knew he did not want to go there ever again, even if he did not know why. He stood up and went to the stove. Every kettle and pan in the shack had been put into service to heat water for a joint bath. He had found an immense oval galvanized tub and dragged it inside; already the interior of the cabin was steamy, the windows opaqued with fog. The tub was a third full. Lauren came to help and they emptied the pots and refilled them, pumping water at the iron sink. One more time, he thought, and they would have plenty of hot water.

"The theory is that you soap up and rinse off before you get in," he said a little later.

He remembered a tiled bathroom with a tiled enclosure of tepid water. The enclosure was two feet square, nearly four feet deep. He had been a man helping a beautiful dark-skinned woman undress, loving her with every bit of his being; he had been the woman sensuously responding to his hands as he undid her robe. They caressed each other, and he was both of them together, feeling her skin under his hands as he gently soaped her, feeling his hands here, there, taking a deep breath, exhaling a sigh. Pouring ladles of warm water over her, over him . . .

He looked about the cabin, for a moment as much in the memory as here. Not the same, he thought, but it would do, and afterward they would get in the tub.

"Just drip on the floor?" Lauren asked in surprise as he helped her out of her clothes.

"We'll sweep it out the door later. What nice fuzz you have on your back. So fine and soft." He ran his hand down her spine lightly and cupped her firm buttock. "What an ass," he sighed.

She caught her breath, just the way his memory prompted, and neither talked for a while. They soaped each other and rinsed each other and climbed into the galvanized tub, where they made love in the steaming water.

His head went under and he surfaced, coughing and sputtering, and then her head went under, and then they both sank. "It's the logistics," he complained. "Too many body parts. Ah, there you are."

Their lovemaking was explosive, and the water churned and splashed out of the tub as they both started to sink again. Corky finally caught his breath and said, "I saw something like this in a movie once and it was romantic as hell."

"Sex isn't romantic," she murmured. "The courtship is, and maybe foreplay, and afterward, but when you actually get to the act itself, romance is out of the question."

"You don't think this is romantic now?"

She was sitting between his legs, her back to him, his hands on her breasts, her hands on his legs, smoothing the hairs underwater. She looked over her shoulder at him, then glanced at the wood stove, the rough cabin, scarred table and chairs, and she started to laugh.

"Miserable woman!" he cried, and slid under the water, taking her with him.

They laughed and played and made love until the water began to cool off; they they dried each other and wrapped up in blankets.

"Sleepy?" he asked.

She shook her head. "I thought I might stay up tonight; you know, our last night and all. If you're sleepy, though, we could sleep a while."

"That's what I was thinking too," he said. He put more wood in the stove, took her hand, and led her to the table. "We should talk a little bit about after tomorrow," he said. "I mean, neither of us is committed or anything, and if I go away and stay, somewhere safe, like Buenos Aires, I mean, you have a great life ahead of you, great future, career. You'll probably make a lot of money, travel."

"And you," she said, nodding. "After you steal enough to get started all over again, you'll go back to drawing, I expect, and find a woman. Someone more suitable for you, a woman who just wants to make you happy without any questions."

"Maybe I'll be a cowboy. Every boy's dream, to become a cowboy. They still have them down there, on the pampas. They live out there for months at a time, make tea in a funny thing. I'll show you." He began to sketch; she watched his face. "It's a gourd with a holder, three legs, and a spoon with a handle that's a straw. Pretty neat. The tea's good too. Good on cold nights on the pampas. It gets really cold there, you know." His voice grew more hesitant as he talked, and finally trailed off altogether. He looked up to see her watching him. She turned away quickly. "Another funny memory," he said, dismissing it.

"All those things I said," she began, not looking at him, "you know, about your hair and your eyes, all those things. I'm sorry. I was wrong. Actually, you're a very good-looking man, really handsome."

He snorted. "I know what I look like. But I couldn't believe you didn't think of yourself as beautiful. That's incredible, that you didn't know it. Probably there's a guy out there good enough for you, but damned if I know where, or who it could be. I'd like to spend the next dozen years or so just painting you."

"You've made me feel beautiful," she whispered. "For the first time, I've felt beautiful. It's a wonderful feeling. Thank you."

His voice was so husky it was hard to hear. "And you made me feel like Superman. I'll never forget that."

After a moment she asked, "Can't you remember anyone who knows what happened to you, how to make it right again?"

He shrugged. "The scientists are denying anything happened. They don't know, and according to them it couldn't have happened anyway. There isn't anyone else." He realized even as he said this that it was not entirely accurate. He could share thoughts with people, but only what they were thinking at the time. Someone had to know what happened, and eventually had to think about it. And that meant that if he tried again, as many times as it took, he might find that person and remember when he came back, if he came back. He felt himself go clammy all over as he considered trying to go "there" deliberately. He had been warned away, he thought distantly, and did not know where that idea came from or what it meant.

"You know what I'd like before we leave this little paradise," he said. "Fresh fish. You know anything about fishing?"

"I know you need some equipment, rod, reel, bait. Or do you intend to dive in and club them?"

"Don't be a smart-ass. When I was looking over the island, before we got here, I saw fishing gear in one of the other cabins. Artificial lures, even. And jars of stuff that looks like it might fool a fish. Tomorrow we'll borrow what we need and go fishing. Okay?"

There was a long pause before she said, "You're not leaving early in the morning?"

"Monday will be better," he said with conviction. "Sunday boaters will be out in force tomorrow. Bad drivers, all of them. Dangerous out there in their midst. Monday will be much better."

"Oh, I think so too! I'd love to go fishing! What do you suppose we can catch from here?"

"Whales, sharks, salmon, red snappers, cod, perch, flounders— You've got the most beautiful eyes I ever saw. Did I tell you that? They're not like anyone else's eyes."

They talked about his past, and hers, and the things they both hated and things they both loved. She was surprised that he hated horses.

"You don't know them like I do," he said. "This time when I was about seven, see, we're visiting a friend of my father's and no one told me there was a devil in the field. I was going to take a shortcut from the creek to the house and I cut through the field and next thing I knew this monster horse was charging me. Red Devil, that was his name. They kept him for stud, made a mint, and that's all he was good for. He charged and I ran to a tree and ducked behind it and he came around after me. For an hour I dodged that devil, keeping the tree between us. Never had time to try to climb it, and I knew I'd never make it to the fence and get out of there. After the first few minutes I didn't have breath enough to keep yelling for help. Horses are dumb and that one was a killer. Dumb and crazy. A rotten combination. I wanted to kill him and would have if there'd been anything to use. All I could do was duck around the tree. They said later it was my red hair that riled him."

They were in bed holding each other. She tightened her arms around him. "What if you had fallen down? He would have trampled you! Oh, Corky. I hate horses too! And then one hurt your father. I don't blame you."

"It wasn't exactly a horse that got him," he said, his face against her hair. "It was a poker game. He'd been drinking and got up to refill his glass and when he sat down again, he missed his chair. Cracked his coccyx. Lost the pot too."

"Oh," she said, not certain if she should show sympathy or laugh. "My parents bought their house when they were newly-weds and they're still in it. Their idea of a vacation is to fly to a resort somewhere or other where friends of theirs will be and after a couple of weeks go back home. Their friends know when I cut my first tooth, said my first word, got potty-trained, everything. My sisters and I called most of their friends Uncle or Aunt this or that. Once I overheard Uncle Jack tell my father they'd better get me a good education, because I sure couldn't compete with my sisters, or even my mother for looks."

"Let's find and kill Uncle Jack," he said.

"Let's put him out in the field with Red Devil."

How could she smell so good, he was wondering. They had used the same soap, shared the water, and she smelled wonderful. When he mentioned it, she insisted that he smelled just as good and they sniffed each other appreciatively, and murmured and talked and dozed and murmured again.

She roused a bit later and asked sleepily what time it was and was content with his answer: February. She fell asleep again.

Rain came during the night and moved on to shore, and when he opened his eyes again fog pressed against the windows. He fitted himself more closely against her warm body and slept.

At two-thirty that morning Trigger Happy stomped to the window to look at the rain lashing the streets beyond his hotel. "Doesn't it ever do anything but fucking rain here?" No one answered. Joe Krueger was asleep on the couch, his arm over his face. Sergeant Carroll was asleep in a chair, his mouth open, snoring. Morris Pitts was at the conference table checking off islands against charts, making notes about what was on each one, what kind of moorage was there. Drissac was rereading the thousand-plus pages of reports that already had accumulated. Notes on the Corky commie and his jockey father and jockey brother and his father's wives, his schooling, companions, everything they could find. Notes on Steele's past, her family, her schools. The Waycross Clinic staff. Friends of friends. Everyone in her apartment building, in the Corky commie's apartment, the store where he had worked part-time. Everyone along each path she habitually took, where she ate, where she stopped. Her correspondents.

Somewhere in that mess, Trigger Happy knew, was an answer, a hell of a lot of answers. And everyone in the fucking Northwest had a fucking boat, Trigger Happy growled to himself. Warren Foley, Peter Waycross, even the wimp Rich Steinman, Morris Pitts. Stan Harlow had made a list of them all and checked them out himself. None of the known boats had been used to transport the Corky commie and the Steele girl to any fucking island. But someone had done it, Trigger Happy muttered. And the fucking navy with their goddamn spies on the waterfront would find out who and where he had taken them. And they'd step in and grab everyone in sight—the Steele girl, their comrades, their bosses, the whole fucking outfit! Except, he thought grimly, the Corky commie would slip right through their fingers and laugh at them. And he was the one with the secret, with the knowledge. He was the most dangerous man who had ever lived!

He snatched up the phone and ordered a platter of sandwiches and coffee, and then poured himself a double Scotch. Before the sandwiches arrived, Captain Drissac said, "I've got something."

Trigger Happy and Morris Pitts crowded around him when he went to the charts and started to search. He put his finger on an island and held it there.

"The other woman, Joan Custer, the one who took Corcoran to the professional village that night. Her father and two associates jointly own half Dog Island. She took Corcoran out there once."

Trigger Happy glanced over his shoulder at the sergeant and Joe Krueger; neither had stirred. He held his finger to his lips. Morris was already at his notes looking up Dog Island. After a moment, in a near whisper, he said, "Three fishing cabins, island's a mile and a quarter by half a mile wide. Two good docks."

They looked at the map, at the town of Blanchard, looked at each other, and nodded.

"Can you get out there with your boat?" Trigger Happy asked. "Even if there's rain?"

Morris nodded. "I've got the best equipment there is. I'll need at least one crew member. You?" He looked at Drissac, who shook his head emphatically. "My man then. He's discreet. When?"

"When can you make it?"

"Just rain, no problem. If the fog sets in, it'll be slower. I'll have to call Ellington, my mate, and that's going to take a little time." It was three then. "Seven."

"I want Sergeant Carroll," Drissac said in a low voice.

Trigger Happy nodded. Room service came with sandwiches and they woke up the sleeping men and told them they were giving up for the night. Stan Harlow came from the other room bleary-eyed; Joe Krueger stretched, yawning, and waved off the idea of food.

"Bed," he said, and stumbled to the door. The others started on the sandwiches and coffee. In his room Joe Krueger yawned again and then picked up his phone and dialed to make his report to his contact in Naval Intelligence. All he could say was that they were onto something, and planned to leave at seven in Morris Pitts's yacht. It was all he needed to say. Then he pulled off his clothes and fell into bed and instant sleep.

# Chapter Twenty-Four

THEY had dumped the water, scoured the floor, and made oatmeal for breakfast. They stood at the door with mugs of hot chocolate and gazed at the fog that hid the entire world.

"It's eerie, isn't it?" she said softly.

"It'll lift before noon." He kept his voice low. It was as if they were afraid of disturbing the uncanny silence the fog had brought to the island.

She shivered and they moved back inside the cabin and closed the door. They sat at the table and sipped the chocolate. "You said that you heard me calling you back," she said after a moment. "Even when I didn't."

He nodded.

"You're going to try to find out where you go, aren't you?"

This time his nod was slower. He took her hand. "After I'm someplace where they can't find me. And you're safe on the mainland. Not here."

"But if you can hear me calling you back, then we should be together when you experiment," she said. "I don't mean that there are ties, or that you have to put up with me, or anything like that. Even if we weren't near each other before, not physically, you were on my mind most of the time, you know. I kept thinking about you, wondering what happened, if I should notify someone. Like that. But what if you go where you go and get lost and I don't know you're gone and my mind is on something else? What if you need a guide for something? I should know when to call you. Or someone should. I mean, it wouldn't have to be me."

He tightened his grip on her hand and did not know what to say. What if he got lost there and she called and called and he couldn't hear her, or couldn't follow her voice home? What if the colonel got her and made her call him? What if they decided she was a spy and put her on trial and he couldn't get to her to help? What if . . . ? Too many what-ifs. "I've been thinking too," he said finally. "Could you tell them that I'm your patient? Say I had a fixation on you and forced you to go with me because I thought no one could see me? You felt compelled to try to help me. I had a knife and threatened you. That line. You know the language to make it work."

"They'll think you're crazy!"

"So did you, for a long time."

"There's no such thing as insanity, only a physiological malfunctioning caused by a physical trauma or disease. There's only behavior."

He nodded encouragingly. "That's the line. My behavior was so aberrant that you couldn't resist trying to straighten me out. Especially since I had a knife. Don't forget that part, that I forced you to go with me. And say a knife, not a gun. A knife's more ominous, don't you think? Besides, they approve of people using guns. Knives make them automatically think nut."

"I didn't think you were insane," she said. "I thought I was."

"But you just said there's no such thing."

"I know. That's why I thought I was crazy. I held two distinct belief systems, mutually contradictory. That's not acceptable behavior."

He shook his head in bewilderment. "Okay, just talk to them like that, and talk a lot about behavior and my insanity and all that. And anything you shouldn't know, try to stay away from, but if you do happen to mention something they pounce on, say you're simply repeating what all I said."

"But that's true. They'll never believe it."

"God," he said in despair. "You're in for such a hard time."

"I should go with you, hide out or something."

"If only you weren't so tall and so beautiful. No one who sees you can forget you. No, we have to do it my way. You tell the truth, except for the use of force. You can have one lie buried in a mass of truths, can't you?"

Now she felt baffled by the direction the conversation had taken. She had started by pleading with him to let her help with his experiments with that other place, but he was willing to talk only about her safety. She was in no danger, not really, but he was. And his danger was real, not simply getting idiots out of his beautiful red hair. She reached out and touched it lightly, remembering with wonder that she had said it was ugly.

"I'll be calling you day and night," she said. "For the rest of my life, if that's what it will take."

He put his finger on her lips. She kissed it. "Let's go get the fishing stuff. One more day of holiday before we have to face the world." He went to the door. "Look, the fog's lifting."

"The fog's lifting," Trigger Happy said with satisfaction. In just a moment the satisfaction had turned into a growl of anger. He looked ahead, slowly turned to scan other directions, and he felt as if he were surrounded by the entire goddamn U.S. of A. Navy. Cutters, landing boats, tubs he didn't know the names of. Even a goddamn destroyer!

They had met at the boat at six forty-five, and Trigger Happy had known it would not be a good day. The boat was too little, for one thing, and too shiny-clean, and somehow suggestive, maybe even lewd in a way he could not define. He looked at Morris Pitts, who had come to greet them. He was too happy, the glint in his eye too bright. Dangerous, Trigger Happy thought. He was surprised. He had not considered Morris Pitts anything but a playboy dabbling in cops and robbers when the mood was on him. But he saw that morning that he was also dangerous. Shifting the action to his yacht, putting him in charge, even nominally as the captain of the boat, changed him. And now what Trigger Happy had sensed as hidden contempt was closer to the surface.

Morris Pitts yelled for his mate to come topside, and introduced him: Ron Ellington, a saturnine man who looked them over carefully and vanished behind the door to the wheelhouse. Before the door closed, Trigger Happy got a glimpse of an array of equipment that reassured him momentarily—monitors, panels of buttons, computers, he didn't know what all, but it was businesslike.

"You three stay in the main lounge," Morris Pitts ordered, making it sound almost like a suggestion. He opened the door and gestured, then turned to head in the other direction. At the door to the wheelhouse, he glanced back at them and said, "Better put on life jackets." And there was that damn malicious gleam in his eyes again. Thus had started the four most miserable hours Trigger Happy ever had experienced. The boat rose and fell, rose and fell, and he was sick; Drissac was sick; the sergeant was sick.

They did it on purpose, Trigger Happy knew without a tinge of doubt. Morris Pitts and that mate of his, laughing at them, hitting the roughest water in the Sound on purpose. He'd get him, Trigger Happy promised himself. He would get that bastard one day.

Finally they had come to a halt, and the boat rose and fell in a slower motion, and the three passengers staggered out on deck to see the world of fog. "We've got company," Morris Pitts said, waving at the surrounding fog. And it had meant nothing to Trigger Happy at the time. Just breathing, sucking in cold air, washing the taste of the last four hours out of his mouth, that had been enough for him. When the fog lifted, minutes after their arrival, he realized what Morris Pitts had meant. The whole fucking navy! Who blew the whistle this time? He would find out, he vowed, cursing steadily under his breath, and he would break that yapping loudmouth into a million little pieces. The mate, Ellington, stuck his head out the wheelhouse door. "Telephone for Colonel Musselman. It's a Captain Storm."

"Go!" Trigger happy ordered, glaring at the flotilla emerging from the fog.

Morris Pitts, Drissac, and the sergeant went over the side to a rubber raft already bobbing in the water. Drissac and the sergeant were to go up the narrow beach to the two cabins on the north side of the island; Morris would go to the solitary cabin on this end.

Trigger Happy watched them leave, then took the phone that the mate handed him. The mate looked terrified; he was discreet, Trigger Happy remembered Morris Pitts saying, but this was a first for him.

"Yeah," he snapped into the phone. The rubber boat was already in shallow water, nearing the beach.

"Told you the fog would lift fast when it started," Corky said with some smugness. "These islands have their own microclimate, warmer and dryer than the mainland. Probably have rain and fog all day, into tomorrow, over in Seattle."

The sun was burning through the wispy fog, drawing up columns of steam, spotlighting the luxurious ferns, concentrating the perfume of the heather into a heady, intoxicating distillation. Everything smelled sharp and fresh and good.

Suddenly Lauren stopped and pointed. "My God, what is it?"

Corky peered in the direction she was staring at, transfixed, and then he laughed. "Banana slug," he said. "Wait a second, I'll get it and show you."

The thing—she could not think what to call it, creature? monster?—was at least eight inches long, moving with what seemed like purpose across a mossy rock ten or fifteen feet off the trail. Corky looked around for a stick to lift it with. Actually it was quite beautiful, with a pattern in dark gold against the bright yellow of the background. He bent over to get it, when he heard Lauren scream.

"If you so much as blur around the edges, I'm going to shoot her head off," Morris Pitts said easily. He had one arm around Lauren's neck, a gun against her temple.

Lauren heard the click of the safety even as Corky straightened up and turned. He heard it, too, she could tell. For a moment there was no other sound.

"What we're going to do," Morris said in his easy, almost lazy voice, "is continue to the top. I believe it's very close now, isn't it? And then we'll go down the other side. And you, Corcoran, will maintain just about this same distance every inch of the way, and keep yourself quite visible, just as you are now. Be careful, both of you, very, very careful. Let's go."

Twice he told Corky to slow down, and each time his voice changed subtly. He wanted to shoot her, Lauren thought, terrified. And he would if Corky didn't cooperate. Climbing the last section of the trail was awkward and slow; when they emerged from the woods, the sun was brilliant, the air clear and fresh. Morris Pitts pulled Lauren to an abrupt stop and told Corky to freeze where he was.

"Look," he ordered.

They were at the peak of the hill, with the water visible to the north and south, and the channel almost directly below them. Everywhere they looked, there were boats.

"Our audience," Morris Pitts murmured. "It's really a shame you chose to be visible today, Corcoran. Has it worn off? Or can you control your condition? Either way, it is a shame. Now what I want us to do is spread out a little bit. Corcoran, over there farther." He indicated a leftward direction with his head and waited until Corky moved, then nodded. "Fine. That is fine. Lauren, I'm going to let you go about five feet this way, where I can keep the gun on you, you understand. Somehow I thought targeting you would guarantee cooperation from him. Another shame, Lauren. To choose this funny little man instead of me. A bad choice, my dear. A beanpole and a pumpkin. That really offends my sensibilities, I'm afraid."

The area on top the hill was roughly twelve feet by twenty, the ground rocky and bare. The way he was positioning them,

Lauren realized, put Corky very near the edge over the channel while she was probably invisible to the observers in the boats, and Morris most definitely was screened from their view by the treetops.

"That's quite far enough," Morris said, and she stopped moving away from him. The gun held on her very steadily. "Now, Corcoran, I have a little present for you. I'm going to throw it. Wait until it lands and then move to it very slowly and pick it up." He reached in his pocket and withdrew something that he tossed to land only a foot or two from Corky. "Now," he said, pointing the gun without a waver at Lauren's head; he was inches beyond her reach.

"Put it on your neck," he said when Corky had the object. "And make certain you tighten it, Corcoran. I want to see the buckle when you're done."

A dog collar? Lauren blinked and squinted. A collar of some sort. She turned to look at Morris, and suddenly she knew he intended to kill them both. The collar must have a beeper of some sort embedded in it, so they could find his body . . .

"We can play this two ways," Morris said, his voice no longer easy or lazy. It grated now. "You can take a dive, Corcoran, and I walk out with Lauren. Or I shoot you both. Decide."

"Corky, save yourself!" Lauren screamed, and dived toward him, remembering for just a second that when he was threatened, his reflex took over. For just a second she caught the look of surprise on Morris Pitts's face; he had expected her to attack him, or run, or something else, not this. Then the world erupted in gunfire and she landed heavily on the rocky ground.

# Chapter Twenty-Five

—YOU mean everything just stopped? Like the perils of Pauline, isn't it?

—Yes, I suppose. That is why we realized the shadow comes into existence right there.

—Boy oh boy! How long's it been frozen?

—The question has no meaning. The shadow existed, does exist, will exist forever, or it never existed at all if we can undo the damage.

—So that's why no one's been able to see past this year? Or see garbage.

—Exactly. Now, look. The woman struck out at him, to make him save himself, of course, and that's where it all stops. We will open ourselves to him, let him come over instantly, without all that fumbling around he usually does before he tries. And you are the only one who will communicate directly with him, unless a problem arises, of course. Then I shall join the two of you.

—And we're going to sucker him into going on through, out the other side? What for? How's that going to unstick anything?

—Believe me, some of the greatest minds have given this problem their undivided attention. We think we may have the answer.

—You're not even sure! Poor sod. What's he done to deserve that? Never mind, no more lectures. For the greater good, all that stuff. I know. Okay, let's get the show on the road.

—Yes. Joan, are you ready, just in case we need you to handle Lauren?

—But of course. The poor darling, ah, the poor darling.

—Right. Here we go.

Corky had been thinking that as soon as Lauren moved away from Morris Pitts, he could make his move, and he knew he would get there before the gun could fire. But Morris Pitts's way could be even better. He would go over the side; Pitts and Lauren would walk out. Only he did not believe Lauren was going to live through this. And that meant, he decided, fastening the collar, that he had to take Pitts anyway, no matter who was watching from the many surrounding boats. Let them think what they would, confirm the colonel's theory, whatever. Pitts would be out of it, and, he felt confident, Lauren would stand a better chance with almost anyone on earth than with that creep. He was watching Morris Pitts very closely; if he shot, Lauren would get it. Corky could move faster than the bullet, but she couldn't. Okay, he thought as soon as he lowered his own hands, jump for the gun. He had to hit the gun and then deal with Pitts, but first hit the gun, knock it—

From the corner of his eye he saw Lauren leap forward; before he could brace himself, or make any countermove, his reflex took over and he dispersed, even before the gun fired, before she screamed and Morris Pitts yelled furiously.

—Hiya, pal. Welcome.

"Where is this? Who are you? I can't see you. Ah, there, that's better." With the words that he could not see anyone, he had seen him. A thin, craggy man in his twenties perhaps, wearing a sweater and jeans. His hair was spiky and white. He was an inch or two shorter than Corky.

—I'm your host, as the saying goes. Supposed to show you around, show you the ropes.

"Around where?" He looked at the landscape: a meadow in the distance with wildflowers in bloom, red, yellows, whites. The sound of droning bees was in his ears; a meadowlark trilled; a fragrant breeze stirred his hair. Behind him was a forest with dappled light, two deer browsing at the edge of the woods. He turned sharply to his host and said, "Crap! Sunday school heaven, is that it?"

The scene changed to a dark and forbidding desert with black basaltic rocks and coarse sand and no living thing in sight.

"And if I think of the angels and harps, I guess I can have them too?" he demanded.

—You catch on a lot faster than most guys. That's the score. You can have whatever you think. Some people start out with the whole scene of hellfire and devils with forks. Some start with the marble halls and heroes. Some with the angels. You got that right. Me? I started with a tropical island and girls. Man oh man, did I have gorgeous chicks for awhile.

"You're dead, aren't you? The others you're talking about are dead, aren't they?"

—Them's the only kind that land here, pal. You score again.

"Where are all the others?" Corky was starting to feel cheated. Was this what he had been trying so hard to achieve, a nutty conversation with a punker? He looked past his companion, nothing but desert as far as he could see. And if he wanted ocean beaches, he could have that, or the island, whatever he wanted.

—In the beginning, how we work it here, is that we sort of keep the newcomer company with only one guy, or girl, if a female comes through. You know, it could feel like a mob scene in a De Mille movie otherwise.

Corky thought then about Lauren, Pitts, and before his eyes the scene opened. It looked like a wax-museum tableau. "What's going on?" he growled, and moved toward Lauren. The scene retreated. It appeared close enough for him to be a part of it, yet excluded him and maintained the same distance as he reached for her.

—It's frozen in time, that's all. There's a little problem in the technical department, being worked on now, I bet.

Corky thought of the boats he had glimpsed and there they were, frozen in the water. A gull was frozen in flight. Sailors frozen at their tasks. A spiffy officer held binoculars almost to his eyes, was already squinting a little, adjusting for them. Water in splashes had stopped, waves did not move. Corky looked again at

Lauren and could not tell if she was dead or alive. Pitts had one foot off the rocky ground.

"Okay, it's a neat trick, and I pay my penny to the man at the gate, or whatever, but turn it back on."

—I can't. I haven't been here long enough to learn stuff like that yet.

"Then take me to the guy who can. Do you have a name?"

—I don't know. We don't use names much around here. I mean, it doesn't seem like we need them much.

His guide had started to walk; Corky trudged at his side, thinking hard. Suddenly he came to a stop. "Where are we going?"

—Wherever you want.

Corky turned back the way they had come. He looked down at himself, normal as far as he could tell. And the guy with the spiky hair would feel solid, he thought grimly, just as the rocks beneath his feet felt like rocks. "Beat it," he said.

—But I'm your guide. I'm supposed to help you adjust, or something. Tell the truth, I'm not sure what that means, but it's a job.

There was something fishy, Corky knew. He sat on a rock, held it with both hands, but he had a feeling of movement, as if he were being nudged gently, almost imperceptibly, along. He resisted and the feeling subsided, then resumed. "Okay, you fuckers," he said, "I'm leaving. That's not what you want, is it? You want me to stay this time, don't you?"

He stood up and looked for Lauren again; nothing had changed. He looked at his guide and thought him out of existence; he vanished.

—I'm still here, fella. I told you, it's a job. I got to stick with you.

"I want to talk to someone about what's going on. Someone who isn't you, jerk."

—So talk. They'll hear you all right.

"Yeah, I bet they will. Okay. What happens if I go back down and finish out that little scene?"

—We are uncertain, no one has ever seen past it.

"You the boss?" The new voice was deep and reassuring, resonant. Corky felt more suspicious than ever.

—There is no boss, no chiefs and Indians. Some of us simply have more experience than others.

"Yeah, and the salary that goes with experience. I know all about that. Who are you?"

—The question is without meaning, Corky. Do you wish me to take visible form?

"Hell no! You turn up looking like Abraham Lincoln and I'll want to waste you. What were you planning for me, easing me to somewhere else like that?"

—That was an error. We thought you would not notice. We are inexperienced in deception, you see. We cannot let you return to your time, but since your body still lives, you cannot become one of us. We hoped to place you beyond time until your body ceases to live, and at that time you would join our ranks.

"Jesus! Limbo! You want to put me in limbo!"

—I promise it will not hurt in any way, mental or physical. You will simply not know anything until you join us, and the time you spend there will be shorter than an eye blink in your perception. One step, then turn around and come to us as one of us. That is all it will seem to you.

"And Lauren? What will it seem like to her? What's she done to deserve something like that?"

—Corky, you have observed many of your contemporaries, you know that what seems agony to them is as nothing in the whole scheme of the universe. You have been able to join only your contemporaries; we have all of time in which to observe and experience all people everywhere. Her time is so brief, her suffering so limited, so insignificant—

"To you maybe. I know what you mean, living through all that garbage people go through and feeling nothing, and it's a rotten system from start to end. If I'm able to change it, believe me, buster, that's what I'll do. Is that what you're afraid of, that something I might do will change the scheme of the universe? Well, so much the better!"

—No, Corky. So much the worse. Without us, they, you, become nothing more than animals existing only for the next meal, the next warm den; you would not even fear the next attack until it happened. Preyed upon by anything larger or smarter than you, ignorant of the past, oblivious of the future, people would become naked apes overnight, and most of them would die, also overnight. Corky, everything in human consciousness is here, everything. Racial memory is here. Intuition is here. Music, art, all creativity is here. Inspiration is here. For more than a million years what is here has been expanding, and each new arrival is a cause of celebration, adding to our storehouse of consciousness. And on that side, people dream and daydream and reach in here to draw from the storehouse. They try a thousand ways to reach inside the storehouse, and a few succeed with some regularity; everyone succeeds to some extent, and eventually everyone adds to it.

"You talk about the past as if it's all one thing. Like a carpet spread out so you can examine the border or the middle or any other damn place you want."

—Yes, it is like that.

"What about the future? Why isn't it like that?"

—It is and has been until that moment that is frozen. We do not know what happens when that moment is unfrozen.

"You know this is nutty, don't you? What can one guy do that big, that bad?"

—That is what we don't know. That is why we allowed you to enter this time, why we would risk luring you into forgetfulness briefly and hope that when your body no longer has energy, the crisis will have passed.

"Why did you wait until now to try to do something? You've had plenty of time to play around with it, find a way out."

—Corky, that moment has been frozen for thousands of years as you would reckon time. This is now for you, but for us it is simply another moment out of time. We do not share your chronology, you see.

"Cripes," he muttered. "What a mess. What a fucking mess!"

—Exactly. You see, we could come back to that moment now and then and consider various options, none of them feasible, I'm afraid. Now, however, your chronology is catching up to that moment, and we no longer can put off decisions. We must do something.

Corky looked at the scene; he thought about minutes before

that scene, and there was Pitts holding Lauren at gunpoint. He looked back, before Pitts had made his presence known. His fault. He had been afraid to use the muscle, make a check of the island. In fact, he corrected himself, he simply had not thought of checking. He had felt safe and secure and alone with Lauren. There he was going after the banana slug. Back before that, back to the cabin, preparing to go on their foray to borrow fishing gear.

"So what happens if I go back to that second, before we even start up the hill, knowing now that Pitts will show? I wouldn't let him get the drop on us this time, you'd better believe."

He could imagine a wise old man sighing sorrowfully.

—That is the disaster we most fear, I'm afraid. You would cause a branch to occur. Everyone has lived those extra minutes, you see. Everyone over there, I mean. They cannot be unlived, undone. You would start a new time line separated from the original one; you would start over, because all of us here are bound to the old line. It took millions of years for us over here to accumulate enough intelligence, enough consciousness to act as a feedback for people over there. It would take the new time line millions of years also. And the other line stops. Nothing can be undone in your past, nothing unlived, nothing recreated. We here would stop also. That is, of course, if it would work out like that.

"Meaning?"

—Another line of reasoning has it that nothing would change. This moment must be experienced because there it is. It must happen because it did happen, will happen.

"I don't get it! I just don't get it! You knew all this was coming, you say. You could see past, present, future, you say. You could have nipped it in the bud before I was even born!"

This time he was more certain of a sighing. He shook his head hard.

—As you say, you don't get it. Past, present, future are your terms, not ours. We are not in time in any sense of the word, my friend. Corky, imagine an infinitely long novel with an infinite cast of characters. You can open it anywhere and experience what is happening on the pages, can you not? The character on page twenty does not know what is to happen on page fifty, but you as reader cannot alter page fifty. If you do not like the sequence of events, you can read some other pages, go to the end, or the beginning, close it and not read at all, if you choose, but the book is finished and exists as a whole, unalterable. No one knows how long it is, or if this actually means we have come to the end of it. That page is stuck; the rest is inaccessible.

"So much for free will," he muttered disconsolately. "Never put much stock in it anyway, I guess."

—No, no. You mustn't think that. Over there you certainly have free will. It just doesn't seem so from over here because free will is bound up with cause and effect and time itself.

"Yeah, yeah. So I can't go back to the past because I didn't, and if I do, everything goes nuts. What if I just let things go on? I mean, I go over the side and never hit the water. You know that's what would happen. I hang out, the way I've been doing, and then reappear and go on from there. Then what?"

—You see, Corky, that can't be what you did, or there would not be the shadowy area. We could simply continue to view events the same as before. And we cannot see past this moment.

Corky frowned at the scene again, yearning to catch Lauren, break her fall on the rocks, save her from the cuts and bruises, maybe even from dying. He tried to get closer and failed and still could not tell if she had been shot, if her eyes were closed because of the fall, if she was knocked out or dead.

"Okay," he said slowly. "I can't go to the past and change things, and I can't go back to that second and just let the action go on the way it's heading, or you'd be able to see me doing it." He felt as if his brain were being churned in a blender. "What other choice is there, damn it? What the fuck good would it do to put me in limbo?"

—Ah, atoms disintegrate, you know.

"Bullshit! If the scene down there doesn't change, doesn't move, nothing happens, and that includes atoms!"

—Ah, yes. Some of us believed that to be the case.

"You don't know! You were going to get rid of me so you'd have even more time to play with ideas. Is that it? You've already had all the time in the world, pal, and so what? You still don't have an answer!" There was no response. "What happens when you try to look at the future, like a long time into the future, not just a couple of minutes?"

Suddenly he felt as if he were standing on the bottom of a muddy river, silt so thick that his vision blurred inches away from his eyes, atmosphere so thick he could not move. It cleared, and once again he was looking at Lauren on the rocky hill.

"You know," he said after a pause, "it doesn't leave much, does it? I guess I must have gone back, no matter what you said. Or I will go back. Something."

—Corky, we could show you the entire history of human life, the instances when life changed because someone there touched someone over here who had an answer, a musical composition, a medical breakthrough, a vision, if you will. We could show you the millennia when people huddled in the cold, thoughtless, more animal than human. They are here, blanks drifting among us, like pauses in thought, the mindlessness of sleep, meaningless.

As the thoughts flowed through Corky's head, the images formed and he saw them huddled miserably in the cold, heads bowed against freezing rain. He saw a youth, a young Mozart perhaps, or Bach, listening raptly, entranced, then writing feverishly. His head was spinning as he saw scene after scene that the voice summoned. Data bank in the sky, he thought morosely, just all of human experience.

—Not only the big, world-changing events, but the small single-life-changing things too.

A man jumped from his bed, instantly awake from a deep sleep, ran to his infant daughter who was choking on a toy rattle.

A woman stopped her car and ran to a phone, made a call to an elderly woman who was on the floor unconscious. The young woman called another number and an ambulance was put into service, medics rushed to the stricken woman.

—You have had such moments, Corky. Everyone has. Sometimes they are wrong; the wrong mind here is tapped, but sometimes they are right. Imagine, Corky, what if the human race is destined to learn to use this vast storehouse in a controlled way, a meaningful way? Is that our destiny? We don't know, but if it is so, do you dare cause the break? Do you dare risk it?

"Cripes!". he cried helplessly. "Knock it off already! I got the point. I really did. Let me think, will you?"

—Yes, Corky. Take all the time you need.

The voice in his head was gone and he felt curiously alone in the black desert of his mind.

# Chapter Twenty-Six

HE had to try it: Building pyramids, sailing with the Phoenicians, walking on the moon, freezing in Antarctica. It was all the same—immediate, accessible, happening in real time over there. He could view it all, or live it, feel it. He could focus on his own yesterday, this morning, a minute ago, and then murk.

He tried it with other people, taking them through that morning, walking with them, driving with them, flying, feeling everything, thinking with them. Then murk.

He looked broodingly at Lauren on the rocks. He saw his own clothes hanging in air, empty. He felt himself, glanced down, nodded. He had thought himself fully clothed, the same clothes as over there too. Lack of imagination, he chided himself. Naturally he was not here in a real body, just a bundle of energy that could think, imagine, travel through space and land where it chose. He began to walk on his black desert that felt as real as any ground he had ever walked on. If he didn't have a body here, he wondered, where was it? All those times when he flew apart, what happened to the tissues, the bones, the blood? Broken down to atoms?

A voice in his head told him that was correct, and absently he said thank you.

Okay, he thought, so he broke down into atoms. Copper, iron, oxygen, hydrogen . . .

—It's a long list, Corky. Do you want them all?

"No. Butt out and let me think, okay?"

—Sorry.

The part that scattered and knew what people were thinking and feeling, that part had nothing to do with the atoms that made up his physical body, he decided, and after a hesitation, this was confirmed with nothing like a voice or even words. But he knew. So it had to be something else that went flying: his mind. A thing separate from his body, after all. He knew Lauren would argue about that, but what else? Again, the feeling of affirmation came. He nodded. How many times had he heard Shelley, one of his father's wives, storming about the house yelling she'd give him a piece of her mind? No answer, he ordered, and went on thinking and walking.

He stopped after a while and made himself a beach chair and a live oak for shade and sat down. He was missing something, he thought, forgetting something that he had intended to consider at some point. He thought of the first time he had dispersed and saw himself leave the elevator with Lauren, saw the laser gun start to swivel just as he stopped at the window. Never before had he joined with himself, and it was spooky, he decided. He could think the thoughts Corky had then, and he was an observer watching himself think those thoughts, maintaining a whole stream of other thoughts simultaneously. It made him nervous. The laser fired and he was flying apart with Corky, and still sitting in his beach chair under an oak tree. "Eerie, real eerie," he muttered.

There was a sigh somewhere and he told it to shut up before it could become words. He played the scene over, this time slowed down, and this time he felt the impact of the laser. He had not felt anything the first time; it had been too fast. He nodded. There it was, right in the solar plexus, like finding a new muscle and having it go into spasm. Involuntary spasm.

He went through all the times he had flown apart, and each time he looked for the sensations, the actual sequence that he had not had time to examine at the moment. Then he examined all the times he had pulled himself together again. That same muscle every time, he thought. He tensed it as he sat there, but not much; he did not know what the result would be if he really used it. He was just testing, he told the voice that seemed to be a worried presence in his mind. It subsided.

It made him nervous to watch himself, to relive bits of his own life, all the while knowing that for the Corky over there each episode was a first and only, a unique experience. Like a film, he told himself when he began to feel queasy; the real thing happened only once, but he could watch reruns forever.

—That's very good, Corky! Very appropriate analogy for your period. Better than the novel I used.

He ignored the intrusion. If it were not for the murk, he would be able to see what happened next with Lauren and him. Not happened! he thought, almost wildly. Will happen! *Will!* But if the book was already written, the film already in the can, whatever was going to happen over there already had happened.

He thought of the day his father had won the Kentucky Derby, and there it was, there he was: Corky the man, reliving the prerace anxiety, listening to the band play My Old Kentucky Home, feeling the tension his seven-year-old self had felt, ready to piss his pants. He willed the scene away.

Will happen, had happened, from here it didn't mean a damn thing, he realized angrily. From here there wasn't any past tense or future tense, only the present, forever and ever.

—Exactly. Except there is a little problem with the shadow, remember. The murk.

Now he understood why no one was allowed all the way in here, at least not until he was ready to stay for good. You sure could find out where the bodies were, where the gold was buried, he thought. So people got a brief glimpse only, and made what they could of it. No free lunch. He remembered the stories he had heard all his life of fortune tellers, clairvoyants, people who foresaw their own deaths, people who prophesied. They got a glimpse now and then and made the most of it, he understood now. People heard voices, saw visions, experienced déjà vu, thought they were being spied on—He thought of Trigger Happy and his conviction that the world was full of spies, that he was being watched all the time. You got that right, pal, he thought with a touch of sympathy.

—Ah, Corky . . .

"Yeah, yeah. The murk. I'm working on it."

He watched Hot Dog keystroke orders to Big Mac, watched Big

Mac's responses. Immortal, faster than the speed of light. "Anyone here who knows computers?" he asked.

—Not well enough. We thought of that. They're all so terribly young, you know, haven't come over yet in any great numbers. The few arrivals have come with blank spots. No help at all.

Not that it mattered, Corky thought. It had been done and could not be undone. Life can't be unlived. Immortal, he thought again, then asked, "Are you guys here immortal?"

—We think so, but of course there is no proof yet, not until the end of the universe, I suppose.

"And you sure can travel faster than the speed of light, can't you?"

—Travel may be the wrong word. I mean without any material body to move, it hardly applies.

He nodded thoughtfully. Faster than the speed of light? Instantaneously was how they got around. Their minds, and his, ranged outside time somehow. So Big Mac hadn't actually altered his mind, just his body, scattering it to atoms, and when his mind got ready, it put them back together. Not mind, he continued; he never had thought of it that way, but as a center, sometimes weak, sometimes strong, but always a center, and he never had thought of it as in his head. It lived in his solar plexus.

"Listen," he said then. "Tell me if I missed something. I can't return to my own past and change anything, or I blow it all up. I can't go back to that one second in time, because if I had done that, you'd know about it. You could have tuned it in by now. I can't go to the future because it's swallowed by murk. Okay so far?"

—I'm afraid so.

"Okay, tell me this. Can any of you go over there and stay? I mean, if you went there just when someone was about to die, could you move in?"

—No, for at least two reasons. Here, communicating with you, I seem to have normal will, purpose, intentions, whatever you wish to call it, but when we are viewing, sharing, we have none. Nor did you when you were drifting in and out of consciousnesses, remember. And the second reason is that the life force is extinguished at death, gone. We do not possess it, Corky. You do, and that is why you cannot simply join us and be done with it. You still have the will to live, you see."

"You bet I do." He remembered. The more of a center he formed, the less able he was to get inside anyone, until the point was reached in which he hovered between being a person and a whirlpool of energy. But there was that point, he told himself; there had been times when he, Corky, had been damn aware of joining with other minds, times when his center had not flown apart. There was no reason to question further, he realized. They wouldn't know the possibilities since they had no will to live, unless what they had was living. But there was one more thing.

"That first time I came knocking, could you have let me in, put me in limbo?"

—Corky, not limbo. Believe me, please, it's an instant only. Although in theory it was possible, we couldn't because that frozen scene had to be reached. But the first time you would have been disoriented, confused; it would have been simple. If we believed it would solve the problem, truly believed it, we could have done it this time. But some of us are not convinced because that would have been interfering in affairs over there. We never have done that, never. You surely realize how halfhearted our attempt was. We hoped you would see through it and make the decision yourself. I believe we are incapable of doing any such thing, actually; interfering and the will to live seem to be interlocked.

"So I have to do whatever is done," he said.

—What are you planning?

"To gamble," he said, and got rid of the chair and oak tree, the desert. He looked at the scene, inches away from him, and out of reach, and then he got rid of the body he had created for himself and streaked back.

"Corky, save yourself!" Lauren screamed in anguish.

Before the shot rang, he made certain that his clothes would go off the cliff, and then he was at Morris Pitts, hitting the gun hand, and he entered him. For a time that was too swift to measure he was a vortex of energy, searching for the muscle in Morris Pitts. And Morris had as little defense against him as

Corky had had the night the laser targeted him. He clenched the muscle, charged it, caused it to spasm. The center that was displaced streamed out in disarray, helpless; Morris, out of control, fell to his knees, and Corky stood up, in control of his own center that now lodged behind the solar plexus in the body of Morris Pitts. He ran to Lauren and examined her head where a bump had already formed. She was breathing almost normally, and already was starting to stir. He gathered her up in his arms and stood with her, in view of the watchers in the flotilla below; then he turned and started down the hill, carrying her.

At the waterfall she blinked and tried to focus her eyes, started to struggle. Great waves of dizziness rocked her and she gave up. In her ear she heard Corky's voice.

"Shh, Lauren. It's okay. You're okay."

Other voices were yelling now and she gave up trying to decipher the words, yielded to the rocking motion. Everything was too blurred, too confusing. But Corky was safe and she didn't care about anything else.

"Can you understand what I'm telling you?"

She shook her head and moaned, reached up to feel a bump that throbbed with her heartbeat, each throb a new wave of pain.

"Listen. Just don't try to say anything. You jumped him and saved me. Got that? He was insane. The ray made him crazy. Not a spy, just a nut. He confessed it all to me. Just nod at whatever I say."

She no longer cared what he wanted her to say, what any of them wanted her to say or do. Somewhere Corky was safe; nothing else held any meaning. She closed her eyes and exhaled a long, labored breath and let herself be carried back to the cabin, deposited on one of the cots in the living room. He gathered up all the notes from the table, stuffed them in his pockets. She closed her eyes again. None of that mattered either.

"What happened up there?" a new voice demanded.

Lauren sat up and waited for the dizziness to stabilize, then with great caution swung her legs over the edge of the cot, prepared to stand up. There was something she was supposed to tell them, but she could not remember what. She could see into the kitchen, where strange men were appearing. One of them she recognized with some difficulty—the fat policeman, the one Corky said was a colonel who wanted to be a general. Before she could get to her feet, Morris Pitts was talking. She frowned, listening to his words.

"He had a knife and she jumped him, saved me. He was a raving maniac. That laser fried his brain. He forced her to come with him because he thought she had done that to him. She was the last person he saw before he got lasered, you know. She was imprinted, or something, and he kept returning to her, demanding that she undo whatever she had done. Poor kid, she didn't have a clue about what was going on, what he was up to."

"You trying to tell me he wasn't a spy? That she isn't?" The colonel's voice was a menacing growl, his fists clenched, his face turning darker and darker red until it looked purple.

"I'm just telling you what happened, what he said up there. Stark, raving mad. He thought you had stolen his sketches of the lady, and he wanted them back, and kept trying to get them. He heard voices all the time, thought he could travel to heaven and back in the blinking of an eye. He said it was up to him to save the world from frozen time." Morris Pitts shrugged and looked slightly bored. "A nut."

"And the invisibility? How did he manage that?" Trigger Happy's voice was so hoarse it was almost unintelligible.

"He thought it was a gift from God. His only explanation. Totally beyond his control. He was as visible as your are when he went over the cliff."

Trigger Happy thought there was a glint of amusement in the eyes of the tall, handsome man before him. The man who had let the Corky commie go over the cliff. He narrowed his eyes. On purpose? If they didn't locate that fuck's body, who'd believe the story about invisibility? No one, he answered himself savagely. They would rationalize the fingerprints in the vault, in his office, the sabotage of the laser, all of it. They'd claim that the Corky commie was a nut with an uncanny ability to sneak in here and there and do his mischief, nothing more than that.

He glared at Morris Pitts, past him at Lauren, who was still afraid to try to stand up. Others had been watching with binoculars and he already had heard the same story, minus details. Witnesses would be ready to support the lie that the Corky commie had kidnapped Steele, that she had saved herself and Pitts up on the cliff. What the report had said was that she had jumped the Corky commie and Pitts had shot him dead. A dozen or more men had seen it all. Already the frogs were in the water searching for the body. "Did you get the beeper on him before he went over the cliff?" he demanded.

"Couldn't see if it was buckled or not," Morris Pitts said, and this time there was no mistaking the mockery.

Next to the Corky commie Trigger Happy hated Pitts more than anyone on earth at that moment. Abruptly he jerked his head. "Get her to the boat. I want this place taken apart board by board before the damn navy moves in. Papers, anything you find." Sergeant Carroll and Captain Drissac nodded and began searching rapidly.

Morris Pitts approached Lauren. "Let me hlep you," he said, taking her arm.

She wavered a moment, then got to her feet, more confused than she had ever been before. He walked her out the door, down the path toward the little beach. As soon as they were out of earshot of the others he said, "Inside every tall, dark man there's a little red-haired man yelling for attention."

She stopped moving and turned to stare at him. He winked. "Look, my hand's bigger than yours."

She swayed and he put his arm around her waist and started to walk again. He had carried her, she remembered suddenly, all the way from the top to the cabin.

Morris Pitts's memories and Corky's memories blended, separated, blended again. When he saw his boat a short distance offshore, he whistled. "Jesus," he said softly. "Look what I got!" For just an instant he almost felt sorry for Morris Pitts, but then he remembered limbo was just for an eye blink of time. The mate was on the beach, where a small boat was pulled up to dry land. Ellington, he remembered, and hailed him. "I'm to take the lady aboard. You wait for the colonel."

In the cabin, the colonel snarled at Drissac to make a note and check out Morris Pitts. Drissac looked resigned, but made the note. He had never disobeyed an order in his life and would not now, although he knew this one was without meaning. He saw and understood the fleeting, suspicious appraisal that Trigger Happy gave him, and knew that his own name would be added to that list. He shrugged, and went back to work taking apart the many cots in the shack. Trigger Happy stamped outside to the edge of the cliff to watch the frogmen and the boats below. They would not find him, he thought with bitter clarity. Everything about this mess had been jinxed from day one, and it was still fucked up. Suddenly he saw himself in San Diego, glaring unhappily at two men with many shiny machines, trying to get a dish with a cube on it to rise. He shook his head sharply, but he knew he would go there; that was his next stop on the loony bin assignment. And he saw himself in a small boat, in the water that looked crowded with boats to the point of an imminent collision. He saw himself throwing out a net, dragging it in, over and over, and he knew the man he saw was a retired colonel. He shook that vision away also and lighted his cigar.

"Goddamn it to hell," he muttered. He knew they were spies, the whole area was infested, the whole world. He smelled them, sensed them with every pinging nerve in his body. And no one was going to believe him. No goddamn fucking person on earth was going to believe him.

Suddenly he stiffened, the hair on his neck rising. A muffled report, like a very distant cannon, reverberated, then another, another. He spun around to see a shiny cannister whoosh against the cliff above the shack, no more than fifty feet away from him. It split open and a whitish fog formed, disappeared. In a fleeting second he experienced his final humiliation. He understood that the navy was knocking out everyone on the island; they were taking over. "Those goddamn fucking bastards—" he started, and then slumped to the ground, asleep.

Corky and Lauren stood at the rail of his yacht and watched Ellington slide to the sand, asleep. There was another explosion, not very loud, not at all threatening. Several landing boats appeared, each with a dozen sailors, heading for the shore. Corky took Lauren's hand. "Let's go below."

Her confusion descended like a stage curtain and when it rose she saw them lounging at a tropical pool with a waterfall. He was drawing her and the drawing was beautiful, hands, feet, and all. She blinked, and they went below.

# Chapter Twenty-Seven

—WHAT a load of crap you fed that poor guy! Infinite book. Data bank in the sky. Hah!

—Now, now. We had to tell him something he could comprehend, you know. And he did turn the page, now didn't he?

—Yeah, I guess. You know everyone over there's been tapping in like crazy? And him, you can't keep him away! It's like he's found a private telephone line to just everywhere.

—Yes. That's understandable. Aren't we all as busy as little bees now that we can see past the murk, as he so elegantly put it?

—I'm the one who called it murk. Remember? And now, no matter what I'm looking at, I can feel him right there taking it all in. Then he draws it. Like that other one, Leonardo.

—Strange that you're always looking at things that interest him that much, don't you think?

—He doesn't tap in on you?

—Once in a great while, but he doesn't stay.

—There's something pretty fishy about him, isn't there? Don't you feel it?

—Well, inasmuch as he was responsible for the shadow, the murk, inadvertently, I admit, but still he was the one who could start it all up again, that makes him fairly unusual. Unique, actually, since as far as we can see, this is the only time such a thing happens.

—Yeah. So why'd you risk so much, letting me stay around when he came over, letting me try to get him to walk on through, the way I did Pitts?

—I told you. We thought you could communicate with him.

—Now I'll tell you what I think. You thought he'd recognize me, that the shock would break things loose.

—Ah, no, not exactly. There are many of us here who like to count things, keep track of new arrivals, that sort of thing. Don't understand the appeal myself, but there it is. .They knew when you arrived, you see, and we thought that perhaps you would recognize him and remember what you did if your attention was directed to him. And then, with his tapping in on you, he would know. Or mutual recognition, or something of the sort, might have jogged a memory. That, or the threat of going into limbo, as you/he called it.

—You would have done that, wouldn't you?

—Well . . . We really couldn't have two of you here, you know. Not if one of you still has the will to live. There was a very real danger that you/he might be tempted to alter the past, a real danger of discontinuity if he did not find the way. Very real, my friend.

—I asked if he was me, or I him, whatever. And you said no. I remember that too. And that was a lie. You shouldn't be able to tell lies here!

—Why not? Anything imaginable, *everything* imaginable, it is all ours. Fables, music, art, science, philosophy, politics. It all is of the mind, all ours to puzzle out, play with, lie about if we choose, reinvent, elaborate on, create. But we would not impose identity on another. It is too private, too personal, too impossible from outside. If you denied him, how could I do otherwise? Everyone who arrives/arrived after the shadow suffered a certain blank spot. That, at least, was real, very dangerous. We did hope you could undo it. Are you positive about him now?

—Yeah. It's me. I didn't make the connection before; he looked too young, and like you said, I didn't remember him, a blank spot. I live a long time, don't I? And Lauren too.

—Well . . .

—I mean, the way they reckon time over there. Okay?

—Yes, you do, and so does she.

—Look. Aren't they great together?

—We were, are, great together, Corky.

—It's you! Where'd you come from? You know what the odds are against finding someone else in this place?

—No. Tell me. But look now. Aren't we beautiful!

—Yeah. We are.

Lauren smiled softly in her sleep, and dreamed of walking hand in hand with Corky, the way he had been before, with wild red hair, blue doll eyes, the way she would always love him most. They walked through a meadow that stretched to infinity, where they had all the time there was.